The Will of my Father

Part II

Emma,

with a heavy heart I write to you. I feel for the world and everything that is happening. We live in a time of great change, and the voice of many are becoming one. Ryan & I have talked about our generation + how rare of a generation we must be. We are filled with the old, while giving birth to all that is new.

— I hope you're staying safe + healthy through this time of uncertainty

with all my hope + Love

P.S I bookmarked your favorite poem.

ISBN: 978-1-951742-23-2   [Paperback Edition]
   978-1-951742-22-5   [eBook Edition]

Printed and bound in The United States of America.

Published by

The Mulberry Books, LLC.
8330 E Quincy Avenue,
Denver CO 80237
themulberrybooks.com

The Will of my FATHER

Part II

DEVEN RIECK

Dedication

To my parents,
thank you for giving me the world,
this and so much more is all for you.

To my editors Willow and Tamara.
Thank you for your passion, endless support
and being part of this journey.

To the misfits, loners, outcasts, rebels, and weirdos
of this generation and generations to come,
this ones for you.

CHAPTER 1

||||||||||||||||||||||||||||||||||||||||||||||||||

mind games

My nightmares arrived that night. Visions of flame and torture erupted into a vast city in some distant future. And yet, it was all too familiar to me. As if I were there. Why was the city in my mind so real? More real than the world in which I had been so mysteriously dropped.

Come to think of it, I hadn't given much thought as to *how* I had arrived here. I remember falling into the body of water near the small fishing village, but beyond that, it all seemed to unfold like a play. Everything happened so quickly. In a short period of time, I had become someone else entirely. Perhaps even a darker version of my former self.

Emily had been taking over my thoughts on and off, for days now. Every time I had night terrors filled with visions of a burning city, she was always there, calling out to me. Evelynn had left for the kingdom the next day; it was now in my charge. My father too, had departed, leaving me with a scroll of instructions. Every morning at dawn, I was to visit the lower lands; say hello to the farmers, whom Father called the spine of the kingdom. Before midday, I was to check the overnight reports with the guards at the Outerwall. After the midday meal, I was to hold a council with the remaining scholars—the ones who hadn't ridden with my father to the far kingdom where I had fought a dragon.

The routine got boring fast; I was in a daze through most of it—halfway involved in the majority of conversations thrown in my direction, scattered as I looked for a solution to too many problems.

1

The scholars were a mix of messengers, artists, and architects from the kingdom. Knowledge was their inspiration and imagination, their gift. Most of these meetings took place behind closed doors. Ideas—both drawn and written—were presented to me concerning the problem of the irrigation tunnel in the lower lands, near the wall where the ancient forest lay. Untouched beyond, and more than just a few hundred feet away, there was a clutter of vegetation that had accumulated. It blocked the water to the lower lands. Each year the knights went in and cut down the vines and overgrown vegetation, letting the water gasp and explode into the lower lands as they provided the soil and crops with moisture. The problem was, the vegetation would grow back toward the end of the year, blocking the water by the time harvest season rolled around. Each spring the knights would have to go back. It was a never-ending cycle that my father didn't seem worried about.

But I wasn't my father. The irrigation plan had been handled by the architect of the group. His stature was thin, and he had the hands of a craftsman. Cuts and scars showed on his skin. A small carving knife hung from his belt. His robes fell loosely on his frame. Eyes blue as a jay's wings fluttered as he blinked, and short blonde strands fell across his forehead. He stood in front of me and spoke clearly. "I suggest we build an irrigation tunnel underground, so we don't have to bother with the plants in general"

"That might work," I mumbled across the table.

The architect pulled a rolled scroll from the bag resting on his lap and walked toward me, bowed when he was a couple of steps away, then waited until I gave the nod of approval, and laid out his design. My mind was filled with ideas. I asked for one of his writing utensils. He looked at me with a smile and handed me a bumpy war quill, then opened his inkwell and set it in front of me.

"May I ask what you are thinking, my king?" his charming, boyish voice rang out.

"What if we didn't go underneath. What if we went around? Why not just go around the ground that seems to not want to be disturbed?"

The room fell silent. "I suppose my father never did this," I added. "Did he?"

The artist spoke up—a tall man who wore a short, rough beard which hugged his cheeks. He had dark eyes that matched his tight brown curls. "No, the king trusted us to do as we thought best. You are very different from him, but in a good way, my king. Not that he was a bad king. Please, don't get me wrong on that matter." He spoke with nervousness.

I laughed at his remark and waved his apology aside with the hand. "Don't worry about it. I know my father and I are different. I think it is because we grew up differently."

Visions popped into my head, blurring my vision. I forced them away, focusing back on the drawing in front of me while I spoke to the council. "Can any of you tell me where the water comes from?"

The architect spoke. "It comes down from the waters in the far North. There are many rivers that carry the water to various regions. Two large ones travel through the kingdom. We made some changes a few hundred years ago, but as you know, the land is always changing, and water is a powerful force which carves out its own routes."

I added a mountain to his design, a tunnel at the top of the scroll, and then two winding rivers snaking down from the tunnel.

"You said you wanted to build a tunnel underneath the plants, but what about the wall between the forest and the kingdom? Are we going to just dig a tunnel underneath the tunnel as well?" the artist asked.

My temples flared. I set down the quill and rubbed my chin as the throbbing continued. I ignored the pain and thought about the possible routes the water could take.

The artist spoke again. "What about the gate? We won't have to worry about the wall if we dig an inleading path down the middle."

I gave the quill to the architect, and he took the scroll, returned to his place across the table, and started drawing as the artist next to him talked things through. It was then that I rose to my feet. I hid my pain from the scholars as I turned my back to them. I walked toward the windows, the rays of light highlighting the dust particles in the air so they stood out in sharp contrast to the war room's dark wood. Out the window, the kingdom was gleaming in the afternoon sun. My thoughts returned to the recurring nightmare and the city on fire. My temples were pounding;

my thoughts erupted with agony as I looked to the far end of the wall and saw the canopy of trees.

I fell to my knees. And fainted. Chaos ensued. There was falling of chairs, then footsteps. The echo of running clouded my thoughts, then two women materialized; Emily and the witch each grasped a side of my brain and pulled it taut. They glared.

The scholars aided me as I stumbled to my room; a voice rang out—a crow's call pierced the silence. Then it was at the window. Its beak poked at the glass as it tried to enter the room. I knew it was the witch. I slept through the night, dreaming again of that futuristic world.

I found myself murmuring Emily's name as I woke to rain the next day, still jumping between this world and the world of my past. I continued to attend to my daily duties.

On many occasions I would take Donte with me. The stone paths' cracks were filling with mud. I didn't like walking in the rain, and I'm sure Donte wasn't too fond of it either. I'm sure he would have preferred to have stayed in the stable and to gossip with the rest of the horses.

I rode across the lower lands until I hit the gray-stoned wall, which matched the clouds in the sky with their bumps, grooves, and puffy edges. The king's guard was with me today. Anytime I came this close to the walls, they joined me. I had met the king's guard just a couple of years ago, when I became king of the realm. However, it wasn't until my father left that I really got used to their presence. In crowded places, they were often the wall between me and my people—a people who still were hesitant toward me. They saw my resemblance to Gregory, and I think that turned some of the elders' respect into a decision to not bother giving me a chance. After the first couple of years, I put faces to the names of the men who wore the knights' helmets.

The leader was roughly my height, with more length in his legs, a shorter torso, and broad shoulders. He walked in front and I rode beside him. He was a year or two younger than me, but it was difficult to tell because he had been a battle-ready veteran long before me. His name was Orion; I often invited him to dine with me. It was in these moments that we learned and taught one another, and developed a secret means of communication through hand and body gestures.

It was an unwritten rule that the king's guard's leader, as well as the rest of the guards, had to meet with the new king—whoever he may be—and develop a language all of their own. Each king is different. Therefore, each language has to be carefully orchestrated. When they knew I was in the palace for the night, it was not uncommon to hear their swords clashing, in that same room I had entered on my first night within the kingdom's walls.

It was also where I had encountered Evelynn. She had followed my father to the Bear Clan's land to counsel with our allies. Orion did his best to fill the void left in her absence. I regarded him as a friend, but I knew in the end, he was just another body that had taken an oath to protect whoever the ruler was. His intentions were aligned with my own, and our friendship grew because of it. When I had first arrived, eyes were on me at all times. Now, however, there was something relaxing in each gaze; they no longer paid me much attention.

I'm sure they would have liked to have stayed indoors today as well. It was summertime. Time flies when you're busy adapting to new cultures and new points of view. Not to mention, when you're busy acquiring insane skills through brutal training by a batshit-crazy older woman with a cane.

I followed the wall until I reached the gate. The two guards and four archers posted atop the wall stood at attention when Donte came into view. I told them to return to their daily routines, whatever that meant. It was the middle of the day. The rain had finally let up by the time we stopped in front of the gate. We dismounted and entered one of the towers at its entrance. A few men were inside, playing a game with stones and coins. Rain dripped from my head and formed a small pool in my crown, only to run down my back like a waterfall when I removed it.

I spoke to the watchtower knights. "Yes, the scholar council won't stop bothering me about the water problem."

Orion spoke right as my final word left my mouth. "Sainath, we saw this problem when your father was here. I can tell you know it's one that can't be fixed. We have torched, chopped, and even poisoned the vines so they would stop coming back, but nothing works. Perhaps we should just let nature be and look for a different solution—perhaps even from this side of the wall?" Orion walked over to the water barrel and started to pour a few wooden cups for the men.

I kept our conversation lively as the eyes of the knights widened, curious as to what action we would take. I was the king and had the final say, but it was important to consider my men's arguments.

"The flow to the lower farmlands," I replied. "They are claiming it's a buildup of vegetation. But something tells me, it's worth checking out personally." I reached for a water cup.

Orion turned around to face me. "Sainath." He was the only knight—and person—who addressed me by my name instead of using my royal title. He continued. "Are you sure about this?" His armor dripped from the rain.

I pushed back my rain hood, and the drenched piece of leather slapped against my shoulders. The chamber wasn't much, but it was warm. There was a large fireplace on the far end that led to the top of the tower, where it released a gray smoke. A barrel of wine rested at the far end of the room. Next to the fireplace were a couple of bags of colored stones. One red and the other blue. I asked what they were.

One of the knights stood up from his stool and grabbed a handful of each. "These are interesting," he said, stretching his palm toward me. "Something the king came up with, umm…your father, I mean. He got them from a merchant in the far East, while the kingdom was still being built. We throw the red stones in the fire. They create a bright red smoke that can be seen throughout the kingdom. It lets the people know to gather what they can and head to the opposite side of the kingdom. Each corner of the kingdom has a tower like this one. The people's safety is our top priority. Without people, there is no civilization."

I nodded, remembering that my father said something similar. "And what about the blue?"

"It's a calming signal. It lets the people know of travelers such as messengers or a stray rider. Just a cautionary procedure, if you will."

I rubbed the blue stone and red stone, exchanging them in my hands before stuffing one of each in my pocket. I ordered the gates open and galloped into the forest with the royal knights. The trail was old, but the forest was far older. That ancient feeling was all around. Trees stood in various patterns, their branches falling haphazardly, with their trunks anchored into the soil. It was quiet with just the noise of the horses' hooves on wet ground creating small waves of sounds that bounced from tree to tree. It only furthered my impression that we were alone in this endless stretch of gnarled bark, branches, and leaves.

A well-choreographed group of nine knights made up the king's guard. I whispered to Donte, urging him ahead of our group. I never had to spur him. My voice, even at a whisper, was enough for him to understand. The clicks of hooves on cobblestone lead us along a worn path, straight to the overgrown vines which blocked that water panel. I looked it over and pressed forward. Hoofbeat gave way to cracks, snapping twigs, and dry leaves as we entered the heart of the forest. At random, a cold breeze washed over us, followed by a wave of hot summer air. We traveled deeper.

The wind became still. The branches were covered in moss and flowers of brilliant colors. For some odd reason, my mind saw the trees as an eerie, Gothic painting. Orion and I rode side by side, motioning to each other whenever various small game scurried into hiding at the sound of our approach. This told us we were the first people to enter this far into the forest in a very long time. Perhaps even *ever*. A doe moved to my left, and a family of skunks lurked by the side of our path. No light penetrated this deep into the forest. It was filled with an abundance of life.

Something caught my eye: a house resting within a tree. It had been partially dug into the small hill behind it. What seemed to be an entrance was covered by the same vines that blocked the water's channel. No windows were visible. I could only make out the door because of the wood showing through the vines. We rode past the house. At this point, I didn't know what I was looking for. The well that was blocked was far behind us now. No-one stopped, as if this house was the least important thing we were here for, even though it was, in fact, the only thing we were here for.

"What is that. Does anyone live there?" I asked.

Orion looked at me through his helmet. He narrowed his eyes in confusion. "What are you talking about?"

I stopped Donte, and the rest of the king's guard came to a sharp halt. "That small hill back there. Didn't you see it? Doesn't it seem odd to you that this whole forest floor is on a flat plane then, out of nowhere, a hill just formed? That is not natural at all."

I looked back over my shoulder, in between the bodies of the king's guard, to the hill. But there was no hill, Only crisscrossing trees and the chatter of two squirrels playing tag where the hill had been.

"You didn't see it?" I said quietly, looking back at Orion.

His eyes narrowed further, and he looked at the group of trees, then back at me. Without hesitation, he nodded. He held up his right hand, quickly making a fist then dropping it to his side as fast as a whip. The eight knights behind us, in one single fluid motion, dismounted and circled me, there might be danger. I took a deep breath through my nose and dismounted too. I was thankful that Orion trusted my instincts. With my right hand flat, I touched my skin and waved my hand in front of my face.

The knights were in defense. No words were uttered. Silence. Until we were safe, we would communicate strictly through sign language. As soon as we had dismounted, the knights split into two four-person groups. They formed two lines of defense with their shields held in front of them — one line on either side of me. Donte was still standing in the middle with me. Orion had a smaller shield which he strapped to his forehand. He tossed me my knife belt. I strapped the leather knife belt around my waist, waiting for any tell tale sound that would betray our enemy's presence.

Our steps became a single movement—right foot, left foot. If anyone heard us, they would think it was just a single person walking through the forest. It had taken many long nights during the winter months in pitch darkness to accomplish what we were doing now. It was a beautiful thing to hear a single step synced between ten men.

The horses trained just as hard, if not harder. Donte and the king's guard stallions had lived and worked together for almost two years straight. We conditioned them to be more like dogs than horses when it came to listening to commands. Our secret language was all done with the hand's touch. When it came to the horses, reading facial expression wasn't in their DNA, so we adapted to this simple but effective means of communication.

Most importantly, there were key parts of their flanks and manes, which we touched with precision so as not to confuse the beasts. The last thing we wanted was disorganization if we were attacked. Where I relied on whispers with Donte, the knight's horses relied strictly on touch. Three taps on the left side of the neck with the hand flat and the palm flat against the neck. Three taps to go on the defensive. Those two years spent living with like minds had done wonders for Donte, and the rest of the horses. Imagine the conversations they must have.

The horses considered Donte, their leader; they saw him as the knights saw me. I gave the touch signal to Donte, who trotted quickly to the horses standing at attention on the path behind us. The most remarkable part was to watch the horses relay the message to one another. They did this by gently nipping each other on the same spot where we had touched them. Three nibbles and a nudge of the nose, and the message had been passed down. The horse trotted behind us in a single file. Half were moving forward and the other half backward. This kept their eyes at a three hundred and sixty-degree visual field for us. I couldn't help but be proud of my old friend.

Tapping Orion's left elbow to signal, "Let me take the lead," he stepped to his right, allowing me to slide ahead of the pack as he fell into formation. We came upon the group of trees that had replaced the hill and home I had seen. The handful of trees looked different from the rest of the surrounding forest. Their trunks split into two, resembling outstretched legs as if they could walk. The limbs twisted into knots before spiraling toward the sky. They stretched in loops and twists at each unnatural turn.

"Well, are you convinced that what you saw was just these trees?" Orion whispered just above that mysterious breeze. Where was that mysterious hot and cold air coming from? I shook my head in disagreement. I walked out of formation, realizing that if we were going to be attacked, it would have happened by now.

I walked up to the tree, to where I thought I had seen a door; my skin began to crawl, and my head started to ache. The tree I approached was in the center of the rest of the odd looking group of trees. The trunk was cracked, and the canopy high above looked like a cumulus cloud or a wild mushroom. My memories erupted from my past life and turned the pages of the book of my mind. Why was the world trying to keep me away from this place? My legs started to jitter, sending out impulses to turn, mount my horse, and return to the palace.

A flock of crows flew above us, and the wind held its breath as they circled, cawed, and landed atop the tree next to the one I was standing below. Then, the wind exhaled. The leaves of the odd trees began to rustle, move, and churn in a radial motion. A shockwave of energy forced me to step back a few feet. The leaves twisted off their hold from the branches and gathered into a cloud of swirling green. Sweat streamed from my head as I watched nature gather to form the figure of a large man, who now stood in front of us.

He was a foot and a half taller than me. Leaves of orange, red, and moss-green made up his body. They rustled, a rough outline of the human like figure which undulated as he moved. My gaze fluttered at the sight, and yet there was something so familiar about this scene that I couldn't tear my eyes away. I remembered seeing the leaves move like that just a year ago when Evelynn and I had shared one last sunset before she left with my father.

"Sainath, move!" Orion shouted from behind me, and before I could turn around to see him, he had already shouldered me out of the way with a thrust. His sword was drawn, and with that, our silent pact broke. The knights scrambled to my side. I rolled to my feet as they put up their defenses around me. They went into Arrowhead formation, with Orion at the tip. I got to my feet. A whistle blew, and the horses rushed over. Donte was already at my side.

With the whistle blown and the formation broken, the knights formed a wall between the leaf giant and me. The twin blades of black meteorite were strapped to the left side of Donte's saddle. With both hands, I grabbed their hilts, my eyes never leaving the figure. I tapped Orion's nose, motioning him to stand back. Donte retreated with the rest of the horses, leaving us to take on whatever nature had in store for us.

The figure finally moved. There was the rustle of the leaves once again as it took a step toward us. With my swords in hand and my knife belt strapped tightly, we waited in anticipation. The formation changed from Arrowhead to Spearpoint. Knees bent and muscles tense, we waited. My salty sweat continued to drip from my face. The princely garments were heavy and restricted my full range of motion.

A calm breeze blew my face dry.

Orion made the first strike. He took a dagger and threw it as if he was hurling a snowball. It hit his target, but it went right through the creature, smacked the trees, and snapped into multiple pieces.

"No, it can't be." Orion looked at me in concern.

I flipped the swords in my hands and slammed them into the rich organic matter at our feet. I looked at the creature as I spoke to Orion. "Stand down; you don't have a chance with something like this. I have faced this before. Well, something *like* this."

"What the hell are you talking about?" he replied. "We can find a way. Let's tire it out. We have it outnumbered. Plus, with your true fighting abilities and my strategic brain, we can take it down together."

The Knights opened up the defense and let me walk in front. "You won't make it out alive, believe me." I murmured as I walked past Orion.

Orion put his sword away and called after me. "Sainath, I have followed you this far, and I trust your instincts. But our duty rests with the crown. Whoever sits in the palace and wears the crown of our people will be defended to the death, so know that if that thing strikes you, I will disregard your word and attack with everything that I have. I'll give you a minute but not a second longer. Do what you think is right. The clocks ticking, young king."

I nodded, then I stared at the grass at my feet, showing surrender to the creature formed from the breath of nature.

CHAPTER 2

||||||||||||||||||||||||||||||||||||||||||||||||||||||

the origin of nightmares

"Well, someone does remember me," the creature said. "I thought this place would have kept those festering memories at bay...I see that you have found a way to reclaim your past. Otherwise, you wouldn't have stopped attacking me. Plus, you wouldn't be so calm right now."

I looked up at the celestial being. "Whoever you are, I want you to know that I do remember you; I remember the nightmares you brought to my peaceful world. I remember the darkness you brought out of me. I remember the final words you engraved in my mind, about a hero who would arrive when the time is right. But I think that time is long gone now. My world has ended, and now I'm in this new place. I can't tell if it's a dream or some twisted fantasy; my mind is playing like a film as I lie in the rubble, bleeding out from the nuclear fallout. You tell me what is going on." I spoke without so much as blinking.

"Sainath," came the response, "your memory amazes me. I thought your brain would still be scrambled. How interesting." The creature looked up at the crows with a sinister frown, and they took flight instantly—disappearing within the leaves' canopy.

The celestial being looked back down at me and bent over. His outer layer of leaves continued to sway around his form. "The reason I am here is that I can't let you near these trees. And here you were doing so well. Such a shame. You see, this tree belongs to another celestial being, the being of naturality and good nature.

12

I am that of violence and war. It is I who gave you the knowledge to create those swords you hold so dear. It is I who sparked the first coals of war in your breast. It was I who forged the idea of armies and worship of gods and goddesses of war. I stoked these fires. My fires. I have ignited and crumbled nations with a mere whisper. All things should end, and humanity is no different. Every great nation must fall. It is only nature in its simplest of forms. In every one of those moments of violence, I had a hand to play, just like I do now."

He walked toward us. I stepped back quickly, not knowing what the creature was going to do. My brain shifted in and out of consciousness; the knights grew as their armor started to shrink around their frames. Orion fell to his knees, weeping as his hands were brought together, and his hand shield twisted inward upon itself. I was twisting his arm at the same time. I shouted, dropping to my knees and holding my hands up in defense. "Please, don't hurt them. What do you want?"

The celestial being stopped and released the knights and Orion before looking down at me. "Ah, that is the same question you asked in your dream all those years ago. Let me tell you what I want. Get on your horse, take your knights with you, and never come into this forest again. Become the king you were meant to be and prepare, as war is coming soon. There is so much you don't know, and your small mind won't be able to grasp the reality of what is going on. That is what I want, and for the future, address me as Apollyon." He turned away from me and walked over to the horses.

I looked at my swords. They lay just within arm's reach. I didn't know if I had enough time or would be noticed if I made a sudden rush to grab them. I looked down at my knife belt as Apollyon extended his leaf-covered hand toward Donte. Of course, Donte kicked up his hooves at the giant. Our eyes met for a second, and I gave a short nod just noticeable to him. Donte neighed and ran away; he galloped back toward the palace gates, leading the other horses to safety. I double tapped my right elbow with my left palm, signaling Orion and the knights to get ready to move or fight with everything we had.

Apollyon was behind everything. I didn't have all the answers, but if it weren't for him, I wouldn't even be in this part of the world. This illusion had kept my eyes hidden from the truth.

Seeing Donte flee agitated the giant to the point that his leaves rustled like a rattlesnake rousing itself to attack. His head jerked toward us, making me and my men draw our weapons. At that moment, I wanted to give the signal to flee. But my anger had been set aflame. It made sense why he was the celestial being of war and violence. I was filled with rage, and my body twitched to move toward him and attack him. It was the same feeling I had experienced in my dream long ago.

Orion bolted without waiting for my signal and took the rest of the knights' horses with him. Apollyon stood with a grin, ready to take on any challenger. He knew our weapons were useless. I had no idea how to defeat a supernatural creature like this, let alone a celestial, who seemed to be the most powerful thing I could imagine going toe to toe with. The way their potential and charm were used to overdose any human being, so he or she acted foolishly was too great of power for anyone to take on.

I hefted three knives in one hand and threw them to distract Apollyon from the others. I didn't need the death of the whole king's guard on my conscience. Plus, I don't think anyone would believe my story if I returned all alone. I would rather die here in the place of my men; they had families to return to even if they hardly saw them. Apollyon absorbed my knives and let them pass through his body. He took every sword and shield thrust with ease, dodging every slash and all the acrobatics of the skilled knights, as well as my attacks. We attacked from every angle, all of us giving the very best we could. His charm over us didn't let up. Apollyon caught a knight by the arm. Grinning, he sucked in the knight's fist and twisted his arm, snapping his forearm in two. The knight was in such a rage that he screamed in disappointment that he had let such a thing happen. He didn't even stop to see the damage in his arm. He fought on with his other arm. Another knight's fingers met with Apollyon's hand. He shrugged his hand to fit between the fingers of the knight.

In the most gruesome way, Apollyon made his fingers expand while they were caught between those of his victim. As he separated the fingers farther and farther apart, there was a sickening crack. The knight's dislocated fingers snapped, then fell apart uselessly. The knight gave a deep breath, broke free of the grasp, and tried to punch Apollyon.

This was pointless. He was going to kill all of us while we fought to our last breath. I didn't know what to do. I dropped to my knees and hands, breathing heavily.

I closed my eyes and talked to myself. "This isn't real. I'm just dreaming again. I will wake up soon. If he tries to kill me, I will wake up. That's how it works, right?"

But it felt real. My heart pounding with adrenaline felt real. My tense, twitching muscles felt real. I walked like a four-legged creature to pick up my swords. They had landed in front of the odd trees. I kept my eyes closed; I felt less rage that way—could pretend it was just a dream. My hands felt around for a sword hilt. I knew I was close. I peeked and saw the glint of the blade, groped around in the grass and moss covering the forest floor. I heard Apollyon's steps coming toward me; I opened my eyes. I couldn't defend if I couldn't see him. As I turned around, Orion's body slammed into me once again. I rolled to a stop a few feet away, landing on all fours.

Apollyon had finally had enough. "Sainath, don't make me kill everyone. Return to the palace and rule your kingdom; this is your true calling."

I snapped my neck in his direction as he was closing in on me. "How do you know what my calling is? Last I checked, I was in charge of my destiny. Isn't that why your gods gave us free will?"

He stopped in front of me. His feet were turned toward my rib cage. One kick, and I'd be a cripple. Still on all fours, I thought about how slim my chances were. What could I say? I took a deep breath.

Apollyon replied. "Maybe in your world this was true, but here, no. Here what I say is how you should govern yourself."

Pain blossomed in my torso as he sent me flying into the bush between the trees. I gasped, trying to catch my breath. Luckily, the brush kept me hidden for now.

"I will give you one last chance to go back to the palace. I would rather not kill you just yet," he shouted as I struggled to breathe. I fisted the grass in my hands and closing my eyes in defeat, and I did what any other human would do. I prayed.

"Dear God, if you are still around, please hear my call for aid. If I survived the end of Earth, please let me survive this too. Tell Emily I said hello and that I could use her sarcasm right about now to cheer me up. It has been so long since I was truly happy. It's just not the same. If this is a test, my lord, then so be it. But save me from this celestial being who is full of darkness great enough that it conjures nightmares. In your name, Amen."

I rose to my feet, cradling my left side. My head peeked over the brush just in time to catch Apollyon looking in my direction. Our eyes met. I still held onto my sword, now dangling at my side. Just as I was about to take Apollyon's offer and retreat to the palace so the knights would survive, I looked over at Orion, who was standing with his sword drawn, the rest of the knights staggering to their feet, weak and bleeding. Their eyes were still alight with rage.

I had to stop this. "Let the knights go, and I will retreat to the palace. After all, you say it's where I belong."

"No tricks. Get going and never return to this part of the forest. I have eyes watching over you, Sainath."

I knew he was talking about the crows and, more importantly, the witch. Now I knew who she worked with. It made sense now. This evil part of this land did, anyway. But what did he mean by my planet Earth? Was I no longer on Earth?

I walked out of the bush and accepted Apollyon's terms. I strapped my sword to my knife belt and gathered my other sword as the rest of the knights came down from their berserk fever. The two knights who had broken bones finally cried out in pain as the reality of their injuries hit them. I knelt by one and helped him to his feet.

I whistled. In moments, Donte came running with the rest of the horses close behind. He had been hiding a safe distance away—also part of our training. Carrying a man home was one thing. Carrying a horse was a whole other story. Because of this, we had decided that keeping the horses from harm was a wise thing to train the horses to do.

When the horses did arrive, we bandaged the broken bones as securely as we could. It would have to do until the palace doctors saw them. The ground trembled beneath my feet, and I ignored it. I just wanted to get the knights home. Once the injured were on horseback, the remaining knights mounted so the wounded could rest on the backs of their riders. The horses who didn't have riders got into position next to their wounded knights. The bond that the knights' horses had with their knights was as strong as that Donte and I shared.

The ground vibrated a second time, so I turned to Apollyon. He shouted, "I thought I said no tricks!"

A fury of leaves shook through his body—the reds and oranges of his leaves buzzed around his celestial frame like a swarm of angry bees. I had no idea what was going on.

"It's not me!" I shouted in return. I smacked the horse closest to me, and the rest took off following the trail back. The knights themselves didn't bother stopping. They knew this fight was over for them. Orion held back as long as he could, then shouted back at me, "Let's get out of here while we still have the chance, my king!"

I agreed and mounted Donte. Apollyon's fury grew. Maybe God was coming to my aid after all. He would find a way to bring him down; I was sure of that.

As we began to sprint away, a vine dashed through the trees and grabbed me right off Donte. It pulled me through the trees, which scratched at my bruised ribs. I didn't have time to call out to Orion. Donte stopped short, twisted around, and galloped at full force—jumping through bushes and dodging trees as if he was the master assassin now. It took just seconds before I was back in front of Apollyon.

"You think you can run from me when I'm talking to you? Your kind has always been a rude species. I can't wait until the time comes for me to eradicate you for good." His eyes were narrow, and his sinister mouth curved into a sick smile.

I drew both swords. "I don't know where this vibration is coming from, and I am not the cause of it. But if you are so sure that it is me, and you want to kill my species off, why not get started?" I spoke with excessive courage. "I'll gladly die. I hate this place. I can't fix it. So, come on. Give me all that you have. I have been ready to die for some time now."

Suddenly, the ground trembled as though struck by thunder, and the forest floor splintered like it had been struck by lightning. The trees parted as their trunks uprooted themselves, creating a massive ball, then limbs—a torso materialized, a bright beam of light at its center. Was this God? I couldn't believe he had heard me.

Another figure stood beside us now. He, too, was a giant. I was caught in the middle of the—one composed of leaves and the other of green vegetation. Flowers erupted from his arms and bark-covered his vital organs if he had any — a face of diamond-patterned vines formed from the mossy head. The giant looked over at me just as his eye sockets blinked open. He parted his gnarled lips and spoke in an ancient voice.

"Duck, young one."

I dropped to my stomach as a spear of leaves shot across where I had just been. The Forest Guardian created a shield with both his vine-like arms, which shattered the leaves in a million pieces. I rolled out of the way; I was no longer part of this fight. My ears pricked up, searching for any sound of Donte. I quickly ran over to him as he entered the clearing. I held both my palms facing him, so he knew I was out of danger and could stop running. He circled me a couple of times, eyeballing the two fighting beings before stopping and nudging me with his head.

"Oh no, you don't," Apollyon yelled. While still trying to pierce the Forest Guardian, he shot his right arm in my direction. I took both swords and parted his arm into two around us, but it wasn't that easy. His two arms reformed behind us. He shoved Donte against a tree and stuck him there with black resin. His arms became tentacles; the leaves were sharp needles, layered in a shingle pattern. The deep reds and oranges gave way to chaotic black ooze that dripped, with every thrust, dousing the forest floor.

My instincts kicked in. I knew I couldn't make direct eye contact with him. Otherwise, rage would consume me. I was light on my feet. I kept moving out of range and, more importantly, stopping directly in front of his gaze. While this was going on, the two celestial beings spoke in a language I couldn't understand. If one thing was clear, it was that they knew each other. It looked like two siblings going at each other. With the amount of fury there was, nothing seemed to be held back. The Forest Guardian took every hit yet managed to block every incoming attack.

I tripped and fell over the root of a tree. The viperous tentacle caught up with me fast; I slashed with my swords as it tried to grab at me. I rolled and threw a knife; it pushed the knife away. I rolled out of the way of another strike as it darted into the forest floor. The root of the tree I tripped overcame to life and wrapped itself around me like a cobra. Surprisingly, it latched itself around Apollyon's arms, giving me time to get to my feet. I backed away quickly, only to run straight into the Forest Guardian.

He looked down. "Stay behind me, young one. My brother knows he can't keep this up for long. He is in my domain. I have more than enough power to tire him out."

"Thank you," I said, still in defense mode as I watched the arm trying to break free from the root of the tree.

"It was wise of you to call for aid; I haven't been called upon by your kind since the early years of your birth."

The leaf spear broke free of the root and came right at me. I slashed it in half again. This time, it had no time to recollect itself. The Forest Guardian grabbed both ends—which writhed like two snakes trying to break free. I dodged out of the way, and he took the two halves of one arm and wrapped them around his forearm, twisting then into the rotation. "Enough of this, Apollyon. You knew it was a gamble trying to bring someone like him into your world. Let it go; you can't conquer everyone with your tricks and illusions."

Apollyon retracted his other arm and turned it into a toxic viper limb too. He sent it flying toward the Forest Guardian, who met the viper halfway and shoved it back to where it started; the arm then picked up Apollyon and slammed him against the ground a couple of times. As soon as the Forest Guardian released his hold, roots from below him sprang up and wrapped themselves around Apollyon like a cocoon. He wriggled angrily as his mouth was covered up.

I put my swords back into my knife belt at my waist, then sighed in relief and looked up at the Forest Guardian. "What will you do with him?"

The celestial being looked down at me, then back at his brother. "He will disappear into the air as soon as he knows he is defeated. He is a sore loser, but through the past millennium and a half, he has come to realize wisdom is more powerful than all the strength in the universe. No point having all that power if your mind is not disciplined to use it."

CHAPTER 3

‖‖

the nature of life

The Forest Guardian released Apollyon from his struggle and watched as his brother was surrounded by a whirlwind of crows that had been hovering overhead for some time now. A twister of black feathers disappeared into the blue sky, and just like that—there was no trace of Apollyon. I looked around the Forest Guardian, who lifted his arm to look down at me as if I was a child.

"Young one, it is safe to leave my side now," he spoke in a soft voice. As I left his side, my head erupted with pain, and I dropped to my knees, screaming.

The witch spoke in my mind. "This isn't over, Sainath. My master may not have a hold on you yet, but remember—I'm deep within the pores of your skin. Your blood is mixed with mine. There is nowhere you can run that I will not find you. I will visit again soon."

Just as I was about to scream for the second time to dislodge the witch from my head, I felt something delicate at my temples. The cool sensation eased my fever, and the witch's voice evaporated. I opened my eyes to find my face covered with wildflowers.

"Young one, lie down. We don't have much time. I must treat that head of yours now that my brother knows your mind can no longer be smothered by the illusions of this world."

I complied and lay down on the mossy forest floor. Large leaves emerged from the moss and wove themselves around me like small blankets. The coolness of the leaves made me sleepy. I didn't fight it and passed out, feeling the vines weave and tangle themselves around the empty cavities of my body.

"Young one, please wake up. I will need your full attention at this point."

My eyes fluttered open. I was lying on a table in a strange room; the roof above was a curve of bark that stretched from one edge of the room to the other. I tilted my head up, but vines at my forehead quickly pressed me back against the table.

"Now, try to relax," said the Forest Guardian. I'm going to take the witch from your mind, so that she may no longer track your movements."

"Okay, I'll try to focus," I muttered. "What exactly do you need me to do?"

The Forest Guardian stretched his arms out. The vines that were around my forehead were part of them. He retracted these limbs until only one remained on either side of my head. The point of each vine touched my temples, then dug into my skull. I shouted in pain, shaking my head back and forth, following my body's instinct to get off the table and flee. I felt the vines drill through my skull plate and hover over my brain.

"Please, young one. I know this is painful, but you must tell me where the witch's concentration is strongest. Where does the voice originate from when she reaches out to you?"

"No shit, it's painful! You just burst through my skull. I feel faint…" I grit my teeth. "But, the voice always comes from the back of my head." The vines found their way to the back of my brain. My eyes widened as they found their mark.

"There, right there!" I shouted in short breaths, as my body dripped with sweat.

It felt tender, like a pimple. "Hold still, young one. This will be over soon."

I shook in fear as the vines pinched the object attached to my brain. I pulled my arms free, but before they could reach the vines at my temple to pull them out of my head, more vines emerged and grabbed my hand away from my head, slamming it back down to my side. My acute hearing picked up Donte neighing nearby; I could hear him running in circles trying to find his way to me.

"Almost there…and three, two, one. Done."

I felt a painful pop that quickly gave way to relief. I felt nauseous as the vines retracted, slipping through my dark skin to reemerge. They clutched a small seed-like projection that had a point at one end. The vines at my arms and torso released me, and I sat up, dizzy. I didn't hold back; I let the vomit come out. As I puked, a black, snot-like substance dripped from my nose.

"Blow your nose until it's clear. I will brew some tea to heal your mind and calm your stomach. Try not to move too quickly. Sorry about the pain."

The Forest Guardian walked away from me, his bark feet tapping against the soft earth. I couldn't turn my head in his direction because the surgery on my brain had sapped all my energy. I was already exhausted from the day's journey. I wondered what time it was and if the knights were on their way back. I had told them to leave me behind, but I was sure that Orion would return for me. It wasn't like him to abandon his king.

"If I told you it was going to be painful, you probably would not have let me do that, would you?"

"No, probably not," I replied between my second and third vomit session.

I slid off the table. The lights in my surroundings were dim. I might have been hallucinating, but I thought I saw small bulbs of transparent gel framed by two small leaves—with what seemed like fireflies dancing within. The sacks of gel acted like a structure, holding it together; this was the light source that bobbed in the air to a rhythm I couldn't hear.

The Forest Guardian walked over and handed me a wooden cup filled with tea; my nose was cleared, and I was able to breathe normally again. The scent of rosemary and sage filled my nostrils as the first gulp of tea entered my empty stomach. I blinked in relief. The pain gave way, and a sense of relaxation coursed through my body.

After my third sip of tea, I looked up at the Forest Guardian and spoke. "Thank you for your help. I had no idea that something like that could even happen. Let alone that celestial beings like you could exist. I feel much better now—light-hearted even. Thanks again. Do you have a name?" I downed my final sip of tea.

"I am like my brother Apollyon and my sister Tamara," he said. "I am the celestial being Asha, controller of nature, and wellbeing. It is I who grew the first trees, flowers, blades of grass, and everything else you see that makes up every individual ecosystem."

I dropped to my feet and extended my hand to thank him properly. He looked at it for a second, then reached out his massive bark-encrusted hand and shook mine. The door was behind him, and its red oak surface made me realize we must be within the group of trees I had been suspicious of earlier while riding through the forest.

"You look famished," Asha said as he took my empty cup.

I turned my weary head and watched him walk to the corner of his dwelling; a bobbing light followed at head-level to give him lightly over a blue flame that burned in the corner.

A bark countertop in the form of semi-circle made up the whole kitchen. Cabinets that were nothing more than shelves sprouted from the walls. I watched as Asha reached above his head. A shelf appeared, and he placed the cup on a flat board of dark brown.

He rubbed the cattails on his head as if they were hair. Without turning around, he asked, "Are you hungry? You should probably eat something. When I shook your hand, I sensed your nutritional levels were quite low with your species' specific needs. Go ahead and sit down."

I looked around the table. "Where would you like me to sit?"

Before I could look back at Asha, the dirt floor mounded up, then crumbled away, and the roots of the trees twisted themselves into a chair of polished white. It was smooth as marble. I touched the cool material before taking a seat. It was smooth enough that I slid around with ease. The arms adjusted themselves to my height and hugged my waist so I wouldn't fall out. A child would have a blast in this chair.

This whole place was filled with strange magic. I shouldn't be marveled by it by now, but I was. Every little detail of this home was exquisite in its way. It was a magic that—for the first time—hadn't tried to kill me. I reached up to my temples to where the moist seaweed was wrapped. I could feel the mouths of small critters tending to the wound around my skull. I felt as though a tremendous weight had been lifted from my mind. My head hadn't felt this light since I had arrived; I didn't have the urge to constantly thought about the danger I was in. The tiny critters acted as surgeons, sewing up the holes underneath and at my temples. It felt odd, but I trusted Asha. If he wanted to kill me, he would have by now—plus, he had come to my aid.

Hopefully, he could fill in some of the gaps that I still had concerning this world and how I had come to find myself here.

Asha's heavy bark feet came over to the table. Did he hold a cream-colored aspen plate filled with multicolored leaves and...fruit? Maybe it was fruit. I took a bite of something that looked like a grape. My mouth expected fruit texture and sweet sugary taste. Instead, I got a meaty plum flavor. I didn't want to be rude, so I forced myself to swallow. I decided not to judge anything on my plate until I had eaten the whole thing. I mixed the leaves and unusual vegetables of various sizes and colors. Asha sat across from me; his chair extended straight out of his body, making him look much thinner. His plate was three times the size of mine.

"It's probably not the kind of food you are used to, but it will heal your stomach since you threw up its contents and ease your throat's rawness caused by exposure to stomach acid. I'm not sure why we didn't add a cellulose structure to your digestive system so you could enjoy these greens more often." His handcrafted a fork from its vines, and he started to feast.

I licked my plate clean, forgetting the world outside Asha's home. I no longer heard Donte's voice. Orion was probably outside looking for me as well. The rest of the royal guard must have arrived back at the palace by now. I set down the wooden fork and pushed my plate away. Asha finished before I did. Putting his hands together, he looked warily at the seaweed wrapping around my head.

"How much longer do you think these little critters will be inside?" I asked. There was an itching sensation. I was pretty sure it was from whenever they walked on the surface of my brain.

"They will come out of your head when they finish destroying the small particles of black magic planted by the witch. I'm sorry, but you can't leave until every trace of me is removed from your body."

He unshackled his hands from his seat, picked up the plates, and walked over to the kitchen wall again. The same shelves that held the cups appeared, jutting out from the walls. He sat the plates next to the cups, and the shelf left our view, shooting high above.

"Thank you for taking the witch from my head, Asha. I know it's probably not the easiest thing to do."

Without moving, he tilted his head toward me, like a dog trying to understand what you just said. He moved his head back and forth, then took a few steps in my direction and walked to the door.

"You're welcome. Your species is in grave danger, Sainath." Asha spoke in a calm voice. His right hand waved over the redwood door on the far side of the room. He could whisper, and he would sound just the same; this place—his home, I guessed—echoed pretty much every note that shook free from our throats.

The itching sensation stopped, and I felt a million walking legs forming at my temples. Asha walked over then. The weird expression on my face must have given my feelings away. He reached out his hand. His palm became a bowl the color of cooking spinach; the pinky and thumb elongated into tracks with high ridges along the outside, but the center remained smooth and deeper than the tips. The fingers looked like long, thin slides—the kind you'd find in a kid's park.

The seaweed recognized its creator and unwound from my head. It slid down his fingers into the bowl of his palm. I watched it slither through the bowl and down the wrist, then the shoulders, to find its home around Asha's neck, where it stopped. The slide fingers rested at my temples. Asha spoke to the critters that were at the entrance of my temples on a hole no bigger than a needle's head.

"Come one now, one by one. We don't want anyone following over the edge, now do we?"

The critters left my head, sliding down each side on the slide fingers and into the bowl that made up his palm. A couple dozen of the smallest insects I have ever seen rested in Asha's palm. I leaned in after his fingers had retracted to their normal massive size. The bugs had shiny skin which appeared black from a distance, but once I got closer, I noticed they flashed neon green as they caught small rays of reflecting light. They each had four legs and looked like ants. Some stared at me.

Asha lowered his hand to the ground. His palm opened up from underneath, and the critters dug into the ground, disappearing in the smallest ant hill mound I had ever seen.

"Fascinating creatures, they are. Be grateful you got to see them. They are very shy. I had to give them some incentive about you still being alive, so they wouldn't recycle your brain while they were in there."

"What?"

"I had to be very specific in my instructions to only deal with the infected area. They only emerge when the stench of death looms into the air. They recycle any and every kind of dead body. Breaking down the tissues, muscles, and even bones into ground-like fragments, then taking them underground to feed the soil. It's all a part of a cycle, like many things."

"Well, I'm glad you told them I was still alive," I said. We laughed.

There was a knock on the door.

"Ah, that must be the knight. And I feel two sets of hooves outside. I suppose your horse is also waiting for you, so our time has been cut short. I know you have a lot of questions, Sainath. Please be patient. Keep your head to the ground. We will meet again."

I opened my mouth to retort, but he stopped me. "No, go. There is a war to prepare for, young one." He made his way to the redwood door, then opened it to reveal forest that shone in the sunset.

"Oh, wow, I must have slept through the night," I thought as I walked past Asha. Donte ran up from around the hill, and I could see Orion not far behind. I waved, readying myself to introduce them to a much nicer—and more helpful—celestial being. Before I could turn around and call Asha out to meet my friends, the door disappeared, and the trees once again blended into the rest of the forest. I pressed my lips in acceptance and embraced Donte as his head smacked into my chest. I knew Asha would have loved Donte.

Orion came around the tree. "Finally. I circled this place a couple of times. Where were you hiding?"

"I wasn't hiding anywhere. Wait, only *a couple* of times?" I spoke out to Orion. "Did you not notice I was gone all night?"

"All night?" Orion looked confused. "As soon as I noticed you and Donte were no longer at my side, I turned my horse around and came right back here. I only arrived a moment ago. Donte got a whiff of you, so here we are now."

I stepped away from Donte and walked up to Orion. I looked him over, searching for wounds. He was scraped up, and his cheek was still freshly bruised from the fight with Apollyon. His brows had dirt rubbed through them.

He was telling the truth. I took a step back and looked around. The ground had healed; the scorch marks from the battle between the two celestials were no longer evident anywhere. I walked around the hill, trying to find the entrance, looking for that redwood door. But it was gone. I made myself go back around to Orion. He waited for me to say something.

"I don't know how to tell you this, but there was this other celestial being who fought Apollyon. They destroyed the ground here—" I ran over and acted out the fight from both sides. "Asha came out of nowhere, and defended me, told me to get behind him. Then, he just ended the battle by summoning roots from all these trees around us. Apollyon was trapped and eventually disappeared—with the witch's help—but then my head forced me to my knees again, and Asha—"

Orion held up his hand to stop me from speaking. "Asha is the good one?"

"Yes! And he took me in and removed the witch's voice from my head…I guess she planted some corrupt seed inside me. That's how she was able to keep track of our movements. After that, he gave me tea, and we ate a salad and talked for a bit. Just as I was about to ask him something important, he said the two of you were here, and it was time for us to depart."

I stopped acting everything out and looked up at Orion, who had a look of disbelief playing across his face. "Sainath, I know you have been under a lot of stress. Ruling a kingdom in your father's absence may be too much for you. Let's go home and have the palace doctor look at you, okay?"

"You don't believe me?"

"Sainath. I believe that a fight happened. I think you might have fainted afterward, and you might have dreamed of the final moments. That's all. I heard the battle as I was riding back here, but as soon as I arrived it was finished with no sign of any struggle. Maybe you killed Apollyon, and the fact that he was a celestial might have done something to you. I have never killed a celestial, and until today, I thought they were the stuff of legend. Oh!" His eyes shot open. "Don't worry. Your secret is safe with me, young king, who is too humble to admit he killed a celestial!"

"No! It's not like that. His name's Asha, and he said…He said—"

Orion put his arm around me and walked us over to Donte, who was grazing in the path where the battle had taken place. I took a deep breath and mounted him. I felt sick to my stomach at the thought that no one would believe what I had just lived through. Maybe it *was* just a dream. After all, time had slowed to a crawl out here compared to what I had experienced in Asha's tree home. Orion tapped me on the knee and then mounted his horse.

We rode side by side along the path. I looked over my shoulder at the hill of trees. Nothing happened. I was half-thinking Asha might appear and prove my story true, but there was nothing. We rode in silence until the gates of the kingdom came into view.

Nightfall and half a moon greeted us by the time the gates swung open. The tower guards gave us a wave. I swallowed my pride and put my king face back on. The kingdom was loud with the hustle and bustle of wives setting tables for supper and with chatter as families reunited after the day's work. Children returned home after being outside most of the day. Livestock was rounded up and closed into pens in the lower lands. I dismounted at the stables. I patted Donte goodnight and left Orion's side as the palace doors opened for me then closed in his face.

I slept in peace for the first time in ages.

A few months passed before I could get away from the kingdom and back into the forest to see Asha. I still had questions that burned inside of me. I needed to cool them off with some answers. I could try to go to Tamara. Why would Orion and the rest of the kingdom believe in her existence but not in Asha? Did they only believe what they could see with their own eyes, or had they taken my father's word as fact?

Boredom settled across me as what I can only describe as fall weather rolled in, evident in the changing leaf color and the cold breath of the mountain which frosted the morning grass.

The harvest wagons were mounted and sent to my father's allies in lands that I had not even seen. Some wagons returned in days, while others took several weeks. Two of the wagons never returned. Initially, I didn't bother sending a scouting party. Nevertheless, eventually my advisors talked me into it. After the scout team went missing, I gave up hope. I didn't have a large enough force to leave for that long of a time and still keep the kingdom properly protected.

Before the winds of winter set in, I made up my mind to seek out Asha again.

CHAPTER 4

||||||||||||||||||||||||||||||||||||||||||||||||||||

the difference between a king and a leader

On the night before I'd planned to see Asha, I awoke to a knocking at my bedroom door. I got up and opened the door just a crack at finding the face of the soldier who stood guard. A forty-plus-year-old face with a thin, greying mustache greeted me.

"My king, a messenger from your father's platoon, is in the throne room waiting for you. He pleads that it is of the utmost importance that he gains an audience with you. He also stressed that his message is for your ears only."

I closed the door in his face and rested my back against it. Of course, the worst possible scenario crossed my mind. I grabbed my robe, splashed some clean water on my face from a vase by my bed, and opened the door to the immense hallway. I took quick steps while tying my robe. The purple, velvet robe which dragged an inch on the ground muffled my steps. I was barefoot, yet I no longer needed to walk in silence. My days as an assassin were over.

I thought of Evelynn. I hoped she was well. I didn't know which loss I would take worse: My father or this woman I had grown so attached to.

I walked past the dining hall and approached the doors to the throne room. Guards were talking amongst themselves until they saw me. Six of them moved to their stations as I approached; they each bowed as I walked by where they stood in pairs of two. The last two opened the doors for me, and I walked in. Guards stood at every window and on the upper balcony. There were at least forty of them—equally spaced out in the throne room. Archers looked down from the balcony, and a mix of duel swordsmen and spearmen stood at the ready on the throne-level floor.

The messenger stood in the center of the room, patiently waiting for me, admiring the complex beauty of the chamber. He was a long, skinny man about my age. He was run-down and looked ready to drop. He met me halfway, walking briskly. Red locks surrounded his fine face, high cheekbones, and pointed chin. He had rough facial hair. I gestured with a wave by moving my index and middle fingers forward together toward the guards to indicate they should follow me.

Two guards approached from behind. "Fetch a servant to bring food and drink," I said. "And another to draw a bath and ready a room for this messenger." There was a nod from both of them, followed by the clanking of metal boots as they left the throne room.

"Thank you for the kind service, my king, but there is no time for me to rest. We must leave at once!"

I stepped closer to the messenger, so our noses were practically touching. I waited for him to whisper the bad news to me. He was silent. "I'm ready to hear what you have to say," I said. "Out with it."

"Your father has traveled past the Owl Kingdom, but he is stuck in polar bear territory," he whispered. "The ruler of the Bear Clan will not let him through unless he goes through the gladiator pit, with the ruler's son, to prove his worth.

"Every heir to the throne must go through trials to succeed as Bear Clan leader. The last challenge is the gladiator pit, in which the heir chooses a warrior from another clan or kingdom. He has chosen to fight your father. There has long been a jealous rivalry between the Bear Clan and your father's kingdom. Your father is skilled, but he is not young anymore. You must ride for the Bear Clan's lands right away and take your father's place in the pit. As long as it's an heir-to-heir battle, a substitution can be made.

"Your father has pleaded for a two-week training period before he faces the pit. He has done so to give you time to get there. It is a ten-day ride to the cold lands of the Bear Clan. I ask this in the swiftest way I can, my king. Your father will not survive against the 2200-pound son of the clan's leader. Bayard has told me what a skilled fighter you are. And how quick you are. The Bear Clan is powerful but not known for agility. We need your speed."

The messenger bowed deeply and took a step back. I bit my lip and walked to a window. I rubbed my chin as I watched the birds on the marble windowsill.

The rose bushes in the garden lay just beyond them, before the gate that surrounded the palace. Servants came in with food and drink. The mid-day meal was about to begin. The messenger took some bread and dried meat. He put them together and inhaled the food with the hunger of someone who had not eaten in days, sat down on the marble floor, and took a deep breath of satisfaction.

I walked into the dining hall, his words replaying in my head. My plate was filled with fruits and vegetables from the mountainside. There was rabbit meat—roasted in a brick oven and thinly sliced, presented with an orange glaze. Normally, I wouldn't hesitate to eat. Eating alone always bothered me, especially in the vast dining hall. It was just me with the servants standing nearby—waiting for me to finish—and guards standing every ten feet around the perimeter of the hall.

But my nose ignored the pleasant smell of the feast. I read the letter over and over again. A guard leaned over my shoulder. I put the letter next to my plate as he whispered that someone was at the main door asking for me. I rose to my feet and walked with the letter in hand. The main doors of the palace opened at the sound of my footsteps. The large, carved, wooden doors opened, and a face appeared in the gap.

It was Sir Thomas from the stables. He held Donte's reins in one hand; the horse was saddled and ready to go. I smiled half-heartedly and patted Donte between his ears. His eyes were bright and aching for action. I feel the flicker of his muscles as his tail whipped back and forth. The two pikemen who always stood guard against the door approached me.

I looked back at them and spoke loudly so that the whole courtyard would hear. "Men, I am sure the news has circulated by now that my father is undergoing a trial. I have decided to take his place in the pits and fight the Bear Clan's heir to form alliances for what is to come."

Frankly, I had no idea what was to come, but it sounded good to say, so I kept rolling with it. "I am to travel with a small company of men. Who is willing to ride with me?"

The pikemen brothers dropped to their knees and bowed their helmets to the ground, ready to rise when I called them. A few other soldiers came around as well. This was a great sight to see, but I felt as though I were abandoning my post—abandoning the people of the kingdom. Who would make the necessary decisions now? Bayard was called "the heart of the king" for a reason. *He* should be here. Now I was scrambling to find someone to monitor things while I was gone for who knows how long.

Or I might die. It had been so long since I fought like a ruthless killing machine. I was thankful I would have a couple of days to retrain my body before getting into the pit. I didn't know what the right thing to do was. My father had told me to stay put and take care of our people. I needed help. I looked at the pikeman brothers.

"Rise," I commanded. They rose and looked me in the eyes. I rested my hands on their shoulders. "While I am away, you must not open the palace door to anyone. Unless something unexpected happens, in that case, bring in all the women and children. Bring everyone else around the palace. I will leave tomorrow morning. Before I leave the kingdom, I will give a speech to the farmers, which I will hold toward the bottom of the mountain."

The brothers nodded in agreement. I sent them back to their posts and motioned the men who would journey with me to come into the palace for preparations. When the doors closed to the war room, six faces greeted me. This was a good start; it would be a mistake to travel in a heavy-plated knight's formation.

I asked my first question. "Who has ever traveled to the lands of the Bear Clan?"

All the hands went up. "That is good to see. I will depend on your knowledge to provide me with the layout of the clan's boundaries and possible exits, in case things turn sour."

The knights nodded in unison.

The war room had four different tables scattered throughout it. Each one had an indented wooden path attached to it. It gave the impression that a large star was carved on the floor. At the center was a table that represented our kingdom; I knew this because a replica of the palace was placed on a mountain on the far edge of the map, along with the lower lands and the forest, which were depicted clearly on the geographic map. There were details etched into the passages and carvings in the mountain I never knew existed. I would have to do some exploring when I got back.

A large forest was settled on the west side of the kingdom, just as it was in reality. One of the knights went over to the miniature's south wall. A lever stuck out of the ground, attached to a large gear system of sorts. All pieces intertwined on the outer edge of the entire room. They only stopped at the door. The knight pulled the lever. The gears moved and locked into place with one another and started to turn. The tables rattled for a millisecond and then rotated — some counter-clockwise, others clockwise.

They moved toward the center table, which was also rotating. The tables closed against each other, and the room fell silent again. The knights moved over to the table at the far end of the room, which I guessed held the Bear Clan map. I walked over—the last one to show up.

A knight by the name of Joseph started talking. He was an older knight with scars scattered across his cheeks. He looked as though he had experienced some close calls.

"My lord, it's a smart idea to shed our armor before making this journey tomorrow," he said.

I looked at the map. It was a land of white—some dark spots highlighted rock formations. The knight pointed out various areas across the map. "The high rock formations would make a good stop to drop off some supplies if things get hot at the pit. And we can place a second-team here." He pointed to a small cave system a couple of miles from the kingdom.

A massive lodge stuck out of the face of a mountain; the entire kingdom was enclosed like a basin surrounding narrow peaks.

"The Bear Clan is known for its ruthless guards and vulgar torture methods. We will be watched the moment we enter the kingdom. If any private words need to be shared, I suggest we do it at nightfall while the majority of the guards are distracted by the pit games. The games will commence the week before we arrive. Then the pits will be cleaned until they are spotless and hollowed out again for the final match against you, my lord."

I nodded, looking at the ice-shaped pit. The Bear Clan's palace overlooked it from an outer deck hanging off the mountain's side.

Dolton jumped into the conversation. He was young—around my age—and fresh out of knight training. He was smart and observant; I could tell this from how he watched Joseph gesture to all the possible hideaways, enemy attacks, and plan B protocol.

Dolton instructed with a calm voice. "This is where we will camp. The lodge is large enough to house all of us, but the Bear Clan is superstitious about pit fights and won't allow knights to accompany you. Rest assured, my lord, I have an idea of how we can be at your side for anything we haven't anticipated. Servants are allowed to follow the king—to send messages back and forth between your father and yourself.

"I figured we could use this to our advantage. The Bear Clan knows the faces of most of our knights since many of us trained in those peaks. All but myself. The knight group before me discontinued the peak mountain training when the Bear Clan began to make their tests more gruesome than necessary. After all, it was supposed to be survival training, not a series of funerals. Their elder trainers won't know my face. I will dress as your servant and be by your side if you need my aid or messages relayed to the rest of the knights."

I nodded in approval. Joseph and Dolton went back and forth in a discussion of sleep schedules, eating, and training. The meeting lasted almost five hours. After the final details had been discussed I felt a lot better about entering the Bear Clan's kingdom.

Morning came, and the knights were ready at the main gate. Sir Thomas brought the mounts up all at once. He truly was a horse whisperer. Donte didn't need to be led; he knew a journey was about to begin. I wouldn't have been surprised to learn he'd dreamed about it. Dolton came forward dressed as a palace servant. He still had his weapons strapped to his horse, but without the knight's armor, he could easily pass for one of the help.

However, he wasn't stocky like the rest of them. His frame was narrow, and his limbs long. He had short, dark brown hair and narrow eyes. His fingers were long and could easily wrap around my wrists one and a half—or even two—times. He addressed me with a quick bow before reaching out to his horse. The rest of the knights, including Joseph, stripped out of their armor as well. Instead, they wore knights' cloaks in the king's colors.

I knew we would have to cross the desert I had almost died in before we reached the harsh, colder lands. Multiple fur coats were stuffed into everyone's side saddles. An additional group was going to ride behind us. They would leave tomorrow and drop off supplies at the plan B station we had decided upon the night before. They were ordered to hide everything, then return to the kingdom.

I called Donte over and unsheathed my blade. It was cold to the touch. But the energy remained alive in the blade. What strategy would I use to drop a 2200-pound beast with thick fur, claws, and teeth? I would have to watch out for those teeth; that was for sure.

The knights mounted, and the crowd parted so we could ride through. Countless hands brushed my legs, and flowers and grasses were thrown at us. I felt strong, healthy and ready for another journey. Nevertheless, a sadness settled in me as the large gates to the kingdom closed, and we found ourselves looking down at the mist-filled mountain path that led into the desert. We rode rather quickly through the mist, without even resorting to asking Tamara for her aid.

We hit the desert sand in a matter of hours. Then, we slowed down to a steady stride and kept up the pace so the horses' hooves wouldn't be burned by the scorching sand. We passed the tree where I was found. A single crow's feather blew across our path and was carried away on the back of the afternoon's desert wind.

We reached the desert's halfway point in three days, but we still had a long way to go. While we rested one evening, I looked to the east and saw the forest outline that Donte must have carried me from when I fell ill. I brushed his neck as he rested his head on my lap. The knights did the same thing to their horses after having watched me do so the past couple nights. Late night conversations would start under the vast sky of stars, keeping just enough light around us to see the outline of the trees in the distance and any abnormal figure that may try to ambush us. The camp slept soundly every night—myself included.

Every day, the heat japed our energy levels. The game was scarce, but luck was on our side. We always had enough food, and hay was packed for the horses; we rationed, and they didn't eat much. For the most part, they drank water from the small puddles we settled near at night.

I was the last to fall asleep, often thinking about Evelynn and how she was doing. I wondered if she was all right in the cold climate. I laughed at the thought of her beating the piss out of some rude bear who thought he could take her on.

Dolton was always the first to wake. He would gather wood from the bare trees that were scattered across the land, then return with a couple of bundles for the next time we made camp. He was playing the part of a servant to the extreme. While we were riding side by side, he admitted that he wanted to be as convincing as possible. The Bear Clan was known for not tolerating liars and cheats. With that in mind, I was thankful for how seriously he took his role.

CHAPTER 5

~~~~~~~~~~~~~~~~~~~~~~~~~~~~~~~~~~~~~~

trial by ice

We arrived in the Bear Clan's territory half a day early. We stopped at the plan B site and put on our extra layers. It was freezing. I put a coat on Donte, and the knights followed my lead. I sent Dolton ahead to let the king know we were coming shortly—after all, he was playing a servant, so I figured I should reinforce that as much as possible to protect him. Without hesitation, he disappeared into the lightly falling snow.

We rode after him a couple of hours later. His tracks were still fresh when the gates of the Bear Clan's kingdom came into view. There was a gentle snowfall. If I were here for any other reason, I wouldn't have minded dismounting and exploring the scenery. It was a beautiful place. Too bad, it was ruled by a ruthless Clan. Gates made of pure ice created a blurred picture of the kingdom; the ice was virtually transparent. The doors opened, and large heaps of snow fell in front of us. A horn blared to announce our presence, followed by the tread of heavy approaching the gates.

This was the first time any of them seen me before—other than the messenger who had been at the dinner with my father a few years ago. Being tired from the journey was an understatement. I was in the midst of falling asleep when Donte stopped at a massive stone lodge.

It made my kingdom's main building look like a stable. It was built on the side of the great mountain. The entire village was surrounded by a chain of small mountains. We had ridden into a basin that had only one exit. If we had to escape, it was not going to be a space we could leave at the last moment. I couldn't believe the size of this place.

The snow continued to fall as my knights circled me, and, as one, we walked up the icy steps. Large doors made of stone stood in front of me. Two guards guarded the main entrance. It took both of the large polar bears to open just one side of the door. To my amazement, it also took another two pulling on it from the other side. An older looking polar bear stepped into our path.

I could tell it wasn't much warmer inside the great house. The breath of the elder bear gave that away. He spoke with a snarl barely masked by his words. "Please hand over your weapons. We can't have you enter otherwise."

The captain looked at me. I nodded my head, approving the request to hand over our weapons. The rest of the knights did so in unison. Dolton had anticipated this might happen and suggested we carry a small throwing knife in our fur boots. We handed everything, but the small unidentified blades over to the guards. It wasn't until the bear nudged me that I handed over my twin swords, my daggers, and my throwing knives. I kept one knife inside my boot, just in case.

The halls were decorated in red and gray. Large, gray stone tunnels spread out through the great house. All of the kingdoms were connected by a series of tunnels. It was a vast network. The Bear Clan's leader knew what was going on at all times without ever having to leave his fortress.

I looked up. Two more floors were yet unexplored. There was a large animal carcass on the table to my left. There was seating available for six or seven polar bears. For men of my size, we could have fit twenty men around the table easily.

A large gathering was taking place. I saw other humans around the house, but they seemed to be of lower rank. Slaves. It was sad and disrespectful to witness. I could feel my men's tension. I walked out of pace and rested my hand on the captain's shoulder. He slowed down so I could have his ear.

"Keep your guard up," I whispered. The captain grazed his right eyebrow with a hand. The rest of the men saw the mute signal and tightened the circle around me. This gave me some strength and support in my limbs. It was freezing. If a fight did break out, it wouldn't last long in this weather. We needed to warm up. My instincts were taking in everything. This world was new and uncertain. I couldn't believe the end of our journey had led us to such a cold-hearted place.

The throne room was nothing short of dull. It was carved from a single large boulder on which a massive bear sat. He was twice as large as the rest of the bears around us—some of whom were feasting, standing guard, and whispering about us. Regardless, every single one of them had one eye on us and one eye on their battle-axes. Most wore silver armor. Very few wore red, which I guessed meant they were the select few who made up the royal guard. These bears were around the throne.

As if that large bear needed to be protected. He looked like the mother of all the little bears who gathered around him like children. He was blind in one eye and had a mark of red paint in the shape of a half-moon stamped on his forehead to indicate his leadership. Their symbol for a crown, perhaps?

After walking for what seemed like half a mile, we finally stood at the steps of the throne. The leader of the Bear Clan had flakes of gray and black in his fur. He was the only bear in the room whose pelt wasn't pure white. His voice echoed off the rock walls. It hurt my sensitive ears. I could feel his vocal cords vibrate throughout the great hall.

"Welcome, young king. I have been wanting to meet you for some time now, especially after what my messenger said after visiting your kingdom."

The old bear struggled to move out of his throne. He was slow, but I could tell by his large muscle that he shouldn't be taken for lazy. I wondered how old he was. My curiosity was taking over now, but I was raised by my father in another time and the world and taught to be respectful to all walks of life.

My body was frigid, but I made an effort to bow to the old bear. My knights followed me, their movements in sync with my own. The hall fell silent, and I could feel the vibrations of the large paws of the bear as he tackled each step until he and I were on the same level of ground. I had thought he was massive from a distance, but now that he was toe to toe with me, his size took my breath away. He bowed to me as my head strained to look up at him.

Although I wore no crown, the respect he showed me made the entire hall bow to me and my knights.

His voice thundered again as he spoke. "Sainath, correct? It is a pleasure to meet you. Forgive me, my memory is not what it used to be, but I am wise in my old age and have learned much from times of war and peace alike. I am the ancient ruler of this clan. If you don't know what that means, I suggest you visit the witch who lives at the edge of your kingdom. She can fill you in on who the ancient leaders are. I have prepared rooms for you and your knights. Don't worry, and they are much warmer than the rest of my house."

A chuckle rose throughout the hall. The polar bears raised their chins to the rock ceiling with a tickle in their ribs.

"Silence!" The old bear raised his voice until it was a barely contained roar. "Forgive me, young king. My followers were not raised with as much respect as the old clans were. Please get settled and join me in the feast hall. I will have dinner prepared for you and your men."

He bowed again and rested his hind paws by dropping on all fours. He was as long as he was tall, covering my entire group when he landed on all fours so that we vanished behind him. The walls echoed with each step that he took, resounding until he disappeared into the tunnel behind his throne. A couple of the red-marked, armored polar bears walked down from the throne and motioned for us to follow them.

The knights fell into position around me like a theater curtain falling to conceal a stage from the audiences view as we started to walk. I was concealed from the crowd again, just as I had been when I first entered the great house of the leader of the Bear Clan.

The tunnels were of pure ice. They looked transparent, but the images I saw through them were blurred past recognition. Then, I saw the end of the tunnel where there was a row of human-sized doors. Doors of beech wood. A human slave waited to greet us.

One of the guards who had led us this way said, "This is the king's quarters. The rest of you will find your accommodation in the hall."

My captain and I exchanged looks as my men departed. The formation broke apart in a millisecond as I entered my quarters. The door closed behind me.

The warmth was a shock to my body. Even the floors were heated. The black stones felt lukewarm against my boots. I unlaced my boots and felt the warmth on my frost-bitten feet. They burned intensely. A large bed of dark wood and cream bedding was fitted with the large furs of animals I did not recognize — a single window-lined the room just above my headboard. Outside, the snow was still falling in a gentle wind.

A giant tub was right next to my bed. The steam from the freshly drawn bath made me smile. I stripped quickly and lowered myself into the near-boiling water. My muscles retracted and relaxed several times.

Once my body was fully warmed, a knock sounded at my door. I reached for my left boot, where I had left it at the edge of the tub and slipped the throwing knife into the bathwater, clasping it tightly.

"Come in," I said.

It was one of the slaves. He was dressed in nothing but a gray overcoat. I looked down at his feet; they were frostbitten to the core. The nerve endings looked dead, and the entire cell reproduction cycle had probably gone completely numb. I could strike his feet with my swords, and he wouldn't even feel it.

He entered with his head down. A breath of cold air evaporated in my warm chamber.

"My king is ready for you to join him for dinner this evening. Do you need help getting dressed?" He held fresh robes in the colors of my kingdom; the purple was a little off, but I supposed I couldn't help but be grateful for the effort the old bear had gone to in showing me this comfort.

I told the slave to wait outside as I exited the tub and dried off. My mind gave way to a flashback as he closed the door. I saw myself in the slave trade. The men with tall hats appeared, then the woman in the white dress, holding her bone cane. Her evil smile and devilish eyes pierced through my vision. I shook the image from my mind and dressed, thinking of the moves she had made on me. She had been old but moved quickly. It was the last time I would ever underestimate someone because of age. I wondered if the old bear had the same quickness to his movements. Was he hiding great strength—trying to seem fragile?

I got dressed and left my room. The slave and two of the Bear Clan's guards accompanied me to the dining hall. We took the tunnel back to the throne room, then walked past the giant chair and through another tunnel across the chamber. It wound behind the throne room. There were no doors that led to the dining hall, just an arch of ice.

I bowed deeply to the old bear, who sat in a massive chair just inches smaller than his throne. A large, stone fireplace was lit near my seat. My knights were standing—waiting on me, no doubt. I sat down, and they did the same. The old bear clapped his paws together. The movement was so forceful; the air hit me even across the 50-foot table that divided us. The doors behind him opened, and the food was brought to the tables. Plates were nowhere to be seen. Instead, we were given crude bowls. They had been hollowed from stone. Or small boulders, more likely. There were no utensils.

I felt like a child at the adult's table. To pick up the drinking mugs, you had to wrap both hands around them, for both the weight and the height of each mug was formidable.

The feast was oversized, just like everything else around us. We ate our fill, and it seemed like we hadn't even made a dent in the food. The good news was, we could talk at a normal volume because the chatter, laughter, and eating were loud enough from the other side of the table that we quickly realized it was a useful opportunity to check in with one another. We could do so without worrying about being overheard.

I knew bears had poor vision and excellent hearing, so we didn't talk about my father, though I wanted to. I was in the old bear's kingdom now; I shouldn't speak up too soon. I was in a precarious position. This kingdom didn't care for outsiders. That much had been evident as soon as we had arrived.

Eventually, the old bear rose, wiping his paws in his fur. He spoke across the table. "Sainath, I hope you and your knights enjoyed the meal. Now that we have eaten our fill let's discuss the real reason you are here."

I perked up. My eyes widened at the realization that he was finally about to reveal my father's location. I nudged the captain—who sat at my right—and he wiped his eyebrows once again. All the men rose in their chairs. The tension in the room was palpable.

"Your father, King Gregory, is being held just beneath the pits. He does not stand a chance against my son. I thought about letting him go since we are allies. However, it is a tradition as old as time that anyone who crosses my kingdom, which is not a polar bear must pay honor to my people. My people enjoy entertainment same as anyone. They enjoy some gladiator sport, is all. From one king to another—You know how important the people are, right?"

I cleared my throat and spoke. "I do understand what you are saying, and if I understand correctly, I may fight your son in my father's place. Is that right?"

"Yes, young king. That is true. And as you are here, I should tell you my name. I am an ancient ruler—this is true. I was here before names became of any importance. But since you are going to battle my son to death, I will tell you just before you enter the gladiator pit."

"What does it matter what your name is, my king?" I spoke with a questioning look on my face. He knew *mine*.

"I will tell you in due time, young king. Now get some rest. You will have exactly one day to train and no more. If you want to make the most of it, I suggest you stay up all night in the pit, training. This fight won't be easy. My son is the best fighter we have—well, one of the best fighters we have. You see—look around you."

I scanned the room. All I saw were the white flanks of polar bears. Some were armored while the rest were sitting at the table, along with the royal guard in red, the members of which sat with the old bear. I gave the king another questioning look.

He laughed, and he stood, this time with ease. He took a deep breath and shouted, so his voice reached the roof of the grand dining hall. "Every polar bear, male or female, is my child. Hahaha!"

My eyes went wide as I scanned the room more closely. It all made sense now. This was why they all looked so similar.

"Now you understand how ancient I am? I have lived over a millennium. Countless of your kind's lifespans. Your very existence is a stench in the air." His voice grew calmer; he spoke in a quieter tone while walking. Then he got back on all fours and looked over his shoulder, stopping under the ice arch.

"If you have the fight in you, head down to the pit tonight. Otherwise, you have all day and night tomorrow. I have told my guards to let you roam wherever you like. Even though you may—and probably will—die against one of my sons, you and your father are still my guests. My chefs and servants, as well as my royal guard, will treat you as one of my own." He walked out on all fours, his royal guard trailing behind him.

I sighed in relief. There was no trap. Yet.

My captain spoke up. "Sainath, if you are willing to train tonight, I will accompany you—"

I cut him off just as quickly as he had spoken and walked out of the dining room. The knights surrounded me again, and the house guards tailed us. I walked at a slow pace and went to my quarters, but whispered to the captain to follow me inside. The knights misdirected the Bear Clan's royal guard; then, they spread out to cover the space the captain had been moments before.

I slid past my door with the captain at my heels. Without any suspicion, the rest of the knights continued down the hall to their quarters. I pressed my index finger to my lips to signify to my knights, quite strictly, the importance of remaining alert. I didn't trust the old bear, whatever his name was. It didn't matter.

With a simple, two-handed gesture, I pointed to the captain and myself. I then made an oval shape with my hands to indicate the gladiator pit.

For the duration of our travels, when the camp had been set up, and dinner was eaten, we would sit around a roaring fire practicing our signals. If the captain or I wiped our brows, the knights would know to be suspicious of their surroundings. It meant that they should "pull the curtain on the king." In other words, the circle would collapse around me. Other signs included double tapping my chest and lightly scratching it with my fingers. To anyone beyond my circle, it would look like I was scratching an itch, but all the knights knew this as a signal to look for an exit—and fast. Beyond those three, no other gesture mattered. All that mattered was what signal we ended with. I could scratch myself silly, and it wouldn't mean a thing.

The captain and I spoke in silence for some time, deciding the exit signals. Eventually, I shook him off. We didn't have time for a full conversation in sign language, so I grabbed some cloth and a piece of cold charcoal from the fireplace on the far side of my room. I wrote in short bullet points. My head started to pound, and I realized that if I wrote in my style, he may not recognize the language. Come to think of it, I hadn't written anything since I arrived in this world. I made it simple by using words I knew he would know. "Exit" was number one on my list, while my second instruction was to find out the rotation of the guards imprisoning my father. The third bullet, I had to ponder. I played with the charcoal in the fingers, turning it over several times, until it made the tips of my fingers black.

I wrote it down quickly. He gave me a puzzled look but nodded in agreement. I threw the scrap in the fire, and it reignited the small flames. I motioned for him to wait until the hallway was clear, then to exit my chambers. I peeked out from my door.

The slave was standing across from it. When he saw me open it, he sprang to life. I acted quickly and opened it just enough that my face was revealed but the rest of my chamber remained hidden.

"Please go down to the knight's chamber and ask for the captain to come see me. I must have a word with him."

The slave nodded. "Certainly, Your Majesty."

I watched as he walked down the hall and disappeared into the darkness. I motioned the captain to leave the room and watched him stick to the wall's shadows. None of us had armor on, so it was easy to blend into the dark walls and not be seen. He would be safe.

I closed the door and sat down on the bed, watching the fire fight to stay alive. I threw a couple of logs onto it. The chamber was still pretty warm. There was ancient technology here, but these were modern times. This was a kind of technology from my time.

The knock came soon after. I opened it to find the slave. He had returned with the captain. "Found him, Your Majesty. He was just leaving the lavatory."

I gave the slave my thanks and closed the door on him.

"I spoke louder than I needed to, in order to make sure we didn't raise the suspicions of anyone listening in. "Captain, I think I will train tonight. Ready the men."

The captain helped me don my armor. While he was reaching for the heavy armor, I tried to tell him off, but he was insistent. "But my king, the polar bears are known for their brute strength. If you are not wearing any armor, one wrong slam could end you. And I am not about to carry two dead kings home."

I smiled at the captain's acting. I applauded silently, and he smiled.

A loud knock resounded through the door's wood. I knew the knights were tired from the journey and the heavy meal in their bellies. I ordered whoever was at the door to come on in. The captain finished strapping my fur boots to my feet and tying the cuffs at my wrists.

A large bear entered. He ducked his head, but was able to squeeze into the room, which was dwarfed by his presence. He was part of the royal guard, by the look of the red half-moon on his armor.

"Young king, your servant had notified us that you are training tonight instead of tomorrow?"

I nodded in approval. The bear opened the door, and I walked out. We were joined by other members of the old bear's guard. I was covered in fur from head to toe, but it was just about the only thing that was going to keep me warm in the pit. I had a feeling the pit would be made of solid granite or something. Maybe a giant meteor. That would be really cool. We stopped outside the knights' chamber. The captain entered and closed the door behind him. I could hear the clatter of armor as they threw their garments about, pretending they were rushing to get dressed, when in reality they had known this was the plan all along. We agreed that if the old bear gave us extra time at the pit, we would be prepared.

They knew I wasn't going to wear armor. They all knew I was a killer—they had seen it. This wasn't our first adventure together. I stood, breathing calming, satisfied with my men.

The door opened, and there they were. The royal bear looked astonished at how quickly the men had geared up, even though they had had an hour to do so, in secret.

We walked to the end of the hall and back outside. The snow had stopped falling. I was a little cold, but I knew once I started training, I would warm up quickly. It was the darkest I had ever seen this world. Only bright stars lit out path. The bears moved silently across the snow. While our feet sank into the snow, the bears' seemed to hover over it. We were definitely on their turf. If anything were to happen, fighting in daylight would be our best option. I had to focus on my hearing just to pick up the long scrape of fur against snow, each time their paws lifted. Other than that, they walked almost as though they were invisible.

The houses were dark and plain; they looked dark gray and black due to nighttime conditions. The gladiator pit was at the edge of the kingdom: a shiny oval bowl. The stars' glow bounced off its surface. At the edge of the mountain chain that made up the walls of this kingdom stood the pit. It was twice as large as the Bear Clan's house and three times as tall. Large steel doors opened as a torchlit path guided our path. The royal guard stopped at the door and handed us off to another set of guards.

Just two of them. They were wearing colors of silver and white, and had faces like newborns. They were young. It was easy to tell by their small size. They only stood about a foot taller than the rest of us. We knew we could take these guys on, if it came down to it.

The pit was divided into four levels—the first one was underground, and it held the fighters. Cages of various sizes lined one side of chamber. I could see beasts in them: large cats and vicious, horned animals too. On the opposite wall were other humans who, by the look of it, were fighting but looked like they hadn't seen other humans in a long time. They reached for us as if we were imaginary.

One yelled out, "Are you real!?" as his fingers brushed my shoulder, only to be snapped in half by one of my knights. Poor guy.

I was walking in front. I scanned every prisoner for any sign of my father, but none of them were him. These guys had lost their minds. My memory triggered, and I thought of my own cage at the house of the old woman with the cane. I had sympathy for these prisoners, and if time allowed, I would free them.

We turned a torchlit corner into a space in which no cages stood. Instead, large tables and a prominent staircase rose to the surface of the pit. A cold breeze crept down from the surface and slapped our faces with kisses. One side had random weapons, while the one on the right held all of our weapons. Everything was accounted for—even my knives. I strapped on my two swords and knife belt. Then I gave the signal and training began.

My sparring partner was another human, one of the men from the cages. This was going to be easy. The pit was made of dirt, and smelled of rotten meat and vomit. Torches were brought out. It had been a few years since I had fought like this. I wondered if I still had it.

Ice sculpture dummies were laid out in a random pattern. Torches lined the pit. I looked up at the ceiling, expecting the stars but they had all but disappeared under cloud cover.

The human slave had long hair braided to his ass. There was something familiar about him, but I couldn't put my finger on it. He held a shield in one hand and in the other, a rusty sword. I unsheathed my twin blades of ebony and let them breathe the stench around me. My opponent drew a line in front of him and challenged me to cross is. I accepted. The training was gruesome—just the way I liked it. Before the first fight had even ended, I was covered in blood. I had missed the scratches of blades centimeters away from hitting a vein.

The slave was skilled and displayed amazing footwork along with his quick hands. He would thrash with his shield, then come underneath with his sword to catch me off-guard, aiming for my forearm in an attempt to disarm me. I saw this coming. It was a common move used by bandits and knights alike. I jumped into the air and slammed both my feet on his shield, catching him off-balance. He staggered back but didn't give into defeat. We sparred for a good hour before the bell rang, and the doors opened behind me.

It was then that I realized who my sparring partner was. That long hair and those deep-set eyes should have given him away, but no—it was his footwork and the fact that he drew a line and dared me to cross it that made me realize he was an assassin like me, trained in the same style. He was one of the three who had walked out of that evil virus of a place where we had been trained to kill.

As the bell stopped ringing, I remembered that I had left him on that hill overlooking the creepy barn. His mind must be long gone. It seemed he was doing exactly what he had been trained to do. Exactly what *we* had been trained to do. I turned away, thinking of how I could fit him into my plans for freedom.

I looked back at him. I knew he could hear my whisper. "If I can, I will free you again, old friend."

The slave's ears pricked up at my familiar voice. *He remembered me.*

Just then, the old bear walked out on all fours. He gazed over at the slave gladiator, who dropped his shield and sword, then knelt in the dirt to demonstrate the deepest respect for the old bear.

The old bear came toward me, turning his back to the slave. "I was watching you for some time. I was resting when I heard you wanted to train tonight. You surprise me, young king. You have some skill to your fighting as well. Come, let's go see your father."

I sheathed my swords and followed him back underground. My knights stood on the right side where our weapons had been laid out. They followed me. I was armed and so were my men. I wondered if the old bear knew. I could sense the eyes of the captain inches away. We walked in a tight rectangle that didn't have a back wall. As if it needed it. We walked in unison. My days as a prince had served me well because it had taught me to walk with our fellow men. To hold your character in a room full of strangers. I think it was a good thing that I had given in to my role wholeheartedly.

We turned a blind corner that led to another set of steps, then to a single dug-out cavern. One torch was lit at the end of the room. It was damp but warmer than the gladiator floor. This cave setting kept a constant temperature. It was almost too warm for me. I was dripping sweat with each step.

My father had his back to the light. He was sitting in a wooden chair. Neither chains nor guards were around. The knights stood at attention when my father rose and came into the light. His glamorous, deep purple robe dragged on the clay floor. I had not seen him for a couple years now.

He hadn't been beaten. In fact, he looked happy and well fed, judging by the vigor in his walk as he moved toward me.

"My son, you have come. Thank you."

I only nodded, since I couldn't say much with the old bear in the room. The old bear now spoke out of turn. "Now that the two kings are together again, I will let you get back to training, young king. You will need a few more hours if you think you will stand a chance in the pit with my son."

I looked at the old bear and took in his sheer size. I looked at the ground that he took up. I looked at the men I had. The skill I had on my own. For the first time we had the old bear in the corner instead of us. This could be our best chance to take him and escape. I began to reach for a sword. Just as quickly as I did, a hand was at my forearm. My father's hand pulled my forearm back my side, and he spoke quickly to the old bear.

"Ursa, please let me have a moment alone with my son so I may prepare him for the fight. Last words and encouragement. You know how it is. We have been allies for so many years. And I know how you are about traditions."

The old bear nodded in approval. He took the steps back to the gladiator pit. A couple of the knights took to the entrance while the rest took to the steps, and the captain stayed next to me. The knights faced us, staying in eyeshot. They were ready for a signal of any kind. Using peripheral vision was now second nature to them.

"Sainath, the battle you are about to face will challenge you physically more than anything you've yet experienced. Be ready. I wish I could tell you which son you will be facing, but I'm sure you have learned that the majority of this kingdom is composed of Ursa's own blood."

He took a deep breath and walked past me up the steps. I followed him, my knights staying right behind.

We talked into the early morning about the culture of Ursa's kingdom. How old it really was fascinated me. Ursa was talking to a couple of men with a sheet of paper at the gates of the pit. I wanted to stay and train some more, but sparring with another human wouldn't do much good. I decided a good few hours of sleep would be the best thing for now. After all, my father did say this would be my most physically demanding fight. The sad thing was, he didn't know about the fights I had already been in.

Come to think of it, I didn't think he knew much about my former life as an assassin. I judged almost every bear that I saw in the early morning sun as though they would be my opponent. The fight was scheduled for late in the afternoon close to twilight and would end once one of us fell. If, for some reason, the fight went longer than that, torches would be lit and it would continue on a night floor, whatever that meant. I gave in to sleep as soon as I entered my room. I had a few hours to sleep before I needed to be at the pits.

My father was roaming the grounds under close watch. He wasn't a prisoner, but he didn't have complete freedom either. After all, his mission was to get out of here and ride to the ends of the known world, to where he would meet Evelynn and Bayard. He had called on me to make this happen. I wondered why he sent Bayard and Evelynn ahead of his own party? How strange.

It was a simple test that could end in life or death. I had been promised a fair fight with death as the final option, if my father did something extreme—like trying to escape while I was fighting. That would end in my death, for sure. I knew he wouldn't do that. Would he?

The thought haunted me as I walked to the pit, the captain at my side. The rest of the knights were just where they should be. It was the end of the day by the time I had strapped on the fur gauntlets and shin guards. The fur had been heated over a slow fire. It was toasty against my skin. I started to sweat but was warmed to the bone right away, at least. I was excited to get this over with so I could go home, or possibly, travel with Father. I wouldn't mind seeing Evelynn.

Her face came to me as the pit gates opened. The roars of 120,000 bears bounced off every inch of the colosseum. I had my twin blades—one in each hand—and a tough hide shield wrapped with steel. The other end of the pit held my opponent. But I didn't see anyone there.

I waited for what seemed like an hour. Finally, the crowd stopped roaring and the gates behind me creaked open. I expected my opponent, but instead, it was Ursa. He walked on his hind legs, which was something that he rarely did, gauging by the audience's enthusiastic cheering. Doing so made him look twenty feet tall. He walked on my left side, keeping his one good eye on me as he waved his arms to calm the crowd.

His raspy voice echoed and ached in my ears. "My kin, the entertainment tonight is brought to you by another ally. One who needs to get to where he is meant to be. Too bad we are the connection between the only two roads!"

The crowd erupted into laughter as the old bear raised his arms and moved them like wings to calm them down again. "Because of this fact, we have held the tradition of friendly fighting in this very place for thousands of years, and tonight is no different. The sun is setting. This young king is here to prove himself and to win his father rightful passage out of the kingdom by fighting my son!"

The whole floor started to shake. I widened my stance and raised my shield in defense. I didn't know what was going on. Why hadn't anyone filled me in? Why hadn't my father warned me? About a hundred feet away, the floor collapsed and a white bear standing on a platform rose into the pit.

Ursa smiled at me as he exited the pit. "Good luck, young king. You will need the stamina of a bear to survive this. Win or lose, you and your father are free to go. Remember—this is for my people. Make it interesting, but I warn you, do not kill my son. This is entertainment, not an execution. My son knows the rules as well. This will be a fair fight."

He said this with the gleam of a half smile that flashed briefly, showing nothing but his gum line and an assortment of rotten teeth.

Once the gate had closed behind me, I got a good look at my opponent. He was much bigger than the other bears. He had a shoulder guard strapped to his breast plate but nothing else for armor. He held a battle ax in his right paw. I decided this was it, and I closed the distance between us.

The fight lasted a good hour. The crowd was on their feet the entire time. It seemed never-ending. We each had wounds and had spilt blood on the cold dirt. My father was right about the physicality of this fight. It tested my moves. The counterattacks were the most painful part. My muscles were getting fatigued, and I could feel it. I hadn't fought like this since my years of training against the white-gloved servants.

The palace life had made me soft; that much was easy to see. My knights were on the first level of seats. They were watching me, waiting for a signal to get my father out of there and on his way to Bayard and Evelynn. But what Ursa had said just before he left the pit made me think twice about crossing a leader like him. He had been a king far longer than my father and me combined. Older than any emperor I had read about in my history books.

Then again, I wasn't in the same old world. This place played with time like it was a dance partner: leading, following, and at times, twirling lifetimes around so it became tough to discern what was true and what wasn't. I had fought for gold plenty of times, but not for sport like this.

The battle continued. The heavy axe was wearing my opponent down. He had swung it with grace to begin with, but after spending so much energy, he was getting sloppy with his swings. We were both slowing down.

It was an odd thing, to know that fighting for sport meant that I had to win the crowd over. In truth, they decided the fate of this fight. I only had one sword in hand and no shield. The bear only had his battle axe.

It ended with a single slice. When he swung his axe at my neck, I ducked to my knees and lashed out, overturning my wrists at the last minute to ensure my sword would come at a downward angle, which would cause the most amount of damage. I knew if I took him down low in the legs, I could end this long-ass battle.

We were both tired, and I was fed-up of pleasing this kingdom with my blood. I was doing this for my father, and this bear was fighting for his father as well. Was this a test? For the both of us? Since we were both heirs to our thrones, I wondered if the old kings had decided to have some fun with us. Perhaps they had planned to make it sound like my father was in trouble and needed me to fight for him, but when I arrived, to have me find him in good shape rather than held like a prisoner. I felt like I was a pawn in their game.

The sword struck. I rolled backward, away from the bear as he dropped to one knee. Reaching for the sword he grabbed its handle. He tried to pry it free, but the angle meant it was wedged into his bone. If he pulled up or down or in any other direction, he would cause further damage to the leg's tissue and snap his shin bone in pieces. Unless he pulled it out exactly the way I had inserted it.

He threw his axe at me, and I dodged it. I threw my sword down, signaling that the fight was over.

I knew I had gone too far. But technically, I hadn't ended his life or broken anything. But I had a feeling his people would think that I had broken the rules. I had given them a show. What did Ursa expect? That the fight would last a lifetime?

The crowd fell silent at the bear's whimpering. It was then that I noticed how young he really was. If he were older, he wouldn't have cried like that. I stood up and started to walk toward the bear, to offer a helping hand. I could easily remove the sword so that he would only need a few stitches and a brace to ensure the bone healed properly.

The crowd started to boo me for trying to help him. I offered a hand to the young bear, who was crying out in pain. He pawed me away.

"No! My father said this would be an easy fight. That you had no skill. But here I am, defeated by your hand. Don't you get it? I was supposed to win. Not *you*! You don't know my king like I know him. He would rather kill me than see me as a failure."

The tears continued until I spoke to him. I crouched down. His massive head was the size of four human skulls. One of his eyes was easily half as big as my head alone.

CHAPTER 6

reXXX freedom

I didn't know what to say.

The bells of the pit rang out, bringing life back to the bears watching us. Their chatter filled my ears; the ground shook as Ursa walked out, into the pit. It was dark—the only light provided by torches.

I helped the son up on one knee. Ursa jogged up to us on two legs.

"Remove that sword from his leg. I haven't seen a move that well-executed before. Good for you, young king. Good for you. Medic!" He shouted and the crowd fell silent again.

Four bears came forth from the gate behind Ursa, with a stretcher in their paws. They wrapped the wound, and I grazed the blade along the edge of my fur gauntlet to get the blood off. I would clean it properly later. Ursa's son was taken away. After my wounds had been bandaged by my knights, a ceremony in the main hall brought the court back to life. My father was free to pass through Ursa's kingdom and go about his journey.

As soon as the ceremony was over, Ursa and my father exchanged a few brief words of appreciation and, just as quickly, my father was ready to leave. He was heading to the kingdom where I had fought a creature of pure myth and fantasy. My first brush with death had been against such a creature. Although my work here was done, Ursa urged me to stay one more night, so as to rest before returning to the kingdom.

I politely declined. "I must return to my own kingdom."

He understood my emotionless expression. I was tired of this cold weather.

But there were other reasons. I wanted to ask Father if I could travel with him. However, I knew my father would want me to return to the kingdom. I would rather sleep in the desert. I felt the tension of this kingdom shifting around me, and I no longer felt safe closing my eyes within its walls. After packing, the knights and I walked toward its entrance. To my surprise, Ursa joined us—the knights and myself on horseback, Ursa on all fours. However, I still had to look up slightly to see his face.

"Young king, you fought like a warrior. If you ever find yourself in need of aid you have it. More importantly, as I noted before, you have my respect. I have seen many young kings pass through here and die by mistake. I have seen entire kingdoms burn from within. Be careful, young king. Just because people say you are the king and the son of your father, doesn't mean that you are. May I have a moment in private with you?" Ursa demanded, with a look down at my horse.

I looked ahead at the gates opening before us. The desert air rushed in, mixing with the cold air in my nostrils. The horses got a whiff and grew excited to get their hooves out of the snow. I looked at Orion and gave him the greenlight to continue to the gates. The knights bolted forward with excitement, leaving Donte, me, and Ursa in their path of dust and snow.

When the knights were out of sight, Ursa slowed his pace. I fought to slow down, pushing Donte. I had felt his heart sink at seeing the rest of the horses run to the flat desert where the sun was rising. Sooner than later, Donte settled for my new pace. I let the reins go lax and let the four-legged beasts walk side by side.

Ursa spoke when a couple hundred feet was all that was left dividing his kingdom from the outside world. "When you first arrived in my kingdom, I smelled you at the gate. You smell of something ancient. Of magic. I smelled it once before, about four years ago. A great rift in the sky appeared in a fishing village, many moons from here. Reports said that a young man fell through the sky but didn't hit the water. Not the way most objects that carry weight would. This was different, as though the water itself was expecting the arrival, and a wave came alive and jumped against the current to catch his falling body. Then the rift closed, and the search for the body began. My messenger searched along the shore, but nothing. Then, rumors started to spread about a slave who had been bought, but couldn't speak. He seemed scared from some kind of accident. After a month, the rumors died down, and I had time to think. I decided to send orders to that village, to a man on a farm, asking him to keep an eye out for this particular slave. Every week he would go to the market where a new batch of slaves had been sent in to work the fields and docks. This man bought many slaves for me. Some are still alive—working throughout the kingdom—but none of them turned out to be the one who fell from the sky."

I rode in silence, letting him keep talking. I removed my left hand from his view, lowering it down to my boot to make sure my throwing knife was still there. I pulled out the blade and gripped it tight, keeping it concealed from his view.

"Interesting story, isn't it?" Ursa stopped.

I grabbed Donte's reins and stopped him out of respect for the ancient ruler. I didn't look at Ursa. We were nearing the gates to the point where the snow was giving way to dry land. Here, the path breathed a little; there was dust now, and Donte welcomed it with a snort of his nose. I could see the knights waiting at the gate on the other side—all of them looked on from the corners of their eyes, waiting. Orion faced me directly. I could tell he was wondering why I had stopped. He was waiting for me to tap my chest to signal him to come to my aid. Our reinforcements with Dolton were waiting for us, a mile or so away. If I delayed too long, Dolton would come with the cavalry.

I had to start walking through the gate. The last thing I needed was Ursa seeing Plan B coming after him.

"For sure. It is an interesting story," I said, to get Ursa walking again.

He moved without hesitation, ambling alongside. "Around this time," he continued. "Your father lost his son and sent his most trusted advisor to find him. Bayard, who—did you know—was also a knight? Before his body became old and fat?" Ursa laughed at his own remark.

Meanwhile, I counted the steps with each blink. One hoof after the other.

I spoke only when his laughter had receded. "Don't talk about Bayard like you know him."

"Young king, you are protecting people you *yourself* don't know. Haven't you ever wondered why Bayard picked you, why he brought you back to a kingdom where you clearly don't belong?"

Ursa stopped at the gate's entrance. I could tell the desert heatwave was getting to him because of his suddenly labored breathing. He lowered his head so our gazes were level.

He glared out of his good eye. I tightened my grip on the knife. He spoke through his rotting teeth, his words just above a whisper but still quiet enough that the knights couldn't hear. "Young king, you are a king, but you are also a mistake. You look like King Gregory and have mastered his body language. But have you ever looked at the small differences between the two of you? Let me tell you what I have noticed as I watched you interact in the chamber under the pit. I had to make sure you were the real deal. Gregory's true child is dead. I would know. My assassins killed him—after they killed his wife—but let's keep that our little secret. In the time that you have been here, I have come to believe that you are he who fell from the sky. You may look like Gregory, but you fight too differently. Here's what happened." He narrowed his beady eyes at me and grinned. "Bayard took you in, gave you a label to fill that empty head, and put you into a story in which you don't belong!" With that, he turned around and walked back to his cold-hearted kingdom.

Donte finally bolted through the gates. I didn't stop him. Orion and the knights twisted the horses and jolted into formation behind me. Dolton met us, mounted and ready, but I didn't stop. I pushed Donte even faster across the desert heat. I was furious and had no clue which side of the story to believe. I had thought Bayard was my friend. I had thought the kingdom actually gave a damn about me. I desperately needed answers. I had to go see Asha and nothing was going to get in my way this time. I spoke only when I needed to. I told no one but Orion about the words that had been uttered by Ursa's ancient mouth.

We arrived back at the kingdom, thanked the men for joining us on the journey, and dismissed them along with everyone who had been part of the war. I was alone, looking at the geographic land, touching every groove and dent in it, feeling the reality of it. It all felt so real. The drapes on the windows, the water I had drunk filling my insides. The wounds from the battle. The bed and voices of my people. Was it all an illusion?

I couldn't tell. Orion tried to talk to me as I checked in on the men during training. I sparred with him and opened up about the many questions I had.

He stopped almost instantly when I told him about Bayard. "Come on, Sainath. Don't you think Ursa is just a sore loser? And maybe he's just toying with your emotions as a leader to get you to make a mistake, just so he can get the better of you. I have known leaders like him and have fought men like that myself. It's all a psychological game to distract you while they take advantage."

I signaled that I was done by dropping my wooden sword. Orion did the same. "Either way, I want to go see Asha and see if there is any truth to it."

"You're the king. If it will help to put your mind at ease, then so be it. When would you like to go?"

Orion picked up the swords and put them on the rack behind us. I looked over at the archery kit laid out around us, as he shed his torso armor and hung it on a wooden dummy. He started unbuckling my armor while a couple of servants helped remove my thigh and wrist armor. I couldn't get out of it quick enough.

CHAPTER 7

the heartbreaking truth

Winter had arrived the next morning and with it, Bayard. I wrapped my old friend in a hug and ordered a vast feast in celebration. When the feast had gone well into the night and the dancing had begun, I asked about Evelynn. Orion and the royal knights had forgone their armor in favor of civilian robes. I watched many of my men dance with their wives—who were more than happy to hold their husbands again. Children of all ages danced to the music, seeming to think that being closer to the instruments meant they were better dancers than the rest of us. Orion and his fiancée strolled over as Bayard and I were catching up.

"My king, my fiancée would like a dance with you. If you will permit it, of course." Orion spoke in the most formal way I had ever heard him. Around the civilian population, it was key to remain in character. Consistency was vital to ensuring people felt safe. I stood, set my chalice down, and bowed.

The dance floor was cleared. A light snow fell, and the drapes were drawn to let the winter stars peek into the palace. Orion's fiancée was pretty, with golden locks and freckles scattered across her forearms and cheeks. Deep dimples appeared when she smiled. She wore a cream dress with white pearls framing her neckline. My crown was back on my head as I took her hand into mine and respectfully danced to the music. Orion danced with a little girl while talking to Bayard; the two lingered around my chair.

Orion's fiancée stared at me in awe. "My king, you are light on your feet. Orion says you are a great leader to him and the rest of the knights."

The song hit its chorus before I replied. "Orion makes it easy to lead. He is devoted to training. I feel at times I am learning from him much more than he does from me."

"You are too kind, my king." With the final strums of string instruments, the song came to its resolution. I took her hand and presented her back to Orion, who twirled the little girl one last time, then let her run off to join the other children.

I saw the concern on Bayard's face as I thanked Orion's fiancée for the dance. With a deep curtsey, she thanked me for the dance and my kind words. Orion held himself to his formal methods by bowing deeply, while reaching out his hand. I gave mine to him. He kissed it lightly and shouted as he came back up, loud enough for the whole hall to hear him.

"To the king!"

The crowd erupted with the sound of claps and cups being raised in toast. I lifted my own cup in response and drank with my people. Bayard set his down and walked over the fireplace. I walked over without raising suspicion. The people of the kingdom knew Bayard was the right hand to the king. I looked into the flames. The inner cape of my robes turned from dark to light purple in their light, which jumped around the fireplace.

"Bayard. How is Father, and where is Evelynn? I thought she was traveling with you."

Bayard didn't look away from the fire. "She decided to remain behind and ride back with your father. She's a better fighter than I am. A messenger arrived a few days before you father did, and gave us a detailed retelling of your fight. Well done, Sainath. I had no idea you were such a skilled warrior. You should have seen Evelynn question the messenger to make sure he was talking about our Sainath! She misses you. She wanted me to tell you she will be back in spring at the latest, as winter makes it difficult to travel in these mountains."

I nodded at the flames and released a breath of relief. It reached the fire and made the flames jump. "I'm glad to hear that she is well. I was getting worried. I will send a messenger to her as soon as we can. And Bayard, there is something you should know. Something that Ursa said, that's been bothering me ever since I returned here. I just haven't had time to deal with it as I had duties to attend to which had accrued in my absence. You know how it goes."

"That I do, my young king, that I do. Come, I want to show you something."

Bayard walked out of the hall and turned toward the throne room. I signaled to Orion to carry on the festivities, and raced after Bayard. Dolton met me at the door, ready to stand by my side. He would make a great royal knight one day. He already had the instincts of a seasoned knight. "My king, is everything okay?" he said from the doorway.

"Yes. Please join the others and let Orion know to watch over the people. I will be back soon. Make sure everyone returns home safely. It has been snowing for some time. Summon the carriages to take the children home. Thank you, Dolton."

Dolton disappeared to speak with Orion. I waited to make sure the message was relayed. Orion gave me a nod from across the room. I nodded in acknowledgement and left with Bayard at my side.

"Get dressed. We are going outside."

He looked pretty determined. I dressed in my winter garments and reached for my swords which rested on the chair in my room, but Bayard knocked and entered before I had given him the okay to do so. "You won't need those. Come quickly."

"Everything okay, Bayard?"

"Yes." He smiled his heartfelt smile and motioned for me to follow.

We greeted the knights at the door. The pikemen brothers talked to Bayard for a bit, hugged him, then let us outside. The snow mixed with the wind from the mountain and swirled in the night sky as we walked past his home.

"How is your wife? I didn't get a chance to speak with her at the party. She had her hands full, telling stories and making sure everyone was well fed."

"That's my wife," Bayard responded. The wind picked up as our elevation increased. As the palace disappeared out of sight, Bayard met my pace and finally said what was really on his mind.

"You should know—you are not the son of King Gregory. When you arrived here, let me guess what happened to you. Stop me if you have heard this before. You were unconscious after the plane went down. You woke up here, in a world you did not understand."

"Bayard, how do you know that?"

Bayard kept walking, until we reached the north side of the kingdom. It was night. The brightest stars I had seen since arriving illuminated the sky. Bayard ignored my question. The moon was bright and much larger than I had ever seen it.

"After that, I'm sure you noticed markings on your arms and got spooked by what might have happened to your body." I nodded again, but he didn't need to look directly at me to know I was agreeing with him. He kept his old blue eyes trained on his feet. His breathing became heavy as we started to climb the mountain.

"The marks, I'm sure, went away before you could really examine them, and then, before you knew it, you found yourself in the slave line. Surrounded by others. Sold to eldritch creatures you had never seen before."

I stopped and looked at him, but he kept walking. "Bayard, there were only humans. I only saw creatures when I arrived *here*, or close to here, I suppose."

Bayard stopped and looked down from his incline on the mountain. Twenty paces separated us, but it felt like a whole lifetime now. I wondered what he was trying to tell me. Ever since he had gotten back from the other kingdom, our interactions had felt shallow, stilted even. Perhaps he didn't think I was doing a sufficient job of maintaining the kingdom.

"Sainath. You were given that name at birth, correct?"

I nodded as he waited for me to catch up.

He continued with his story. "After a remarkable turn of slavery, you were knocked out by something you cannot understand. The air was heavy and your mind faint from the newness of it all. Our minds have this fascinating trick when we need familiarity in foreign places... they need something to latch onto, to find comfort. But you found something, didn't you?"

"If you are talking about the peasants, then yes. They took me in and realized there was more to me than the collar around my neck."

Bayard stopped me and turned my shoulder so I was forced to face him. "Once a slave, always a slave, Sainath."

I narrowed my eyes at him, turned, and resumed walking. "You're wrong. They gave a damn about me in this new world. A chance to start over."

"And where exactly are you?"

"I don't know exactly," I admitted. "Someplace during a different time period, I suppose. Am I dead, Bayard?"

"See, that's a tough question to answer. Let me finish, and I will leave you to figure that one out on your own."

I nodded and we continued ascending the mountain. I could make out a figure ahead.

It was Tamara, no doubt about it.

"After the peasants—who I'm sure let you go fearing for your safety—you decided to turn in the opposite direction and return to the very town that had put you in shackles in the first place..."

I nodded; I couldn't argue with that. The peasants had let me go and told me to head east, but I had retraced my steps.

Now, a deep breath took the place of words. "Please stop me when you hear this."

I pressed my lips and kept walking toward Tamara's shimmering figure.

"You were keen enough to know you wanted to do something—to prove yourself. A dark energy called you to a house on a hill, overlooking the town. The gate was open to you, and more bizarrely, the front door?"

"All right, yes. I felt that it was a bit odd that everything had just fallen into my lap. Is that what you want to hear?" I spoke louder than I had anticipated I would.

A couple breaths later and we were face to face with Tamara. Our beards had frozen into fine icicle threads. It made our faces resemble a frozen sun with rays spreading in various directions. The left side of my mouth was starting to crack in the cold. I had been licking blood from my lips for the past five minutes. My lower lip was raw and felt tingly.

"Hello, young man, and hello, Bayard," said Tamara. "Thank you for doing this. I know it is not an easy burden to bear. Please, come in from the white winds."

A massive fire erupted right behind her, and wooden chairs fell into place around it, followed by small game appeared on a spit. The ice started to melt from my hair. I could hear the water from the roasting squirrel sizzle as the moisture of its skin dripped into the flames, then evaporated in their immense heat.

"Take a seat, warm up, and for goodness sake—Bayard. Hurry up with your story, or I will finish it for you."

Bayard stepped forward so he was nose to nose with Tamara. I never noticed how big Tamara was. She was taller than any man, but I noticed she would often bring herself down to the height of whoever she faced. Was she trying to be fair to us humans?

My thought was interrupted by Bayard. He yelled, spitting with force into the goddess' face. "I wouldn't need to be here—I wouldn't even *need* to be telling him the truth—if you motherfuckers would just be honest. Tell us how it is. But I suppose even honesty is beneath the mighty and all-powerful. Isn't it?"

Tamara grew a foot taller than him. "Bayard, of the soil and ocean salts," she hissed. "Do not test the goddess of humility and compassion, for it was I who granted you your voice, and with it, the power to speak with conviction and praise. Do not attempt to use my gift as a weapon against me."

Bayard didn't stand down. "Why keep the truth from the person who could have saved us, if you fools had just put him on the right path in the first place? But you have all these trials one must go through. Look at him...really *look* at the creature I have had to watch over!"

Tamara stepped past Bayard and looked me over. The fire was burning the squirrel in front of us to a crisp. I wasn't hungry anyway. I watched as the skin charred from amber to charcoal. I finally looked back at Tamara. I could feel she was looking right through me.

"Bayard, take a seat, and calm yourself. Your story is not done yet." Bayard levitated momentarily, then his body settled into a wooden chair, and a bowl of food appeared next to him. "Eat something before you tell the rest of the story. I would hate for you to forget something. And listen up."

Bayard took the bowl in his hand and lifted a spoonful of stew to his mouth. I could smell carrots and caramelized onion with golden potatoes. Bayard kept his gaze on us while he fought to regain control over his body. Then Tamara let go, and he landed to my right, so he and Tamara were a mere couple of feet from each other. She walked around the fire and through the flame. A snowy wind protected her as she moved. The squirrel disappeared and a raw one took its place.

She shrunk until she was the height of a little girl. She looked up at me as she drew near, like a curious child would before asking what your name was or if you would like to play with them.

"Bayard, I do see him, and do you know *what* I see?"

Bayard wiped his lips with his hand as he continued to eat.

"I see a being made of the earth he was formed from," she said. "The dark soil that once grew food in abundance."

I looked down, and, to my surprise, realized I was naked, though I didn't feel so at all. Tamara stayed in her childlike form, walking in circles. She faced me and shrank so she was only slightly bigger than my big toes.

She touched one. "I see the million miles walked and endless lives of small creatures in the fields, grasses, and pastures that these feet have encountered."

She expanded to my size and looked into my face. "I remember these eyes, Bayard. Did you know each human's eyes were crafted from a mixture of the characteristics of that individual's soul? The eyes of this human are filled with brown and gold specks. He is one of a kind, as you all are. I wish you would take more pride in your individuality."

I spoke as she looked into my eyes, "Tamara. Why do you no longer call me a king?"

"Correction, Sainath. You *were* my young king. Now that has passed. Now, Bayard. Finish your story so I may wrap this up and continue to address more important matters with Sainath."

Bayard frowned. He set the bowl down and watched it roll into the snow and dissolve to powder, adding to the slight slopes that had now formed around us from the wind's constant blowing. My clothes reappeared on my body. Not that it mattered. I felt the same with or without them. I sat down to hear Bayard spill the rest of the beans. He cleared his throat with a hoarse cough and continued where he had left off.

"When you entered that house overlooking the fishing village, you met a small woman. Innocent-looking until angered, correct?"

"Yes," I replied straightening my posture in the wooden chair.

"Good. Next, I imagine things got dark. You lost your mind and your body was broken just to be molded anew into something fiercer—something that stood a chance of surviving in this world."

I stood up. "Yes, I remember it. Yes, I have heard it before. But *what* does this have to do with me *now*? I survived, didn't I?"

"Hmmm. Yes, you did. Let me finish and make my point."

I pursed my lips and sat down, reluctant to listen to my own past all over again. I didn't want to be reminded about the brainwashing I had undergone or the torture my body had endured through those circles. Images of white gloves flooded my mind; I still remembered landing that single blow on the servant. That had been my only moment of relief. Other than leaving that cursed place for good.

"Let me guess, although the training was gruesome—at best—you learned, and you learned *quickly* that this world is *not* remotely like your past world. Perhaps it crossed your mind before you had been completely submerged. Before you'd given up control of your thoughts. Perhaps you remembered that you had lived another life, walked another path. Loved others, had a family that you called home.

"After you walked out of that house, you didn't care what you did as long as you could breathe another day. But being a foreigner in a new world, where does one begin? With the only thing you have been trained to do, of course. With your heightened senses and muscles capable of being locked and loaded instantaneously, you were ready to become a killer for hire. You had a good run, but it didn't help your mind recover the memories you had lost. No, it only suppressed them more. You found comfort in doing what the old lady had taught you to do. You thought you were fulfilling your purpose, until you met your first friend. Donte, with his sleek mane and flickering tail. It took a creature on four legs to teach you humility again."

"That was lovely, Bayard," Tamara spoke, bringing Bayard's story to an end. "I will take it from here. Sainath, will you walk with me just a little farther? There is something I would like to show you. Something that will make you understand your position and, more importantly, why you—of all humans—have a big part to play in the fate of this planet."

She walked by my side, maintaining the same height as me. The peak of the mountain was just a few feet away. A passionate kind of energy invigorated my senses. I found myself wanting to see what was at the top, and even more anxious at the prospect of seeing the landscape on the other side. I was curious about what Tamara had in store. As far as I knew, my world had been wiped out from nuclear war, and I was one of the few left standing. Even so, I couldn't doubt the facts. But *how* did a place like this exist? If the world was all but gone...

I had spent the past couple years wondering if this world was a place the government had developed for the "rebirth of humanity," but if that was the case, why was everything so primitive? Why were there no guns?

It was like a place hidden away, forgotten, and almost completely isolated from the rest of the world—tucked into a space which no ideas or technology could penetrate. A place time itself had forgotten. Yet everyone believed they were living in the present. Was I the only one who believed that there was something seriously wrong with everything here?

My feet stopped at the tip of the peak. I looked out at the landscape and my breath almost froze mid-exhale. It was glorious beyond measure. The barrier of the kingdom ended on the other side of this mountain. The stars were just an arm's length out of my reach. I could feel their intense heat, like a million and one suns spread across vast distances yet filled with so much energy that they radiated heat waves that dispensed over trillions of miles. What I was feeling was only the remaining fragments of that pure energy.

Tamara interrupted my train of thought. She didn't walk. It would be more accurate to say that she floated. I had almost forgotten she was there at all.

"Here is the end of the kingdom. You have been here a handful of years, in Earth's measurements. You have experienced headaches and your memories have resurfaced on and off. I remember designing the gift I had given you and later passed on to your kind on Earth.

"Are you talking about the soul?" I looked away from the landscape and devoted my full attention to her.

"Yes. it only took me a million Earth years to create such a thing— from energy and star particles. Don't you get it? The Wikums were created from the planet that was created for them. We created them from the trees and plants that thrive on the planet where they spent their whole lives. Asha hasn't told you the Wikums' story yet. I will leave that to him. He enjoys telling that story. I think it's his favorite of the multiple species and worlds that we have brought into existence. Did you know Asha was born from the first light in the universe? It was through him that the rest of us came into existence. Don't ask me who created us. *I* don't even know that answer. Look over here."

I followed her white arm where it pointed to the east. "See that large star there? Glowing with the faintest hint of a red hue?"

I reached a hand over where she held her finger. I pointed at a red star. It was no bigger than a 4h pencil head next to my finger.

"That one?"

"Yes. That is no ordinary star, Sainath. It's the planet you call Mars. And just a hand's breadth to the right of it is your home. Earth."

71

My nose tightened and I my eyes were suddenly moist. I pointed at the dimly-lit star just two stars away from Mars. I stared at the low blinking of...Earth. Tamara kept speaking, but I couldn't focus on her words. I could only focus on trying to make sense of where the hell I was, if not on Earth.

"It normally shines brighter, but sadly, there is nothing left. It will take half of one of my own kind's lifetimes, just for the radiation fall-out to disperse and the atmosphere to come full circle once more. I'm afraid that by that time, your sun will go supernova and vaporize Earth. Life won't have a chance to start again. I'm sorry, Sainath. None of us wanted this to happen." Her brow furrowed. "Except Apollyon. He believes we need to start another species and with it, a new world."

I looked away from Earth and turned around in the foot-deep snow. I didn't stop walking until I reached Bayard and the crackling fire. Tamara floated, pacing back and forth behind me. She was looking at her feet, continuing as though she were reading from a script.

I couldn't look at her.

I shouted, "If you gave a damn about us—if you actually cared so much about who we were to you, why didn't you do something? Why didn't you save us from our own destruction?"

I grabbed her shoulders and shook her body. I knew she was letting me do so, which made it worse. My voice broke, but I kept going. "And if you saved me, why couldn't you save my love and my unborn child, at the very least?!"

Suddenly, Tamara grew out of my hold on her shoulder, then shrunk back down, calming herself. She floated atop my fur-bound boots and spoke so softly; she might as well have been a hundred miles away.

"Don't you think I wanted to? Don't you think all I wanted was to come down to Earth and rally as many of you as I could in my true form—to scoop you all up and bring you here? Don't ask me such things, Sainath of Earth. I am the celestial being of *compassion*. I know of such matters better than anyone.

"We made a promise that we wouldn't interfere. We gave you everything: gifts of our own creation that took far longer to craft than any invention the human race could ever dream of forging. Asha, Prima, Apollyon, and I each added a piece of ourselves into the creation of the framework that is *you*, Sainath. The Wikums were made from their own planet—but you, Sainath. You and the humans of Earth were created from the stars and Earth. You are made of dirt, water, and the elemental textures and colors of everything combined. Your eyes are stars and planets yet to be discovered. You were made in *our image*. Be proud of that. As for you personally, and why you were saved—"

"Wait. Before you answer that," I pointed behind me but kept my gaze fixed on her celestial figure. "If that is Earth, then *what* is this place?" I was shaking. Tears ran down my face and dripped down my right index finger, to the ground where I pointed, between us.

"I was going to end this speech with that, but if you must know now, this is another planet entirely. Let me show you something else. Did you ever wonder why these barriers are in place, and how they intersect depending on their natural environments?"

"I thought those were just to distinguish the kingdoms from one another," I said, struggling to maintain my composure. "You know, like countries."

"You are partially right. They are in place, because without them you would die in the time it takes to let out a breath. The temperatures outside these barriers are extreme, to say the least. This is the home of Apollyon; it is his creation, from the ground up. He is the youngest of the four, yet the most ambitious. Your species found out what he is really capable of, unfortunately.

"He was the only one who had anything ready regarding a second start for humanity. As you can tell from your time here, this world is still beginning. And history tends to repeat itself, so of course, kings and creatures of various forms battle for territory. I'll admit, violence is more prevalent here than on Earth, and the risks are even higher, but what do you expect from a new world that still has no intelligence beyond its own appetites?"

She stepped back and traced her fingers above the snow. Floating before me, she watched her feet. "I'm sorry to say there is no time machine for you to jump into and escape to another planet. Reality might be strange, but that's beyond the bounds. We may seem unreal to you and this place, far-fetched. Maybe it reminds you of something you read in an imaginary tale of myth, but this is as real as it gets. Look—behind those rolling mountains, beyond the barrier. Do you see? That's the end of this planet."

I looked, squinting in an attempt to discern the far edges of the mountains, but I saw nothing but darkness. No snow caps. Nothing. "Wait, you said this is just the beginning of this planet...The people here are first generation?"

"Essentially, yes. The animals you see were given human characteristics. All along, the plan was that Asha and Apollyon would create a world where animals and humanity could co-exist. We tried it out on your planet, and for a while it worked. Many things worked. It was when the little things fell apart that your kind became doomed. Asha holds great pride for the animals and plants that roamed your world, but your species got greedy. Too great a population and too much preoccupation with power. In the last fifty years of your existence, you wiped out all the significant animals that had once held power in their domains. We knew the next generation of humanity wouldn't believe big cats or elephants had ever existed. Your children would think you were telling them another fairy tale about animals who once lived in harmony with humanity.

Asha, Apollyon, and I decided that Earth had to end. It had become a cancer that was spreading to every inch of a world we had created for you. Yes Sainath, we do feel. You know what hurt the most? The worst part was knowing Earth had been the quickest planet of our creations to perish. So, before you judge us for not saving your species, take a look at what your species has done to itself, and then ask me if you deserved to be saved in the first place."

I took a deep breath. I couldn't face Tamara. Not after that statement. She was right. I didn't know what to feel, but the dark memory of a nightmare Apollyon had sent me all those years ago on Earth impressed itself upon my mind. He had warned me about Earth's end. He blamed me too, just as Tamara did now. The skin across my face tightened in anger at the wrongness of it all, and anger erupted like a volcano. With heavy steps I walked toward Tamara; I knew I could hurt her with my fists but sometimes, words hurt even more. I wanted her to feel my wrath. I grabbed her by the shoulders again and shouted. Her starry eyes stared back, unafraid.

"If we were created in your image and you gave us gifts to thrive and expand to the point of our own destruction, then why *for fuck's sake* did you create us in the first place? You knew we would end our own existence! Tell me—I *have* to know. What made you and the other celestials change your minds about us? I get it, we had been entrusted to care for a planet that had given us everything. We took it for granted. I—"

I blinked. Looking down, I realized I was still gripping Tamara's shoulders. My knuckles had turned white. I wanted her to give me some sort of reaction. I wanted her to feel the pain I felt. I looked up at Earth's faded light, at the realization of the distance of an astronomical number of miles I couldn't even begin to understand. I shuffled my feet in place and looked at my feet. Softly, I said, "I'm sorry."

CHAPTER 8

i begin to believe in magic

Tamara gently steered my shoulders and we began to descend. I could see Bayard's shadow dancing on the ground as he paced around the fire, waiting for us.

"I can understand your anger, but what has happened is now in the past," said Tamara. "Originally, we celestials were hesitant to create you. At least, I was. We were about to give numerous gifts to a species that wouldn't even survive long enough to travel across vast star systems. We didn't change our minds in creating your kind, Sainath. We don't change our minds; it's not in our nature to debate the what ifs. That's an emotional trait we do not possess. Humanity sealed its fate. If it makes you feel any better, know this. I witnessed you firsthand when you arrived on that mountain across from us, when you took shelter in my home. Watching you evolve to who you are now, standing before me...I must say, you are full of surprises. Because you have shown me the strength of your humanity, compassion, kindness to nature and animals alike, I have formed a new conclusion about you. That is why I want to offer you something. Something that might just save your species from annihilation."

Tamara stopped for a moment, her arm draped across my shoulders as if we were close friends. *Did my humanity really rub off on her?* I searched the expressionless face of hers. I couldn't tell.

"Sainath. As my time with you is coming to an end, I must tell you this one thing," she said. "Well, a couple of things. One. You are not the son of King Gregory. Two. Your destiny is not to rule this place or anywhere else, but to start humanity again. There are others here like you—don't forget that—they just don't have their memories from Earth back yet. I'm sorry about the brainwashing, but we didn't want anyone to remember what they had experienced in their last moments of Earth.

"There is a planet that is worth investigating. Prima has been there a few times. She is many miles from here; you would pass a dozen planets before running into her. Prima and Apollyon have very different philosophies on how humanity should begin again. Apollyon wants to restart humanity just as we did before, but make the creatures of land and sea equal in intelligence to the human species. Prima, on the other hand…she has the power of creativity. She influenced humanity to progress at the rate that it did, so she blames herself the most for your species' downfall. She fled and wanted us to come with her—saying humanity is doomed and that we should just find another rock whereupon to develop a brand-new species, just like we did with the Wikums. She is trying to mask her feelings concerning how much she adored your species."

I stopped at the fire and sat down. Turning around in my warm, wooden chair, I looked back at the smallest dot in the night sky, which flickered with the slightest sign of life only when I strained my eyes. I felt tremendous guilt, but there was one thought that kept coming back to me. I had loved many in my lifetime. I had a great family and a few dear friendships. I had been happy and lost it all. And now…was I here to start humanity again?

"Sainath."

My neck snapped back; my attention drawn back to the moment. Tamara paced in the firelight as she finished her tale.

"Prima believes in starting over, but I don't think we need to do that. I know Apollyon, Asha, and I believe in a second chance for humanity. Prima gave you one of the greatest gifts, as I mentioned. Before your DNA was even written, you were chosen for the gift of creativity. After you were born, Prima watched over you. She nurtured you and oftentimes was your muse. That is why you would be the perfect messenger to go to her and show her that humanity deserves a second chance. What do you say?"

I stood up and wrapped my heavy fur coat around me. It was black with purple stripes on the back, with gold cuffs and feathers which decorated the neck. It was the king's robe. My imaginary father had worn it, and now, so did I. I had known deep down that Gregory wasn't my father. Tamara had said there was a resemblance, but that was all planned. Everything was planned.

"If I do this, will you do something for me?" I replied softly.

"If it's in my power, I will fulfill whatever you desire." She floated upon my feet, and moved so our noses were almost touching. Her frosty breath erupted from her mouth and dusted my lips with tiny shards of ice. "What do you wish?"

I looked back into her hollow, white eyes that sparkled liked a hundred stars. I wondered if she was completely hollow on the inside. She and the rest of the celestial beings were made of stars, she had told me before. This knowledge made me curious, but I focused on the moment.

"If I do this, will you bring Emily back?" I whispered as the ice melted from my lips. My gaze stayed fixed on the stars in her eye sockets.

Now her gaze dropped to my feet. "If you do this, I don't know if I can bring her back, Sainath. The afterlife is a whole other thing. It's a place we celestials don't travel to. And if you think we are strange beings, then you haven't seen anything yet. The beings that guard the bridge between the realms of the living and the dead are creatures even I wouldn't want to face." Tamara spoke without looking up at me.

"But you guys are like gods!" I piped up. From his chair, Bayard looked up and then away quickly. He looked around as if he wasn't listening. Then, he got up and turned his back to us, looking down at the kingdom and the numerous torches which lit its stone paths and homes.

"Sainath." Tamara floated from my presence to circle the fire once, only to turn back to me, twisting her neck to look over her left shoulder.

"You may see us as gods, but even with all my power and wisdom, I failed the single greatest creation known to the universe. The things that lie in the world of the dead would crush me; even if I could rally the other three celestial beings, we are no match for that world. They have existed longer than anything known. Think about that. There is always some creature dying. Sainath, no one I know has even tried to cross into that place. I wouldn't even know where to look. Some say it is high above us, on clouds of its own.

"Your own species called it Heaven. Other myths and legends say it's below our feet. And even more don't believe such a place exists. We can only interfere with living souls. No matter how close they are to death. It's an unwritten rule. The Unknown is a terrifying thing, Sainath."

She still stood a few feet from me. I gave a deep exhale and nodded. "I understand."

I walked past the fire, toward Bayard who looked just about ready to walk me back to the kingdom.

"One second. I didn't say we were finished."

My body lifted on its own, my head twisting to meet Tamara's attention. These four celestial beings had such tremendous power, I couldn't imagine a greater force in a whole other place. If the place actually existed.

"I'm sorry I can't aid you in this," she said. "I may not be able to cross over, but it doesn't mean you can't."

Looking up with hope, I asked, "How?"

"If you are serious about bringing Emily back, there is something else you should know. Not everyone we brought back and brainwashed turned out like you. Actually, only two others survived the body conditioning. Some were lost to insanity and have been wreaking havoc on this small planet. Apollyon has been letting this go on because he enjoys violence. Why do you think he included his own puppets in the brainwashing? To test everyone until they broke. He will let this go and on, claiming this is how humanity started. Though I agree—with some parts of it—I disagree that war should begin this early. There is a war coming to your false father's kingdom. I'm sorry but you have another decision to make. You can either fight in the battle or abandon the kingdom to its fate. That is the last thing you must know."

Asha said something similar...

She released her grasp on my body and I sat down again, trying to absorb everything she was telling me. "We really should have broken up these conversations, Tamara." I spoke bluntly to lighten the load.

Then I saw something in the celestial being, a funny movement of her mouth. I couldn't believe it. Tamara was on the verge of smiling.

"I can't tell you what that feels like. I am jealous of your kind, Sainath. Oftentimes I wish I could be one of you. To know so many emotions. To be able to feel so much toward everything you see and hear, to me, is one of the greatest gifts bestowed upon your kind. All thanks to yours truly."

She bowed delicately. Later, Bayard told me this was the highest praise from a celestial being, a mark of deep respect when conveyed to a member of a lesser species.

"I know Asha pulled away the dark veil—the one Apollyon had put in place while you were still on Earth, so that you would see nothing but darkness here. Asha lifted it from your mind, but forgot to draw it from your eyes. They are still foggy."

My lips curled in confusion. "I can see just fine, thank you."

She floated to me once more, and raised her white, nail-less fingers. They stretched into my eyes.

I didn't feel any pain. A burst of cold water filled my sockets and flushed them out. I fell back, blinking wildly. Above, the sky was luminous. The stars no longer appeared like white lights. I could actually see the various colors in each individual star. The night sky was like a painting, coated in brushstrokes of various hues and textured pigments. It wasn't a black canvas with little dots on it. All this time I thought the night sky was dark, but in truth it was completely the opposite. I wish I could have had this sight on Earth.

One vertebra at a time, I lowered my head to see mountains around me, then the fire. Its flame was filled with blue and yellow, framed by an outer layer of orange and red sparks. The wooden chairs gleamed, bouncing light reflected off the fire.

My robe was suddenly more purple than black. I was sparkling like the stars. My hands were filled with small cuts that held light inside. I took off my cuffs and rolled up my coat sleeves, mesmerized. My marks were there: the scars that I remember seeing when I first arrived here. These claw marks ran around my arms like a serpent, gleaming with light that was almost blinding.

I finally rested my eyes on Tamara. She was a child again and looked the same as before. Her size was the only thing that had changed. I looked at her doubtfully.

I asked, "Why is everything else so incredible now, and you are now ordinary?"

"It is because, now that I have given you another gift, seeing my true form would completely blind you in less than a second. So, from now on, when you see me, I will appear in this form to you. Whoever else sees me will still interpret my form as the bright star you once knew me as. Now, turn around, and take a look at your friend as I have one last gift for you."

I moved my feet slightly and looked at Bayard. He was much smaller now too. His brown jacket had shrunk to a vest with an air-force logo on it. Military boots appeared at his feet, although his gut stayed the same.

"Tom?' I said, reaching out to touch the brown leather jacket.

Tom turned around and embraced me. "Well it's about time. I thought I might be stuck in that skin in your eyes for a long time. Thanks Tamara."

Tom rested his shoulder against mine. He even smelled the same. Remarkable. I stood a step back and looked him over. He seemed perfectly fine. His arms were sliced up like mine. We compared the length of our serpents.

I couldn't believe Tom had been here this whole time.

"He arrived just a year before you did," Tamara said, anticipating my question.

"How is that possible? I swear he was dead before the plane crashed."

"Mostly dead, but not completely. Just like you, he arrived, survived the brainwashing, and was set free. Tom was watched over by Asha. His complete tie to the natural world blossomed when he arrived. Even when Tom was a child, he had a better connection to the animals in his backyard than to his family. As he grew older, he found he could calm the nerves of frightened creatures. Tom was born with the gift of communication. Because of this, he was a good resource for the king of this realm. As I'm sure both of you know, the human species are on the lower end of the food chain on this small planet."

Tom spoke. "As much as I like my old name, I think I will stick with Bayard. It seems to be more fitting for this place. That part of me died with his wife and children. I would rather have my Earth name rest in peace with them, if you would be so kind, Tamara."

"What?" I said, surprised.

Tom turned to me. "Sainath, do not worry, friend. My memories from before I came to this world will still exist. I won't forget how hard we fought for a better world. Two strangers at the edge of a dying world. May our adventure continue, friend." He smiled from the side of his mouth.

Tamara stayed in her childlike form and floated toward Tom. She floated up until she was eye to eye with him. She let her head touch his, then spoke in a quick whisper I only heard because of my acute ears. "Name that made this vessel what it once was, be gone. Return home to those you hold dear. Awaken the other half. Vessel. Take form. Become the man, Bayard."

She stepped back. At first nothing happened. Then, Tom's flight jacket grew until it reached down to his shins and fur sprouted around the collar. A beard started to grow rapidly on his face. His glasses flew in the air and floated right above him. Bayard was back.

"Bayard, is there anything you would like to say to your former self before I send its spirit to Earth?"

Bayard reached up for his glasses. They brushed his hands softly like a close friend or pet. Bayard nudged his glassed with his face and said, "Goodbye old friend. Tell the kids hello."

With that, the glasses zipped this way and that, zigzagging in various directions.

"What are they doing?" I asked Tamara.

"They're trying to find Earth. They're having a hard time because it is now the dimmest star within reach. I will help." She floated forward.

Bayard and I watched the child-like celestial being rise up above us. The glasses were still flying around in a frenzy. She grabbed them as they zoomed by her, turned in a 180-degree rotation, and pointed as if showing a friend which direction to go. "Tom, fly straight until three stars fall in line at 45 degrees. Take the middle star, and you will arrive back home."

The glasses nodded in midair and zoomed off like a bullet shot from a gun. Then we were alone again. The fire was dwindling.

"Sainath, my time with you is officially coming to an end. You have a decision to make. Fight the battle for this kingdom or leave for Prima's world and convince her it's not too late to give humanity another chance."

I looked at Bayard. He looked at me and then to the sky, toward Earth.

"What if I do both?" I said.

"I had a feeling you would say that. Remember, if you choose to attempt both, I can't guarantee your safety in battle."

"And you could if I left to go find another planet?"

"No, but I could keep you alive far longer."

"Fair point," I responded.

The fire burned out, and Tamara vanished in the cold wind. The blizzard's harsh winds attacked us while Bayard led the way back to the kingdom. By the time we arrived in the great hall, everything was covered in a foot of snow. The feast was over and the lights, dim. Bayard and I walked to one of the guest rooms. I really didn't want to drag snow all across the palace or wake the resting knights.

"Do you think Tamara is upset that I didn't give her a straight answer?"

Bayard didn't look at me. He stripped his heavy coat from his shoulders and rested it upon a rack near one of the fireplaces in the room. The throne room was adjacent to this chamber.

The palace was quiet. Guards stood in their normal positions. I heard a flutter of footsteps above as servants moved along the halls; someone must have alerted them that I had returned.

"I don't think Tamara knows what anger is. I might have arrived a year before you did in Earth years, but I had been in this world for almost ten years in its own rhythm before you even arrived. Time is always shifting, moving at various speeds, although it never seems to slow down properly. Asha found me washed ashore and divulged everything that was going to happen to me. He said it was a test, and you know how stubborn I can be. If there is a challenge, you know I will rise to it."

"Yes. Absolutely, Bayard!" I thought seeing him transform into Tom and then back to Bayard would make me feel differently toward him. But he was still Bayard to me, with Tom's memories intact. No wonder we had become quick friends.

"After I had undergone these exact tests—or trials, I suppose you could call them—I worked with Asha to heighten my abilities, and through it all he taught me healing techniques against the darkness he said would arrive when you stepped into this world."

I looked up at him as he helped me remove my wet clothes. I smiled to myself. After ten years of being here, I could tell he had become completely accustomed to their culture. I was no king. I just play the part that Apollyon wanted me to in this world. Yet, here he was, taking my drenched clothes and treating me like royalty. He continued talking as he took my boots off. I let him do what he had been set on this planet to do.

"Once I finished with Asha in the very forest that you visited not too long ago, he told me to find a way to become close to the king of this kingdom, because this area was created last. Humanity was the last species to arrive here. That is why there is a war coming. It's Apollyon's doing. He has been sending false messages back and forth between the kingdoms. He wants humanity's path here to unfold as it did on Earth.

Asha told me we would need to come together and fight if we want humanity to have any claim on this planet. After meeting your false father and this realm's king, I learned what I could of this place. I also discovered that you and I are united by a far greater purpose. I think that is what Tamara was trying to say. It is ultimately your decision to fight or flee. Asha told me it would be my role to aid you on your journey. He said I could bear some of darkness for you, which I have been doing since the witch awakened."

I stopped Bayard with a wave of my hand. He closed his lips mid-speech and bowed. Just then a knock sounded at the door. Bayard got up from the floor we were sitting upon—our shadows dancing on the cherrywood flooring of the great hall. The drapes were drawn, and occasionally a vibrant flicker or crack in the flame would erupt, causing my shadow to cling to the drapes for seconds, then shrink closer to me as the fire calmed.

A servant entered, carrying bowls of hot water and clean rags. "My king. Shall I draw you a hot bath? You must be frozen to the bone after being gone for so long."

"Please do. Two baths. Bayard will be staying here for a little longer. If that is all right with him."

Bayard looked down at me. "Yes, my king. That would be all right. And thank you for your hospitality. My wife is surely asleep, so she shouldn't fuss too much if I arrive a little later."

The baths were drawn. Bayard got in, and water flooded the tile floors. The bathroom was on the second floor of the palace. White marble tiles spread around in a circular formation. There were two baths, which could be removed, and room for more to be brought in, should the occupant so desire. The hot water came from the second kitchen just across the hall. This made it easy for servants to transport the hot water, since there were no faucets or pipes—just oval canisters of some sort of metal. A wooden block was set inside to sit on. Various blocks were stacked along the wall to accommodate whoever was using the baths. I grabbed a rather tall block and set it down. I wanted to sit high; my lower back hurt from walking up and down the mountain.

I don't know how Bayard didn't feel any pain. He rested his eyes and let his head roll against the lip of the bath. We faced each other, half an arm's length between us. A couple of serving girls entered. One washed my shoulders while another tilted my head back and started to wash my hair. No care was given to the amount of water flooding the marble tiles. A single drain planted between in the middle of the floor carried all excess water away.

I tilted my head back and enjoyed the feeling of every single strand of hair gathered and released in the servant's small hands. She didn't say a word. The bath house was quiet, and it seemed all was peaceful. I knew Bayard had fallen asleep when I heard the rumble of breaths begin in his throat.

I was very tired. I had traveled many miles on both foot and horseback in the course of just a few months. My mind was exhausted, both from Asha and Tamara. I didn't know why I hadn't thought to ask either of them the pressing question, as I was now sure they would know better than anyone else. Plus, I was pretty sure Bayard had been about to tell me something important before the servant came knocking.

Who was the witch? And why was she after me?

My brain flooded with both conversations I had shared with those celestial beings. I mulled over their thoughts on my species and the future outcomes they wanted me to pursue. I let my mind become fully drawn to Asha and Tamara's words. My brain kept coming back to the Wikums. I pondered how they must have lived. I was so relaxed I didn't even notice someone else had gotten in the bath with me.

My eyes were still closed, so at first, I figured it was a third servant. Wait. Why would I need three servants? My eyes shot open.

Bright green eyes met my own.

My hair was pulled tight behind my head, so I was held in place. The servant washing my shoulder clasped her hands around my mouth and the third shoved me under the water as the witch let go of my hair. I splashed frantically to get Bayard's attention.

"Hello, Sainath. We are alone again. Don't spoil it. We have a lot of catching up to do."

I was running out of air. The sheer weight of the witch was surprising. She was always in the form of three women or a crow. You wouldn't think either of those would be that heavy. But multiply the average weight by three, and add a hefty sized bird to the mix, and well, I guess the weight made sense then.

My new eyes could see her clearly underwater. Her black hair mixed with strands of gold that lit up the water around her. Her eyes glowed that unsettling, deep green hue. She didn't blink—just stared at me. Her voice echoed through the water as she opened her mouth to speak.

"You have been up to some big things, haven't you? It *has* been a while, Sainath, since I last talked to you, when I showed you the world you could conquer. You must have forgotten all about that because here you are, talking to celestial beings. I thought you were on humanity's side. Now here you are, about to do favors for the likes of them!"

I gave her a strained look as the water's pressure lessened on my body. I floated up to the surface, and the witch followed me out. Whether she was in the water or out seemed to make no difference. She looked exactly the same. Her face was completely dry, and her skin still shone like gold.

"Sainath…" her voice trailed off as she crawled toward me. The other two manifestations disappeared.

I looked over at Bayard who was snoring, fast asleep. "Bayard!" I yelled, but he didn't respond. I screamed, "Guards! Anybody!"

No one came through the doors. I was alone with this evil spirit who shared my bathwater. I settled down. When I really thought about it logically, I wasn't too scared of her anymore. For the longest time she hadn't bothered me—not that I was complaining.

Our legs were intertwined like vines along a tree. As always, she knew how to seduce me.

I relaxed my shoulders and spoke in a conversational tone. "Tell me something, witch. Yes, I met with Asha, the celestial being of nature. He took your darkness. He even told me as he did so. If that is true, how are you here now?"

"Fool, I am darkness," she replied. "You may live in a kingdom of light, but there's still a fundamental law of balance. Darkness cannot exist without light. Sure, the good-for-nothing Asha took the darkness from your mind which made keeping up with you difficult, but I knew you would have to return here eventually. I just had to wait for the right moment, but…"

She reached out and touched my chest. Her fingers melted into my flesh. "There is still plenty of darkness here." She grabbed my heart between her fingers and squeezed. I screamed in agony, grabbed at her hand, and watched it come out of my chest like a knife pulled free from a wound. Her hand dripped black goo, which mixed with the lukewarm bath water, turning it the color of a swamp. Her body was cold against me—not icy like Tamara's but cold enough that I realized whoever she was, she was better informed about the celestial beings than I. Far more aware than she let on.

"You see, the mind could be clear as a cloudless day, but the heart remains full of darkness. And yet, nobody would expect *you* to be a terrible person. But look at what is inside you—you are corrupted. She took the same bloody hand and placed it just below her collarbone. Her breasts were buoyant on the water's surface. She reached between them, into her chest. Immediately, black goo sprayed forth. She was filled to the brim with it.

"You have made your point," I said with a deep breath.

She removed her hand and shook it out on the floor, then rinsed it in the water we were sitting in.

"Now, that is done. Since everyone is telling you what they want from you, let me tell you something that I know will guide you to my side." She put both hands on the lip of the bath, one on either side of her body. She edged her hands toward me, leaning forward. It didn't take long for her to close the distance between us.

Her rotten breath took me back to our first encounter. The golden strands of her hair were alive on their own and moved toward me like snakes. They brushed my skin. Her eyes dimmed down, the green dulling until it looked almost natural. Her skin was chilly to the touch as her hands clamped onto my forearms. Her legs moved around my waist and locked behind me. I was all hers again.

"Now that I have your full attention, I want you to know something, I couldn't help but overhear your chat with Tamara. You want your poor beloved back, but no seems to be able to help you fetch her. The only option you have of saving her is by going alone into the Unknown. No human has been and returned. And as much as I hate the "compassionate queen of light" you see her as, Tamara is right. It's *far* too dangerous, even for celestial beings. What makes you think a mere mortal such as yourself stands a chance?" Her black lips brushed against my own.

"Let me guess," I responded. "You are going to help me where they can't. And in return you want me to be chained to your side to ensure the new world is created in your image, rather than that of the celestial beings."

"My, my. Someone has been using their ears more and their mouth less, hasn't he?"

Her left arm reached for my hair and started combing it back with slender fingers as her right hand aroused me further.

"I will help you," she whispered, "I will travel to the dimension of souls and reclaim Emily for you. All you have to do in the meantime is win the war that is coming to your doorstep! Only if you win will Emily be returned to you. But," she stopped thrusting and pushed her tongue into my mouth. Abruptly, she pulled away, and whispered in my ear. "Win at all costs. Your species must survive. Unlike Prima, I do believe you deserve a second chance. I have guided your blade before, but I won't be on the battlefield to save you if anything happens. This is a risk, but if you want Emily back among the living, I don't think it will be a problem for you."

I moved her off of me. She retreated back to her side of the bath. "If what you say can be done, then I will do it. On a couple conditions."

"Fair enough, Sainath. I am listening."

"Okay." I looked over at the slumped form of Bayard's sleeping body. I don't know how he had slept through any of that.

"First thing, you can't let anything happen to Bayard. He is my only connection to Earth—the only person on this planet who I know is real. He must live through the battle."

"Done." A flick of her wrist shot a ball of blue, concentrated energy in his direction. It covered his body thinly, like a mucus membrane. Then it dissolved into his skin, and he was back to his normal, pale-looking self.

"I can't save him from a sword, but he is protected from all poisons or illness. And your second demand is?"

I nodded in agreement and returned my focus to her. A moment of silence passed between us.

"Tell me who you are—who you *really* are. Or, who you once were before you arrived here. Did this place change you into something else when you arrived, like it did with just about everything else? Did you go through trials like I did too?"

She stood. Her naked body was completely dry. A dress of silk and gems appeared like a fog to clothe her body. She stepped out of the bath and looked down at me. I thought she might cast a spell or something.

But nothing. She stood there. Her eyes swelled. Bowing her head, black beads of tears fell and shattered like glass with every drop. It was like hearing a pin in the quietest and darkest of places. It was lonely.

Finally, after watching a rainfall in its most potent form, she whipped her hair back and looked down at me. Her face dried as if it had never known a single tear.

Then she spoke. "How dare you ask me such questions. Do you not know I could break you in so many pieces that even the celestial beings couldn't put you back together again? However, I count you brave for asking such things, so I will not break you today, Sainath. Instead, I will answer your questions in due time if you must know my story.

"After you have won the battle, travel to Prima and do Tamara's bidding, if you wish. Prima will share insights as to how I became…this thing you see in front of you." She gave a wave of her claw-like hand. Water surrounded her and with a splash, she was gone.

My natural instinct caused my gaze to dart to the small window in the left corner of the cream-colored walls. I waited for the crow's call, the sound of which my ears had grown so accustomed to. Its absence today caused a wave of fear to wash through me.

I had made my decision. I would take both proposals from the witch and Tamara. If there was a remote chance of seeing Emily again, I had to take it. I would fight and find a way to Prima. Maybe it was the wrong choice; It certainly was a long shot either way, but the only thing that would make me happy would be seeing Emily again.

Bayard rustled in his sleep, tilted his head forward, and looked around. With a stretch and a final yawn, he came back to reality. I still didn't know how he had slept through all of that. The witch must have cast a spell to block his senses while still keeping him in a deep sleep. I wondered what he had dreamed.

CHAPTER 9

the voices of war

"Good lord, what time is it?"

"I'm not sure," I said, looking at Bayard with a puzzled expression. He got up in the bath and called for a servant to come with his clothes. A knock arrived shortly after, and a woman entered, brown eyed and fragile limbed. She carried Bayard's heavy garments. She bowed to me before setting the clothes on a stool on the opposite side of the room, near the door. She handed Bayard a towel.

"Would you like me to bring your clothes, my king?"

Just as I was about to say yes, a horn sounded from the main gates. I knew the call.

I sprang from the bath right leg over left, rolled out, landed on my feet, and jumped up to the small window ledge. I looked out at the far watch tower, searching for the color of its smoke.

It was red at the main gates. Without looking back from the window, I replied to the servant. "No, not my clothes. Grab my armor. Bayard, dress quickly and get your wife and yourself to safety. On your way out, release Donte."

I didn't hear any footsteps. I jumped into a squat, still naked. "Did you hear me! Get moving!" I shouted so the guards outside the halls could hear.

Bayard put his pants on and was out the doors, leaving them flung open. I could hear Orion's distinct footsteps ascending the stairs. He turned the corner, pivoting on his sword. It skipped across the wet marble before catching on one of the grooves in the tiles and turned on a dime. The king's guard stood behind him in the doorway.

"Sainath! Here!" He threw me my twin swords. "You will need these, regardless of your choice. I'm with you, friend." Orion bowed deeply, and the king's guard followed, bowing in unison. "Tamara came to me in a dream and told me the choice you have in front of you." A servant came running in, and dropped armor at my feet. Another servant followed and started to dress me. They strapped on the back of the chest plate. A flexible black garment was its first layer. It was fresh, newly made. I had never had to put it on before. The horns continued to blare in my ears.

I looked up at Orion, who was waiting patiently for my command. My first thought went to Gregory and what he would do.

Protect the people. Without them there is no kingdom.

I could hear his voice in my head. The only opposition I could think might be attacking us would be Ursa and his Bear Clan.

Tamara was right. This wasn't my battle. I could easily flee and be fine. But regardless of this world and how fake it felt, I still gave a damn about the few humans who were here. Even if they had been brainwashed and morphed into something else.

I could hear the shouts of my people.

I looked ahead at Orion and the guards as the final strap around my shin guards fell into place. I sheathed my swords. "Where is my knife belt?"

"I couldn't find it, my lord." Orion spoke under his breath, looking at the window beyond my shoulders. He felt the cries of the people just as I did.

He should be king instead of me. He had all the great qualities and not a hint of darkness in him. Unlike me.

"Go," I commanded. "Open the palace gates, and ensure the people find shelter in these walls."

Without hesitation, Orion and the king's guard bowed and dashed through the doors. I heard shouting as the people crammed into the palace. I ran downstairs and met up with Orion at the entrance. The palace guards were stationed in mass numbers, waiting for me. I didn't say a word as I took the back exit out of the palace. Before descending around the palace toward the front gates, I turned around to see that the couple hundred men who protected the castle had followed me out.

"Half of you stay put here. If we fail to hold them back, you are the last defense for the women and children—your *wives* and your *children*. With every breath of your lungs, stand your ground and protect our most valuable assets to this kingdom and its future. Our people."

The palace guards gripped their shields and slammed their spears on the palace steps with one booming clap. Then they retreated back into the palace, barring the exit gate behind them.

"The rest of you are with me!" The mixed colors of the palace guards and horses blurred as knights mounted them, led by one black stallion belonging to Orion. I heard Donte running up the stone path.

I swung around his neck and mounted. Nudging his hind quarters, me and a hundred knights rode toward the main gates, dodging the people as they scrambled for the palace. I was thankful that whatever lay outside the walls remained there.

We arrived at the gates, just as the sky was bright red from every Watchtower within the kingdom giving off the same signal. They had all sent up the signal, far into the sky. Our allies in other kingdoms had to have seen the plumes of smoke by now too.

The knights got into four rows of twenty-five, exactly. A few other knights started coming up from the lower lands and other areas surrounding the kingdom, once they heard I was at the front gates. The stragglers were pikemen. They took their places in the front of the first line of knights on horseback.

I dismounted, signaling the men to stay put. Orion followed suit, chasing me up the steps to the gate's watchtower. It was time to see what exactly Gregory's kingdom was up against.

Archers greeted me on my way up. I could hear the roar of the army at our gates. I looked up over the wall.

A mass of white covered the mountain below. Ursa. The sore loser couldn't accept defeat at my hands. I knew he wasn't happy with how his little game had gone. But I didn't think he would assemble such a force just to prove his power.

Ursa was easy enough to point out. He stood on top of the cave I had first inhabited a few years ago. I wondered where Tamara was. She was the protector of that cave. Had she abandoned it or was she defeated? It didn't make much sense since she was a celestial. There was no way she was gone, I decided.

I looked deeper with my clear vision. Ursa had recruited the lizard creatures. I had fought one of them when I first arrived. They were specialists in poison and favored the long bow with throwing knives. I had firsthand experience with their techniques from that time in the forest when Donte had been stolen from me.

My skin crawled at the sight of a massive group of them. Their lengthy bodies and pointed chins were marked with distinctive black gashes, which ran along their legs. With brown vests and black facial hair, they seemed hybrids of lizard and man. Many of them were short-range fighters, but a few archers stood in their ranks.

Beyond that, I looked past the bears and saw a herd of slaves from the Bear Clan. They wore collars on their necks. I remembered them. They didn't want to be here, but they would be the first of the casualties when the battle began. I knew they would be picked up and used as shields by a large portion of the bears. One of the archers came to my side. A Peregrine falcon's feather stood straight up from his helmet. The rest of the archers wore the same feather; however, theirs dangled down on the right and left sides of their helmets. This placement told the commander which hand was favored by each archer. Some shots were better suited for left-handed archers, compared to the traditional right-handed approach. This was a simple yet effective way for the commander to give orders. He would call left feather or right feather. I looked down on both sides of the wall—the Peregrine falcon archers were a mixed bunch. The commander with his single, erect feather stood to my left, while Orion stood at my right. They were one of King Gregory's first allies to hear the call and must have traveled through many moons to get here. Bayard was right, false messages were probably sent by Apployn forces in order to create this mess and the Peregrine Falcon clan must have intercepted one of the messages and had sought it out to make the journey in secret. King Gregory had told me about the Clan and just how like the bird of prey, they were the top of the pyramid when it came to secrecy and disrupting vile plots. They see it all, always in the back corner of dive towns and kingdoms alike. They were known for being the greatest archers across this planet. I wish we could be meeting on other terms besides war. I was curious what their homes looked like and just how the ally relationship started between the general and Gregory. They lived high in the tundra filled mountains and valleys on the other side of the planet.

"My king, we have clear shots at the first line as well as at Ursa," said the commander. "Give the word, and we shall end this fight before it even begins. Beyond their ranks, we have identified all the lieutenants. Our main concern is the lizard people. Everything down to their spit is toxic to us. Beyond that, we think we can keep the casualties to a minimum."

I nodded. Looking out over the white and green mixture of the army, I spoke. "It doesn't matter if we take Ursa out now or later. His people are loyal to the bone. Commander, I have seen his kingdom firsthand, and let me be the first to tell you, every single bear our there is Ursa's offspring. This means no matter what we do, each and every bear will fight for their father until their last breath. As for the lizard people, yes, they definitely pose a threat to us. I suggest we take them out as quickly as possible. They will cause the most damage to us and our people if they breach the walls. Do you have the heavy bows locked and ready?"

The commander looked over my shoulder and I followed his gaze. There were massive bows atop the tower, strapped to a wooden base cemented to the tower itself. Arrows were made from a whole mass of trees. The bow was fashioned from a triple thread weave, each thread composed of fibers of a material foreign to me. It glowed blue.

"Yes, sir. The ancient bows are locked onto rows of at least thirty bears."

I turned and looked at the commander. He had a tight gray mustache which rested high above his lip, right below his small freckled nose. His round eyes had a green tint to them. He didn't smile. He had a slim frame and went by the name Zahel.

He looked serious as he spoke up, his lips set in a thin line. "Each of the large bows can pierce twenty to thirty men in a single shot."

I was shocked at these statistics. I looked behind Zahel and saw the massive weapon with an arrow the size of a tree trunk locked in position. Two feathered men nodded my way.

"Zahel, stay on guard and keep your bows ready. I don't want to start this war. Perhaps Ursa will come to his senses and stand down. We will wait until he makes the first move. Until then, have the archers take rotations. I don't want anyone getting sleepy on the wall. You are our first line of defense."

"Yes, my king." I touched his leather shoulder on his drawing arm. "Midday is already upon us. During the hottest hours of the day, the bears will be at their weakest. When night returns with its cold, windy breath, so too does their strength. I will be back here by then. I must check on the rest of the towers to make sure this is where his army's efforts are most concentrated. I don't want anyone sneaking in."

"Yes, of course. I will command my archers as you say."

I brushed past him and hurried along the wall, toward the next tower. I stopped just as the steps down to the gates came into view.

"Orion," I took a deep breath. "Ride past the far gates into the forest and ask for Asha's aid. I know you don't believe in him. Nevertheless, you have followed and trusted me this far, so I ask that you trust me once more. Ask Asha if he has anything that might render us immune to the Lizard Clan's poison. Even if it only protects a handful of soldiers, that could be useful. Take the remaining messengers with you, and have them ride through the forest to the Owl and Sparrow Clans. Ask for their aid too. Each bear down there outnumbers our men four to one. You've seen how long it took me just to bring down one."

"True, and you are one of the best fighters I have ever seen," he said as we approached the tower's final steps.

I leaned in so my voice was reduced to a whisper. "Just between us, if we don't get aid, we won't stand a chance. Even *I* don't know Ursa's true power. I worry he may have killed Tamara when he took that cave."

"You don't think she is really dead, do you?" Orion's voice rose in pitch.

"Keep that to yourself. I don't want anyone losing their grip on reality. We must keep every man at arms full of courage. Now go. If Asha has something to offer us, we need it."

Orion raced down the steps. All the knights of the kingdom were stationed on the inner walls, all around the kingdom. I estimated there were about ten thousand men. Up until this point, I had no idea the army was this vast. There was a weak point near the forest, however. An open gap. Seeing this told me two things. There was either a large army that surrounded ninety percent of the kingdom, or the knights were just following protocol. I hoped it was the second option.

There were around three thousand men at the front gates. The red smoke had stopped. The sun was piercing through the thick red clouds, and a breeze blew in from the west. It was warm, and I was thankful for it.

The next tower in my path was near the forest; only one other lay beyond it, on the forest's outskirts. Archers stood at the ready—arrows gripped in hand, bows held tightly. My presence was known shortly after. My steps resounded on the wall; everyone else stood still, rocking from foot to foot in an effort to ensure their legs didn't fall asleep. I turned sharply into the tower. A few men were inside, busy adjusting their bows, while a couple of blacksmiths crafted arrows. An archer dashed past me and grabbed two bundles of arrows, then ran back to the front gates.

The men stopped their work and looked at me. Their veins twitched visibly in their necks. I could not tell if the prospect of the end of this war was lingering in their minds, as they stood in their semi-circle encampment within the tower. They didn't say anything. I felt like I should say something to calm their nerves. What would my father have said? What would King Gregory say? My mind was blank.

I nodded in approval. Then I asked a question. "Have you heard the commander's orders?"

"Nothing yet, my king," said one of the blacksmiths, looking up from his work table. It was strewn with stone arrowheads and bundles of shafts made of various kinds of wood. His hands shook but quickly returned to his table's edge to brace themselves. He was young. Maybe only a teenager. His arms were thin, and the man next to him was not much bigger. I could understand why they were scared now. They were just kids. Most likely the sons of seasoned archers.

I backed out of the tower and found myself on the edge of the wall once more. I decided to look back down the way I had come. I took a closer look at the young man who had run past me with bundles of arrows. He was already coming back again. He was even younger than the two men forging the arrows. The dome of his helmet jiggled with each stride. He ran past me again and sat down immediately as he entered the tower; he moved with so much anticipation, it was as if the battle had already commenced, and his sole mission was to supply the archers. I walked back into the tower and looked at the boys hard at work.

"I know all of you are scared, but please know that this battle has not even begun yet. Please do your best to relax. I have given the commander orders to stay alert until Ursa has made the first move."

The young smith stopped his hands from shaking long enough that he could speak up. "Who is Ursa?"

"Ursa is the large bear in the middle of the horde, camped atop the collapsed cave."

"I can feel his energy," the smith said. "And it makes me want to run away every time I'm on the wall. It's scary."

The little boy in the corner raised his head and reached out his hand. I looked down at him with my golden eyes. He was blind in both of his. Most likely, he'd been born that way. I bent down in a squat and removed my gloves.

I remembered Emily teaching a blind five-year-old to dance. What the child could hear was remarkable. To the blind, music was something experienced a whole new way—the environment took on the qualities of a song. When I went to pick Emily up one night, I had met her student.

It was a winter afternoon. My mittens were still on when I reached for her hand. Emily came to my side and removed my glove. "If you want her to see you, you must go bare-handed. You must touch her hand with your own."

I didn't know that it would make a difference. But I believed her, and the little girl giggled as our hands touched.

This situation was no different. I removed my battle gloves and reached for the child's hand. We connected. I could feel him. He was small, but he had a great awareness of space, of his world. In a split second, the boy smiled up at me.

Then, just as quickly, his smile turned to a frown, then an expression of terror as he slowly pulled his hand away from mine.

"You carry the same energy as the bear—" his voice broke. "The bear on the cave of whom you speak."

My cheeks were hot. I slipped my glove on, ignoring the nervous glances which had returned with renewed force. I left the tower, biting my lip. I didn't have time to explain. It wasn't like I knew much more than the blind child did. Did I? I continued along my path.

I looked over at Ursa. He stood his ground. His ground troops were getting bored. A few of them rolled their necks in frustration and a few others started walking around, taunting the archers. I knew that tactic wouldn't work with these kinds of men, especially after seeing how disciplined Zahel was.

I remembered when Ursa had said he was our ally. Now he was at our gates. It was because he didn't think I belonged in this world with the rest of them. Was this planet so fragile in its beginning—so nebulous— that something as simple as that could so drastically change the course of his feelings?

The forest came into my view. There was a canopy of trees, lush with leaves of varying shades of green. The last archer stood at my right. Now I was completely in the open. My guard was up; a single well-placed arrow from one of the Lizard Clan's archers would ignite a war I wasn't entirely sure I wanted to be a part of anymore.

Next, the tower came into my view. The clouds had dispersed, and the sun brightly lit the sky and made the metal plates on every man's armor on either side of the wall gleam. The bears would seek cover soon. The day was hot, the snow on the mountain melting quickly. The breeze steadied. The world had become still, and I felt like the fastest object moving on this planet.

The men in the tower greeted me. They were the same soldiers I had met a few months prior; they had given me the rocks that gave off blue and red smoke. I asked about Orion.

"We let him through about thirty minutes ago, my lord."

I sat down on a little wooden stool and took my gloves off to let my hands breathe. "How come there are no men protecting this part of the wall?"

"This wall never really needs protecting. The forest—and whatever lives within—takes care of any living soul before it has a chance of seeing our beautiful faces." The elderly men laughed together, and I joined in.

The sense of relief that laughter provides the human body is like medicine. Does someone laugh when they want continued pain or added stress? No, we laugh to reduce such things. This was one of those moments. The joke wasn't even that funny, but laughter tends to spread once begun.

A cup of wine was brought to me. Compared to the rest of the men on the wall, these did not fear death. They were the oldest of the knights: grown fat, dirty, and bearded because of how problem-free their work had been. Hence, their lack of exercise too. A handful of the men were equipped with double axes. The thought of our own men creating a circle around the kingdom came to me.

"Why are all the men spread out? I haven't seen the other half of the kingdom's walls. Has the army surrounded us completely?" I asked as the first gulp of warm wine hit my stomach and immediately eased my shoulders and brought them down in a relaxed slump.

"The knights are just following protocol. The other half of the kingdom is probably waiting on your arrival, my lord."

I shook my head. "You are probably right, I know you guys don't have to worry about it here, but once this thing kicks off, lend your aid wherever it may be needed. I sent Orion to get help because I have a feeling we will not stand a chance once the front gates are overrun."

My hand tipped the clay cup, and the wine poured like a mini waterfall in front of my men and gracious hosts. "You—all of you in this tower— are veterans. The oldest knights in the entire kingdom, I am sure of it. Pick up your axes, strap on your shields, and walk with me. Just your presence out on the wall and on the field will give much needed courage to the many young men who have never seen war. Many of them won't live to see another day."

The last drop of wine dripped to the floor as the men strapped themselves up. I led the way out of that tower, the five of them following at my heels. Our steps were like thunder now. Before we were even in earshot, heads were turning. I looked down the wall and saw a few archers turn to watch us from a distance. My chest plate was outlined in gold and purple. It shot rays of blinding light, reflecting the sun back at the sky.

The last tower was in view. I looked down at my men, who now resembled the ones at the front gates. I pointed at the soldiers ahead. The veteran knights broke formation and waddled down the steps to greet the men below. I stopped the last knight in his tracks. He turned to face me.

"Yes, my lord?"

'Move all the men from this end of the kingdom to the front gates. Open the gates and bolster our force against the vile troops who stand at our wall. Do not make any mistakes. Hold the line until you see me. If they have not *yet* struck, before night fall and you don't see me arriving, you have my permission to unleash everything we have. Now go!"

I let go of his shoulder. These five men were the stuff of legend. Every child in armor had grown up listening to stories about them. It was time they fought alongside their heroes.

I surveyed the land. There was no threat to this half of the kingdom. The land beyond this wall was barren, with sharp peaks and a straight drop to the base of the mountain. Not to mention, there was a frozen lake on the horizon and then nothing but a range of mountains—one of them was the very mountain I had climbed the day before last.

Then nothing. From what Tamara had hinted, there was a sheer drop off the planet's edge beyond these mountains, directly into space. There was only one way into this kingdom, from what I knew, but now I was wondering if there were technically two.

I gathered the fifty archers who stood on the wall and told them to follow me. As we abandoned that final tower, I turned to face the kingdom and saw the massive army making its way across the kingdom and past the palace. They were led by the five knights. This was a good sign. Nevertheless, an uneasy feeling overcame me as I took the final steps into the green, grassy fields of the farmers' district. It didn't feel right leaving our north side exposed like this.

The archers stopped. They formed two rows of twenty-five on either side of me. They waited for me to take charge. "I need five men to stay here to keep a watch on our north side."

The archers looked at one another. Before long, five men approached, their bows in hand and quivers full. I stopped them briefly as they went to pass me on the steps.

"You have enough signal rocks?"

"Yes, my king. At least two barrels of each."

"Good. If you see something suspicious—even if you don't believe it—toss the entire barrel in the hearth. If the battle erupts at the front gates, no will be turning around to see the signal."

My king," one of the archers looked up, sweat coursing down his leather helmet. "Throwing that much ignition rock at one time will blow the top of the tower clean off…"

"Precisely," I said. "It will be loud enough for us to hear over the battle and come to your aid. Off you go now."

The men ran up the stairs. When I looked up, they all bowed deeply, their bows at their chests. I bowed to the young men, then mounted a stray horse tied to a post on one of the farmer's homes. She was a draft horse, but still moved faster than I could on foot.

The sun was getting ready to set as the front gates came into view. A couple thousand men turned and created an opening for me. I leapt down from the draft horse and let her wander back home. Orion was at the front gates with Donte in hand. Catching a whiff of me, Donte yanked himself free and trotted over. We met halfway, as usual. I think he secretly liked that.

Together, we rode to the gates. Orion was waiting and so were the rest of the men. I could feel the uneasy attention as I walked through. "Did you get a chance to meet with Asha?"

Orion nodded in acknowledgement. "You know what that tree-talking loony told me?"

I looked at Orion. "Continue," I said, rushing his story.

"A hero doesn't arrive when he is most needed. Rather, at the last minute when all seems lost."

I tilted my head and squinted at Orion. "That's it? Nothing practical about helping us? Not even a small piece of advice?"

"Nope."

"Well, did you ask?"

"*Of course* I asked. He already knew the war was coming. I told him I had come on your behalf, and that we needed help to turn the tables on this war. All he did was say that mystical line and melted back into his magic trees."

I could hear the frustration in his voice. "I'm sorry I failed you, Sainath. I know how greatly you were counting on his support."

I didn't say anything. I let it go. "Let's focus on the next few hours."

The last of the sun's light was vanishing. All I knew of war was what I had read about in history books during my previous life. I had no firsthand experience. Never had I engaged in anything more than my assassin training and solitary killings. Nothing of this scope. Upon arriving on this planet, I had been trained in hand-to-hand combat, but never in the strategies of full-out war.

A somewhat scary feeling came over me, but a rather pleasant excitement too. If I died here tonight, there would be no reason at all for me to carry out the celestial beings' plans. I could simply pass on, and my soul would go wherever Emily was, and that would be the end of it. I looked up at Zahel who kept me in his peripheral vision, awaiting my signal to send ten thousand arrows raining down upon our enemies. They would darken the sky much more quickly than the approaching shadows of night.

I nodded to the captains who stood behind me, preparing to lead their various squadrons within the massive army. Another couple thousand were already beyond the walls, waiting for me as well. This was it. I looked deeply into the setting sun. The veteran knights would give the signal any second now. I looked over at Orion. He smacked his shielded fist to his chest and bowed his head to me.

"Orion, were you born of this planet, or did you arrive here?"

"What the hell are you talking about, Sainath?"

The veteran knights gave the signal. The gates creaked open for us. The army followed behind while a thousand men stayed inside as reinforcements.

"Zahel!" I shouted to the sky above me. We entered the protection of the wall, moving hoof by hoof. "Commander of the Peregrine Archer Legion, let your wrath rain down upon this vile force that dares to challenge us to such games."

For the first time, I heard Zahel's true voice—A raspy, thundering cry that echoed off every stone and vibrated through each feather on every archer's helmet. "My brothers of the legion, may your arrows fly with the speed of the heartbeat of the Peregrine falcon. We are the first sight our enemies will have of this war, and we will be their last. Let our enemies know the terror of our skill!"

With one loud clap, thousands of arrows locked into bowstrings. There was the sound of dragging leather as each archer drew back their bows, followed by another clap from what I imagine was the commander bringing his hand down with such force that it broke the sound barrier as he swiped his padded thigh. The clap echoed and just as I got to the front lines, the sky became pitch black.

I looked from side to side. The royal guard surrounded me, followed by the rest of the knights. I took a step forward. From here on out, I had to let my instincts take over.

I looked over at Orion who had taken his place by my side. I heard the veteran knights step up. I drew one of my swords and waited for Ursa to charge us. Waited for that moment when he and I would fight. Orion's horse shifted beneath him, and Donte danced in place. The horses were ready. I looked over at Orion's face one last time, then drew my black steel sword and raised it to the sky. I pointed it at Ursa, who unleashed a roar that I felt across the hundreds of feet that separated us. He was nothing more than a white and gray dot in the distance.

The arrows were still journeying above us as I spoke to Orion. "Stop me if you have heard this story before."

CHAPTER 10

*living with the
choices we make*

The arrows hit their mark, and the battle erupted in a mass of roars and taunts. I suddenly wished I had my throwing knives. I could have hit the lizard people before they had a chance to notch their arrows.

I lost the royal guard in a matter of minutes. The hacking and clashing of swords concealed the voices of the men who fought. The bears broke through our defenses but met the archers on the wall before even having a chance at the gates. Taking out one bear at a time was an exhausting conquest. Each bear easily outweighed and outmanned us four to one. It took all my speed to bring them down to their knees. I let the knights take it from there.

Donte was on his own; I lost him in the first wave of clashes with the enemy. I used my agility to my advantage and brought down many enemies. A few of us stood there, gasping to catch our breath. We had made it through the first wave. I looked around and saw the second wave already striding toward us. This was going to be a long night.

It was a clear night, at least. Stars shot their beams of light down upon us, as if the battlefield were a stage and each soldier just an actor playing at war. A half-moon shone down.

It was only with my new eyes that, looking over my shoulder, I was able to witness a second light in the sky. It must be a second moon. I couldn't believe I had never noticed it before. Then again, I had never known to look for a second moon. It was slightly dimmer than the one directly overhead. With its green tinge, I wondered if perhaps it was another planet.

An arrow whisked past my right shoulder. I looked in the direction it had come. A poisonous stench announced the arrival of the Lizard Clan, as they advanced on the right flank of the kingdom. One of them broke formation and lunged at me. A knight intercepted and took the next arrow square in the chest, then dropped, paralyzed in seconds. I grabbed his body by the shoulder plates and dragged him back behind our line of defense, across a barrier formed from the piled corpses of dead bears.

I heard another arrow flying toward us. I stopped dragging the body so I could focus on it. I wondered—could I catch it? Like I used to with throwing knives? It had been years since I had done anything advanced like that. Instead, I raised my meteorite sword and deflected the arrow right before it hit the tip of the blade. It bounced off the metal and changed its trajectory forty-five degrees, deflecting into a bear who was about to swing his axe at me.

I knelt over the knight and snapped my second blade from its sheath and crossed both swords at the hilts where they were the thickest. The next arrow wedged itself in the dirt right before the bear landed at my feet and brought down his double-bladed axe. My blades took the full force but not without my entire body sinking a full foot into the blood-drenched snow. I kept my strength in my legs, just willing my body to keep me alive. The knight was right under me and couldn't move. His quivering eyes seemed to be praying that my own body wouldn't be the last thing he saw, falling on him as we both died.

A falcon arrow screamed past my ear and stabbed into the bear's elbow. With a roar of pain, the bear looked up toward the wall. This eased just enough pressure on my body that I was able to react. I shifted my shoulder behind me to avoid the axe coming down, and at the same time, released my swords. I pulled my right heel away from where it was crunched against the knight's rib cage. With one fluid movement, I kicked my heel back with a force so mighty that the knight slid behind me, freeing up the ground I stood upon. Bringing my swords down, I took a breath and slid across the soft ground. I moved to the left and slashed with both blades—left over right—as the axe blade grazed my right shoulder into the ground. My mouth full of hot blood, I stood and jumped on the back of the great beast and stabbed both swords through his ears, ending his existence before he even had a moment to cry about it.

It all happened in a single breath. The front line stopped fighting the bears and looked at me. I pressed my knee into the head of the corpse. Then it came crashing down the slope as I removed my foot. There was a splash as my metal boots made contact with a puddle of blood.

A great voice of courage awakened in the men; the knights started to gain some momentum. Copying my movement, my men went for the legs, then stabbed the massive creatures from behind. It still took a couple men to bring each bear down, but now we were much more efficient. I jumped on a pile of bear corpses and held both my swords in the air to catch the moonlight, signaling Zahel to unleash a slew of arrows from the tower archers' bows.

Before I could advance, a large gust of wing shot through the air, drying my face instantly. The 100-foot arrows met their mark, each pinning twenty bears at once, which effectively eliminated the rest of the second wave for us.

I scanned around me. With my sword, I deflected arrows from the lizards; one of them got so irritated with me, I think he unloaded his entire quiver in my direction. He finally dropped his bow and ran at me—suicidal—with his dagger drawn. Right before he reached me, I countered him, flipping his feet out from under his body with my sword. I wiped his scaly feet clean off the ground. He flipped over once before landing on his backside. With one clean stab from my sword, he was as good as done.

I drew in a deep breath, glad I had let my instincts take over again. It felt good to be in control once more. I had missed how this felt. More impressive was how easily it all came back. I had probably killed twice as many soldiers as my knights. The only ones who stood with me, stride for stride, were the veteran knights. Line by line, wave by wave, we brought down bears and lizards. By the time the two moons were disappearing with the morning light, the mountainside wasn't even recognizable. The gates opened at times to collect the wounded and dead, drawn by blue flags from messengers of both sides. The flags indicated a break in the battle to collect the bodies. Even through the brutality of war there was still respect for the dead on both sides; this act of truce surprised me.

I scanned the numerous bodies and looked for signs of Ursa. The cave was half a field away now. Me and the veteran knights were at the halfway point between the two armies. My knights started retreating to the gates, dragging the paralyzed men to the horse-drawn wagons that were scattered across the battlefield. I didn't see the bears collect any of their kind. They just returned to their encampment about a mile from the base of the mountain.

We had lost half of our men to poison arrows. A few hundred more were cleaved in pieces across the land. It wasn't bad in comparison to what our odds had been. Bowing my head, I scraped at the blood-stained ground. Back and forth my boot went, digging deeper into the earth. I just wanted to see something besides blood on the mountain. A few inches below the surface, the bare ground revealed itself to me. A voice carried across the land; it was Orion on his horse. Donte followed, not far behind. A gash spread across his chest. It looked like it had been seared shut by extreme heat. The wound was over a foot long, at an angle just below his neck, where it ran down to meet his front leg. I sheathed the twins and waited for my ride.

The gates closed, and voices started filling the silence the battle had left behind. Any free space at the first half of the kingdom—including the palace—had been converted to white tents for medical aid. Women and families came pouring out of the palace gates when the word spread that the first day had been victorious.

It wasn't true. We had a long way to go before victory should even be considered, but I knew the men's spirits needed bolstering to keep their courage and hope alive to fight through another day. The sky was blue dotted with a few clouds which spread across the small planet.

The bodies would start rotting in the heat if we didn't burn them quickly. Before I could say anything, gray smoke rose outside the gates. I half jogged to the front tower. Climbing the steps quickly, I saw that the dead were already being burned. The remaining knights who had lost appendages were already inside getting attention for their wounds.

"Are you all right?" Orion moved out of the way to let Donte through. I had dismounted at the gates so his wound could be treated, but now he was showing his usual stubbornness. I let him walk at my side as I checked on what remained of the army. It might have looked like we won, but we had only managed to take out about a quarter of the bears. They had caused the deaths of half our men over night, giving the helms of the fallen to their wives and now-fatherless children was going to be a harrowing task for the field doctors and messengers.

"Orion." I motioned him over to the nearest medical tent and spoke softly. "We might survive one more battle going toe to toe with Ursa. We cannot stand anything more. We *must* get aid. Did the messengers from the Owl Clan return? Any news of King Gregory? These men need his leadership more than they need me, let's be honest."

"Nothing yet, Sainath. One messenger did arrive," he said. "We thought we could sneak him past the bears at the base of the mountain. Sadly, they returned him to us on his horse. With his head tied to the saddle. It was the quickest—but riskiest—way to the Owl Clan. Otherwise, we would have had to ride around the mountain chain and then across the desert to reach the back side of their territory. We would be losing more time, and as you said, we might only have one more day in us…"

The royal guard huddled next to the tent where we stood. "Go check on your men. I need to make some changes if we are to hold out for more than a couple of days."

Orion bowed and walked away with his horse. Donte looked at them, then back at me. With a flutter of his lips, he started following me once more. I took him inside one of the medical tents. The men all looked over as Donte was brought in. He lowered his head and finally let his tired legs drop to the ground. After he had sat down, I grabbed a medical kit and looked for some bandages with which to wrap the gash. I touched the wound, and Donte snarled at me. With him sitting, we were eye to eye. I was on the ground next to him, my strapped legs crossed over his.

A servant rushed over. "My king, is there anything I can do for you? Maybe run a bath, or at least help you out of your armor so you may rest?"

Another servant came over. "I can take this beast out of the tent, my king. It doesn't belong here."

I stopped cleaning Donte's wound. I looked up at the servants. The knights stared from their beds where they lay with bandaged limbs. Some ate and drank in the corner of the tent.

I hadn't realized I had created a scene. Nevertheless, I was the king. I spoke without standing and just kept working—picking a length of bandage and cutting it into strips which I then deposited in the small kit that lay next to my left knee.

"This animal that you see," I began, "is not just an animal to me. He has every right to be in this tent. Just as much as any man who fought by my side. He may not be a human, but he is still a knight, just in a different form."

A chuckle grew into booming laughter, which rose from outside the tent. I didn't look up. They could laugh all they wanted. I didn't have time for it. They thought they had won today, but they didn't know Ursa like I did. There was always a Plan B with someone like him.

I still remembered what he had said about how old he really was and all the wars he had fought. No way was this going to end quietly. I had a solid understanding of ancient battles from history class during my school years. Ursa had thousands of years and experience to back him. This was just a test. A test this kingdom was not ready for. Clearly.

I bandaged Donte, but needed a cream from the needles of the evergreen pine to make sure his wound didn't fester. The only problem was, the needles were only found on the forest floor far beyond the wall. Retrieving them would necessitate leaving the kingdom vulnerable. It would take me half a day to go and return. I got up and patted Donte on his head as if he were a dog. This communicated the signal "stay." He whinnied and lay back down.

"Give my horse fresh water and food. Do not move him. And that is an order! I will return for him…soon."

I lifted the flap to the tent and walked out into the open. Circles of men sat in scattered groupings around the tents. If the palace behind me was obscured from vision, it would look like we were in the middle of the battlefield. I went in search of Orion. He would be in the royal tent—where I should have been this whole time. I knew they would accept Donte in a heartbeat; they had seen him in battle and knew he was smarter than any living horse. I knew the connection I had with him.

Two pikemen stood guard at the entrance. It was the only tent that had mandated guard duty. I waved, and the men bowed their heads. My feet hurt in the metal boots, and my shoulders ached from swinging the blades with the force that had been needed to pierce through the polar bears' armor and rend their fur.

Inside, only four men reclined on cots. The knight I had saved earlier was on the edge of the bed, shaking his limbs to coax feeling back into them. He stretched his legs out while a servant massaged his feet. The servant saw me walking from behind and bowed, then walked away. I sat next to the knight. I took in the room; my eyes rested on Orion, who was tending to his men. The rest of the royal knights started undressing to get some fresh air. A few of them left the tent; I presumed they had gone to fetch food and drink. All they took with them was their swords.

"Thank you for saving me," said the knight. "I thought that bear's looming shadow over us was the last thing I was ever going to see." He wiggled his toes with concentration. Patting him reassuringly on the back, I left his side and motioned Orion to follow me out of the tent with Dolton coming out of the tent catching up to us. His armor was bloodstained like the rest of us. The shield he strapped to his back was in half from a clean cut of an ax no doubt. He was standing and eager to speak with me.

He spoke briefly to his wounded, then followed me, still fully dressed in armor. It seemed we were the only three still clothed from head to toe.

"Listen." I turned my back to the rest of the tents and what remained of the army. And spoke sternly to both of them. "I need to go into the forest to collect medicine for Donte's wound. Otherwise, he will be overcome by fever in the night. But I am afraid to leave this place because it will mean that I will be gone for half a day. While I'm in the forest, I hope to run into the Forest Guardian and try to change his mind...if I can."

Orion shifted his weight from one leg to another and glanced at the wall which still glinted with the silhouettes of all the archers, waiting in position. Lezah still maintained his same, stoic posture on the tower, his back to us.

"Do what you must Sainath," said Orion. "But whether you are here or not, I will fight and so will your army."

"So will I." Doltan murmured in.

I unstrapped one of my black swords and handed it along with its sheath, admiring the craftsmanship. Orion unsheathed the sword, and the black blade sang a song in the wind; it vibrated in the slight breeze that suddenly came and left. The sword held its position straight in front of him, dividing the two of us. It was the thinnest sword in the army, light and versatile in both backstrokes and forward slash.

He flipped it in his hands a few times. "I remember how long it took me to master flipping this sword in the air, just to catch it without stabbing myself in the hands."

"You made these swords, didn't you?" Dolton spoke up admiring Orions swordsmanship.

I released a deep breath. "Yeah, it was a long and painful journey during the last of my world travels. Hang on to this and let it be by your side so, everyone here will know you are now in command. It is much lighter than your sword, so you won't have to swing as hard. Let it fly with the extension of your wrist.

The army fell silent and gathered around the royal tent. Orion looked around, then back at me. "Are you not coming back?"

"I do not know, but if I can't find aid soon, you and I both know what will happen to this place and its people."

Orion twisted the sword in his hand—a beautiful blend of wood and metal—and dropped into a stance. He gave it a couple of swings. "Very light compared to my own. You are right. I will take good care of it, I promise. Come back for it though, won't you?"

"Of course. Hold them off for as long as you can. I will return as soon as I am able. Take no prisoners and don't attack Ursa head on. Neither one of us knows how powerful he is; he has us outmanned and in terms

114

of advantages, he has years beyond us when it comes to experiences with warfare. Don't let the men get too soft or too drunk. Keep men alert at all towers. Monitor the rest of the kingdom while you still have time—and last but not least—check on the women and children. Make sure they know what the plan is if we fail." I started walking past him toward the far wall where the forest lay. I shouted without looking back. "The kingdom is in your hands until I return!"

I found a horse wandering away from the tents. She carried the royal knights' blanket. I coaxed her over, mounted, and rode to the forest gates.

CHAPTER 11

||||||||||||||||||||||||||||||||||||||||||||||||||||

a story within a story

The sun disappeared as the tower to the west came into view. The black mare was older, her heavy breathing tended to skip an exhalation here and there. A few archers brought their bows to their chests and nodded their respect for me by way of greeting. I waited for the gates to open. Two levers on top of the tower hooked to a pulley system of heavy chains—and a device that most closely resembled a rolling pin—turned counterclockwise when one lever was pulled. The iron gates lifted and the smell of vegetation assaulted my senses. I kicked the mare's hind quarters to spur her forward, and she bolted with a struggle at first but found her stride about a third of the way into the forest.

It was at the end of the day that I arrived. I feared the worst for the kingdom. The enemy had set up camp at the base of the mountain, but that wouldn't stop them from sneaking around in the dark. The mountain sides were completely dark. Luckily for us, bears have poor vision and depend mostly on their sense of smell to navigate their environment. It wasn't until the stars had shot out and night blanketed the sky that I discovered the mare was exhausted. I wanted to keep going but didn't trust her to find her own way back to the kingdom.

I settled under a tree, hitched her nearby, and rested for the night. I was close to Asha's home. I could feel that the energy of the forest was extremely strong in this area. I had to be near the center or at least close to it. It only made sense that he would reside in the heart of the vast forest.

I prayed for Orion, Doltan, Zahel and the rest of the army that night. I prayed that messengers would bring the word in the morning, a spring in their step from the good news. I prayed that the Owl Kingdom would come to our aid. I didn't know how they might fare on the open battlefield, but from what Gregory had told me, they were the wisest of societies on this planet. I thought about what Tamara had suggested I do about my future and also, about what the witch had said. I weighed the two paths in my head.

I nodded off still praying for the men and Donte.

Sunlight shot through the forest and bounced from tree to tree until a ray smacked into my eyelids, waking me. I hadn't dreamed. I smelled of old sweat and overheated vegetation. I realized many leaves had fallen on me in the middle of the night. The mare stayed tied to the tree next to me, chomping on the grass. I let her eat. I knew we had arrived at our destination. I just needed to convince Asha to come out.

It was early morning. Glancing in the direction of the kingdom, I noted that I didn't hear anything, which was either a very good or very bad thing. I needed to hurry. I looked around for a particular set of trees. They were scattered on the south side of the Forest Guardian's home as they had been before.

I called for Asha as I looked, knowing he would be listening through the trees. It wasn't until I picked two handfuls of the pine needles and stuffed them into the pouch tied to the mare—happily eating her fill of the dewy morning grass—that I let my frustration show.

"Asha, I know you can hear me. Orion has already come to see you, and you told him the same line that Apollyon told me in my nightmare before Earth was destroyed. If you are playing along with him to see this battle through, I swear I will ignite this whole forest so it's consumed by flames after I claim victory, one way or another, with my army. I'm pretty convinced Apollyon had something to do with Ursa being so angry at me. What lies did he tell Ursa to fill him with such rage? He didn't assemble all of his forces against my kingdom just because he was sore about my having defeated one of his sons in a tournament."

I mounted the mare and waited. My ears strained, seeking out a rustle in the canopy or the roots of a tree pulling themselves free from the earth. But the forest was silent except for the rousing birds who gossiped amongst themselves.

I urged the mare forward and started off in the direction of the kingdom. The war on my doorstep was already readying for round two. Just as I found my stride, a branch came out of nowhere and swung me off the mare's back. I flew all the way back to the tree where I had rested the night before. Rolling a few times head over shoulders, I slowed to a stop on my back. Another tree branch reached around like a snake and stood me up. I opened my eyes.

Asha looked down, his head covered in moss and vines. His tentacle hands reached for me.

"I am sorry, Sainath," he said, taking my hand in his own and shaking it. "I have been away traveling to Gregory's aid. After all, this is his kingdom. I heard Orion but could only relay the message that I did because I needed to speak to you personally. Not him. I knew Apollyon's last words to you on Earth would spark an interest poignant enough for you to leave the battle and seek me out. How are you?"

It was early morning. The grass was still damp with dew, and droplets dripped from my fingertips where I had clutched the ground. As I stood, Asha unfurled the vines entangling my body. The vines deposited my full weight on the grass, making hardly any noise. The forest erupted with animals and plant noises as Asha's presence was felt by its flora and fauna. It was like a chorus of children, excited to see their father or an old friend who has been away for a long time. Deer, elk, and smaller game arrived in groups or on their own to see Asha, and if they were lucky, they'd be graced by the gentle touch of one of his large hands. He grew a white, petaled flower no longer than an inch, on the tip of his finger. All matter of wildlife lined up to approach this little white flower. Later on, Asha explained that it was the flower of a tree from the first world of the Wikums.

"Tamara mentioned them, and said it was one of your favorite stories to tell?" I responded, now that we were back in his tree home. Here I felt I could speak more directly. My mind was clearer without the listening creatures who lived just outside of the walls of this inner tree which Asha called home.

"Did Tamara tell you the story of the Wikums?"

"She said you might want to tell it," urging Asha to spill the story to me, and tell me why it was significant to the celestial beings.

He looked at me as tea was being poured by a branch into clay cups.

"Good, you are already sitting down. A quick story, and then we shall talk business.'"" Asha spoke as his chair erupted from the forest floor and the teacups were placed in front of us by the retracting branch resting itself back into position against the far wall where the kitchen lie. His soothing voice began a remarkable story.

"In the beginning, an immense amount of energy took the form of a sphere. In the far reaches of space, there existed a handful of species that were on the brink of war. Among one of the habitat-filled planets was a world filled with peace and instinct-driven creatures. These creatures interpreted the sphere-like figure as a new star forming, but this supposition was wrong. The massive energy sphere was in fact made up of trillions of souls, all glowing brightly like individual stars. One ancient being would later go on to say that he could hear chatter coming from the sphere. Perhaps even words or a fully-realized language shared in the conversation between the souls. As the energy of the sphere grew, many civilizations left the solar system out of fear that the massive energy ball would explode without warning.

However, one particular race of beings decided to stay behind. These ancient beings were simple yet advanced in many ways.

Let me explain. The beings had an odd structure about them because they had very small heads. In fact, their heads were so small, their eyes were mere centimeters apart. There was just enough space between them to fit two fine hairs or one coarse one. Each face consisted of a single tube-like structure that moved up and down when they took in air. The tube stood and extended on top of their head, in which there was an opening like a straw. It flexed and shrunk into itself when air entered, and relaxed and inflated skyward a couple of inches when the air was released.

. They had two arms and two legs. Their arms were like a straw too, but with ridges bound up very tightly. When they reached for something and lacked height, they could unravel their arms to reach their objective.

119

Their legs were the same way, but more useful when in movement. Jumping, they could cross great distances in a single bound. They only ate plants, which may explain the color of their skin. They themselves had three colors to them. Each began white at a young age, then green and soon turned gray with the arrival of adolescence. This particular ancient race was called the Wikums.

For all their intelligence they lacked a couple of things. For one, none of them knew anything beyond what was instinctual, due to their special body structures and their intuition concerning the green planet they inhabited. It was the first planet in the universe that had a wide array of plants on it, and they were the first beings to breathe oxygen—the only ones that had a lung structure complex enough to do so.

Now, here's the twist. The rest of the universe demanded oxygen. Not for the breathing of course, but to fuel their ships for a galactic war brought on by a neighboring planet that quickly saw how weak the eyes wikums were and how easily they could be manipulated in provided fuel for a war that didn't involve them. You see, in the eyes of every other civilization of the known universe, the Wikums were mere slaves that could do only one thing: provide fuel. But, the Wikums couldn't stand up for themselves nor retaliate against this notion, because they didn't know how to do anything other than what was natural to them.

Wikums were missing a vital factor in their lives. It wasn't that they were the bottom feeders of the known universe. It wasn't their work ethic—no way! It was an emotional connection. You see, they worked in silence, only talking if it applied to a problem in the production of extracting oxygen from trees and plants. They mated once a lifetime when their skin turned from green to gray. Wikums were stamped with a number across their abdomen by one of the ten first Wikums. They lived very long lives well into a 1,000 of your years. No funeral or mourning existed among them. Once they died, they simply would be ignored or walked over if they died in the very few paths that existed throughout the planet. Eventually being trampled would flatten the Wikum bodies until they just became part of the ground itself. The remarkable thing was the Wikums would be made up of the perfect amount of nutrients to sprout new trees. It mattered which Wikum it was—female or male—

whichever was closest to their number when a Wikum turned gray was the one they mated with.

However, there was one who believed there was something very wrong with this behavior, something missing inside of the Wikums. It was one who flew too close to the glowing star of souls. The one who believed he heard voices coming from it. Among the Wikums, this one was called 650.5. They didn't have emotions to drive them, so why have names? It was much easier to track everyone's performance with numbers anyway. The numbers were assigned on the day they were born.

650.5 was an odd character and he knew it too. No one else had a half in their names. He was the only one. This was because he was born in the heat of the midday sun, and all Wikums new that the female wikums only gave birth under the second full moon. Yet, as emotionless as they were, none but the elders noticed this odd birth which occurred once more and only once more who was also called 650.5. This 650.5 drove one of the tankers that hauled the oxygen across vast distances to faraway civilizations. Most of it went to the neighboring planet that they were slaves to, but they didn't really mind. 650.5 would often get lost in his work, always looking up beyond the canopy of the trees, deep into the atmosphere. The Original Ten, who were the first Wikums to be born, found him to be clueless and not a proficient enough worker.. They thought, after much discussion among themselves, that this was because he was only half of what a real Wikum was.

So, they took him off the endless green land and demoted him to transport duty. It was a very easy job, and 650.5 liked it. Each destination was preprogrammed. He just sat in the cockpit of the ship and pressed buttons. An onboard AI told him which buttons to push in case of an emergency. Most of the time, he didn't even sit in the cockpit. He would find a window seat somewhere on the side of the ship and watch endless stars pass him by. His other favorite thing to do was put on the radio wave headphones. He could listen to everything that was going on outside of the ship in the vast emptiness of space. Anytime he passed an occupied planet he could pick up the faint buzzing of energy. But the most powerful of the energies was the large glowing ball near his home planet. Since all the other civilizations had up and moved when the glowing sphere erupted into its present size, 650.5 was traveling much farther than he had ever imagined. On his way home, he would take off autopilot just to circle the glowing sphere at least once with his headphones on, listening to its unusual chatter.

650.5 never wanted to land. He wished he could stay in space for the remainder of his life. He didn't want to get paired off with a random female, probably named 650. He had never even met her. But he knew once he turned gray, the elders would pair them together. He didn't want to live like every other Wikum. As stars and space and planets of various colors flew by his window, his hunger to fill the emptiness inside him grew. He ate until he almost burst. He even tried working in the fields again, only to be spotted and escorted out after a few minutes in the trees. It wasn't until he started to turn gray that he realized what his body was missing.

It was a bright morning when 650.5 woke from his tree home and found when he looked down that his skin was changing. He knew by the time the sun set, he would look totally different, and by the end of the workweek he would be paired up with his mate. If that wasn't the worst of it.

He stepped out of his treehouse and looked up at the stars fading in the morning light. He realized in that split moment that his time of driving among the stars was coming to an end. He would be grounded and forced to reproduce before he was allowed to work again.

He walked among his people, watching them at work. Many of them didn't mind that he was staring. As he walked along the base of the countless ladders that stood by the roots of every tree he walked by, a gray Wikum with folds wrinkling his eyes stepped into his path. 650.5 knew this was one of the elders, preparing to lead him to his future spouse. 650.5 gulped a heavy air bubble and almost choked on it, as the elder wrapped his slinky arm around his shoulder and proceeded to walk 650.5 away.

The middle of the community contained a workspace. On each end of the planet lay the segregated communities of the Wikums. Males on one side and females on the other. There was never any trouble; the males and females never snuck off to each other's communities. When it was time, the elders brought the males over to the female side.

650.5 wondered what 650 looked like. Or perhaps it would be 651? He knew whoever it was, it was never decided by a random occurrence. From birth, it was always predetermined that spouses were either the next or previously numbered female in the sequence. He would spend only one night with her, try for offspring, and then they would part ways—never to see one another again. None of the Wikums grew up knowing who their parents were. You could work alongside them all your life and not even know it. After birth, the Wikums grew rapidly and ready to work in just a couple of days. 650.5 didn't like that. He was curious about the females and often thought about becoming closer, knowing them beyond the status of mating partners.

He let the idea drift from his breathing tube as a shuttle came into view. The distance between the males and females was vast, and they needed shuttles to cover it.

The shuttle was gray and had two oxygen-fed fans mounted underneath, and a glass dome wrapped around the top which allowed its occupants a 360-degree view. A pilot was waiting near one. It stood at the height of the Wikums; after all, everyone was the same in all ways and therefore, height was no exception. The shuttle's hood rested just below their chins. Small holes were drilled through the glass so they could breathe freely. The glass door slid off into the body of the shuttle as 650.5 and the elder walked in and sat down. Automatic seat belts shot out of the gray seats and locked them into place. The shuttle rose a couple of feet off the ground, hovered for just a moment and then, like a slingshot, thrust to the east, taking off in the direction of the female community. The elder who sat next to 650.5 didn't say much. He reached under his seat and pulled out a wooden box. Resting it in his lap, he regarded 650.5 before speaking.

"650.5, correct?"

650.5 nodded warily.

"Today is a special day for all Wikums. Today you meet your spouse and hopefully beget offspring to better our people. With more workers we have more oxygen to give away, and so we can continue to exist among the other lifeforms spread throughout our galaxy."

650.5 looked down at the wooden box and realized that the elder was reading from an engraving on the lid. He must have read this countless times. 650.5 was surprised that the elder didn't have this passage Memorized. Now he felt even worse, knowing the elder's words were not even his own. The elder took a deep breath after reading the passage and opened the wooden box to reveal something...not so gray. Nor was it green. It was a color he had never seen before.

It was pure. The fabric looked like it was made of the clouds and stars way off in the distance. The elder gave him the piece of cloth and instructed him to put it across his chest. 650.5 did so and turned his back to the elder so he could tie it for him. 650.5 looked out of the window and watched the blurred trees fly by. He imagined for a moment he was in his fuel tanker up in space; he felt sick to his stomach and the gnawing emptiness expanded throughout his whole body. He closed his eyes to calm his stomach. The shuttle started to slow down and finally hovered in one spot for a moment while the fans cooled as they prepared for descent.

The elder got out and 650.5 followed. The female's community was no different from the male one. Their homes, built in the trees, consisted of single-room settings just like his own. Just a handful of females walked around the community. All of them had just turned gray. Looking around, he couldn't discern whether or not he had seen any of them in the fields; they all looked identical. What did it matter if the elders paired them up? 650.5 felt like he could just walk up to any number of females in front of him and get the same result that society expected from him.

The elder guided 650.5 to the females. The female onlookers watched as they approached. Another elder came forward with a female tailing close behind. The female was emotionless. As their steps got closer to one another, more shuttles started to arrive. Other males were unloaded and paired up with the remaining females.

The elder from the females' side met with the elder from the male side. They talked briefly and nodded to one another, stepping away from 650.5.

The female elder spoke up, "650.5, please meet 650.5." 650.5 looked up from his feet, startled. This female had been given his very own number…he couldn't believe it. How was this possible?

The female elder spoke again, though her voice failed to break the surprise or concentration apparent on the faces of both 650.5s. "This is a rather interesting pairing. Never in our society have we had halves paired together. But since the elders have spoken, this must be a good match to deliver offspring to our community as well as the rest of the inhabitants of our galaxy."

She looked between them, waiting for a reaction to her statement. But neither one said anything. 650.5 looked at the female; she also wore a white cloth but hers had been placed around her mid-section instead of her chest. I suppose it was one way to tell them apart. He looked around at the handful of others who were being placed together. They were all dressed similarly.

The other males seemed a little more cheerful than 650.5, but then again, that was how they always looked. Was he the only one who noticed how boring everything was? How bleak and dull this ceremony was? A funny sensation coursed down his arm. It startled him and activated the spring in his arm. He recoiled—withdrawing it behind his back—and studied the female in front of him. She was surprised by his reaction, and it was clear she didn't know what to do either.

The elders were walking away now. 650.5 didn't know what to do. He looked over at the other pairings for hints. They had taken each other's hands and started to walk to the female tree homes. The female 650.5 was watching another pair do the same exact thing.

How did they all know what to do and yet, the first halves of a whole didn't?

The elders turned away just as they reached the shuttle. Both of them had a look of concern on their faces as the entrance opened and they climbed in. 650.5 watched as the shuttle took off, then reached for the female's hand and held it briefly. He didn't understand the point of it. He didn't feel any different. Was he supposed to feel something by touching another Wikum in this way? It wasn't like physical contact wasn't allowed; it wasn't explicitly against the rules.

However, it was an *unwritten* law. If they did touch another Wikum like the 650.5s were doing right now, they wouldn't get strange looks or lose their shifts at work. The day would continue. The stars would still shine, the two suns would still rise. That's what bothered 650.5 the most about society. There was no dispute and no debate. The empty space in him ached at the very thought of it, of not really knowing any of his fellow Wikums.

As soon as the shuttle left their sight, they both let go of each other's hands and stood there, motionless. The second sun was just about done with its cycle for the day. The female looked down at her feet; they were abnormally small compared to typical Wikum feet. Her toes were still slightly green around the edges, but by nightfall, they would be as gray as the rest of her.

For the first time, an odd but wonderful expression flushed through 650.5. As he looked down at her feet, his lips came together—pressed in a firm line. Then they stretched in an upward curve. 650.5, for the first time, smiled. The female saw this and seemed to find it rather strange.

His expression made her head tilt to one side. She brought her finger up to his lips and traced their upward curve. She repeated the motion over and over again until her lips mimicked his, and she too, smiled. The 650.5s stood and smiled at one another.

Nearby the other Wikums did what society intended them to do. In a few moments they would be finished and head back to their respective houses. Maybe they would see each other at work the following day or in passing as they returned home at the end of their shifts. Some would never see each other again, and even if they did, they wouldn't take notice.

Both the 650.5s still stood across from one another. His smile faded, then hers did too, just as quickly.

The other females would be walking back to their community soon. 650.5 looked behind him and saw the green and gray mixture of his kind returning from the tree fields. It wasn't long before they were being passed by large crowds of females. No one paid attention to them or their shiny white cloths. No upward curves ran across their lips and no one looked at their own feet. 650.5 stared at the female in front of him. His eyes were drawn suddenly to movement beyond her right shoulder.

126

A few of the males were already exiting the tree homes and making their way toward them. However, the males didn't mind them either. 650.5 turned away and started to walk away from female 650.5.

It's not that he wanted to leave, but he felt as though he had failed. In the moments that society had instructed him to go and do what he was born to do, to reproduce more workers, he had fallen short. Why hadn't he done anything? Why had he pushed her hand away?

He followed the other males. After walking a few feet, the shuttles arrived, and the respected elders emerged once more and began leading the males inside. 650.5 watched as his shuttle came down to land. Female 650.5 was already walking back to her tree home. He wondered if she felt just as terrible as he did for not following their society's customs and ultimately, their way of life.

His stomach shot needles of pain into his abdomen. He grabbed at his stomach as the elder stepped out of the shuttle. The elder motioned for him to enter. Then, the glass dome came back over and was locked in place. The fans roared and hovered for a moment before launching forward, returning 650.5 to his community.

On his ride back the wooden box came out again. This time it was flipped on its side, and another passage was revealed. The elder mouthed it once, then started to recite the customary words aloud to 650.5.

"Congratulations, you have succeeded in furthering our existence in the universe and added more workers to the cosmos' ever-needed supply of fresh oxygen."

The elder looked up from the wooden box, turned it over, and opened the lid. He looked up from the box and asked for the white cloth back. 650.5 turned his back to him once more. He untied the small knot and gathered it in his hands. Folded, it was laid to rest in the box, the lid closed tightly. 650.5 looked out of the glass dome as trees melted into the background of the sky. He tried to make himself smile again, but he couldn't.

Strange thoughts entered his mind that night. He could hear the restful breathing of the other male Wikums in the homes around him. He paced back and forth pondering his failure of the day. His mind hurt from thinking so much, for focusing on one distinct idea. He started to wonder again about the other 650.5. She looked like every other Wikum, but then why had she seemed so odd to him? She had the same nose, eyes, arms and legs. It made no sense. He felt a warm sensation overcome him. He pictured her springy legs, and then he pictured her feet, and his lips began to make that magical shape again. He smiled in the dark, realizing he would like to see her again. He fell asleep with the thought of 650.5 in his mind, and the hole in his stomach finally started to close.

Back in her own community, 650.5 woke with the first sun. It beamed through the slits of wood in her home. She woke frightened, with the memory that yesterday she was supposed to have produced an offspring steady in her mind.

She sat up and rubbed her midsection, thinking about how disappointed she was in her actions. Why hadn't she just taken the male's hand and led him to her home like the rest of the females? She felt disgusted with herself, and cowardly at the same time. Bringing one of her thin gray fingers to her lips, she rubbed them. She closed her eyes, thinking about how his lips felt. They had been soft, and she remembered while she was touching his, all she could think about was pushing her own lips against him.

'Why would I want to do something so foolish?' she thought to herself. Close contact alone might draw some eyes. But lips? Lips never touched in the Wikum world. It was forbidden, though no one had ever been told they could or couldn't. 650.5 felt as though it were just another unwritten rule. She had never seen anyone else do it. Now another image popped in her head. She tilted her neck up and looked at the wooden frame of her home and how the small slits in between each wooden piece let in the sunlight. It was like thin strands of a spider web. She reached out and watched as her fingers interrupted the line of light. The image of his lips' upward curve imposed itself upon her mind once again, and she rose to her feet and wondered what made him so different. He was like every other male when he stepped out of the shuttle, with his white cloth across his chest. His hands were the same as hers, and his ears were the same too.

His springs were slightly smaller than her own, but that shouldn't make a difference. He probably didn't work them like she did. Maybe he worked in a different area where he didn't have to reach very far? But he hadn't taken her hand when she reached for it, had he? Nor did he seem to want to come to her home and do what was expected of them. Perhaps he was a little different than the other males. She pressed her lips together and tried to move them in the way he had. She couldn't do it. Her lips stayed in place.

Her eyes flickered with fear as she realized that she would beget no offspring. This had never happened before. Or if it had, no one had ever spoken of it. She knew an elder would soon arrive and check her womb for a heartbeat. The average Wikum was born in just one week and two days later, was put to work. What was she going to do? Maybe it would be okay. Maybe they would decide that the two half-numbered Wikums were not meant to be together, after all. She was sure the elder would summon another male in the next cycle of grays to impregnate her. Then life would return to normal, and she would never have to worry about seeing the new male or the other 650.5 ever again. But in her mind, she couldn't deny that she wanted to see him. At least, just so he could show her how he made that curve with his lips.

A knock sounded at her door. The elder walked in after she had given the signal of approval, to communicate that she was home. The elder motioned her to sit and then lie down flat on her back. The gray hands touched her midsection. They stopped over her womb and paused a few breaths. 650.5 closed her eyes in fear of what the elder would say.

The elder lifted her hands—motioning for her to sit up and inspected her for a moment. 650.5 was sure that whatever happened next was going to go one of two ways. She hoped the elder would just wait until the next gray cycle of males and free her from the anxiety of this examination. The elder turned her back to 650.5 and picked up a wooden box she had arrived with. She flipped it over and read the bottom of the box to herself.

She looked up again after mouthing the words to 650.5. Then, she set the box down and opened the lid. "May I have the cloth back, please."

650.5 stared in surprise, bowed her head, and turned her back to her. The elder untied the knot and folded the cloth in her hands before laying it to rest in the wooden box. She rose and walked to the door. Reached for the wooden handle, she spoke while facing the wooden door.

"Another male will arrive in the next cycle of grays. We will try this again, and we will prevail for it is what is expected of you, so that we may grow our society. This is our work and our way of life. This is a minor setback but nothing we can't overcome. You are released to work in the canopy once the second sun rises, of course." The door opened just long enough for the elder to step out in the sun, then it closed just as quickly.

650.5 lay back down, turned on her right side, and slept until the alarm for the second sun went off. She awoke, still dreaming of the other 650.5 and the magic he held in his lips.

When the first sun rose the next day, 650.5 left his tree home and walked to his fuel tanker. An elder was waiting for him as he grabbed the keys from a small office building. Security Wikums who monitored the area didn't pay him any attention. 650.5 walked up to the elder, who waved at him. This was an odd sight. An elder showing up after the ceremony of the grays was over?

Then it hit him like the light of the mysterious orb which speaks in space. They never fully went through with the ceremony! He never went with her into her tree home. Growing uneasy, he watched the elder. His stomach felt like it was filling the space in him; it quickly expanded to occupy the emptiness he was used to feeling.

The elder Wikum spoke in a quiet tone. "650.5, I have heard from the other elders that you did not follow through with the ceremony of the grays. You should know—this is not a good sign in our society. In fact, this has never happened before, 650.5. The next ceremony of the grays will take place in a few days. I suggest you get your head on straight and join in line with the first-time grays. We can try this again…with another match. I had a feeling putting two halves together wouldn't work out. But the other elders were determined that we should take such a risk every 500 years or so." The elder pursed his lips together until they shrunk. He turned on his heels before 650.5 could say a word.

650.5 watched as the elder walked the steps leading away from the fueling tanker landing pads and got into a shuttle which, shortly after, shot across the tree-topped work area.

650.5 boarded the tanker and waited for the Wikum outside the cockpit to give him the take-off signal. The modules in front of him glowed. He moved his hands toward the launch buttons and paused. He could hear the tanker filling up with oxygen. It would be getting dark soon, and the second sun was beyond the halfway point in the clear sky.

A hand broke through his concentration, drawing him away from the launch buttons. He looked up as the Wikum below waved the green light. 650.5 gave him the okay and pressed the corresponding buttons to initiate the launch. His autopilot clicked on as he cleared the atmosphere and entered the marbled dark and light of space. He was glad the elders hadn't grounded him for what he had not done; he let the automated system take over and moved over to his usual stargazing spot, waiting to catch a glimpse of the gleaming sphere which held voices. He put on his headphones, reclined in his chair, and closed his eyes to the soundless space.

Small beeps echoed through his small ear canals after the first few planets had passed by. His eyelids lifted; his gaze now open to the bright sphere. He jumped out of his chair and reached for the autopilot controls. He took control of the tanker. As he did so, an unusual light flickered on.

"Warning. Off course. Please redirect ship to maintain course."

The automated message repeated itself a few times before drowning out in the background. 650.5 still had his headphones on—he could hear the sphere talking louder and louder as he approached it. If he damaged the tanker, he might actually die himself. He anchored it, cooled off the engines and put on his emergency suit, which was only to be worn if there was a breach. He slipped on the all-gray outfit.

650.5 missed the color green, but now everything seemed gray to him. He unlatched the door and attached his body to a retractable cable. He checked his wrist module and made sure it was calibrated with the tanker's onboard systems so he could pull himself back onto the ship, or if something happened, he could call the ship in for a quick pick-up.

650.5 didn't know what he was thinking. He had already gone against one of his culture's guidelines and now he was about to break another. The loud, warm, glowing sphere hung in the air just a few hundred feet from him. He wasn't sure if it was just a large ball of energy or if something lay at its core. As he floated closer and closer, the voices grew stronger, and the language slowed down to a series of beats. Short and arrhythmic, they had him nodding his head to match their strange drumming. When he was just an arm's reach away, his cable went taut. He couldn't go any farther.

But there was a way. If he unloaded the springs in his arms, he'd be able to touch the intense energy from which these voices vibrated, just out of his reach. 650.5 knew he had to touch the orb. He had made it this far, and a large part of him knew this was right. The emptiness inside his torso started to close once more; the chasm began to shrink until he felt the same fullness as he had in the company of the other 650.5.

With a deep breath, he unzipped his arm sleeve. A cold chill ran up his arm; quickly, he released his spring, hurling it toward the immense sphere. His gray fingers brushed the edge of the sphere ever so slightly.

Suddenly, the sphere went quiet. It grew still. 650.5 retracted his finger, extended it again and tentatively nudged the sphere once more. Nothing happened. *Had he broken it?* He wondered. The glow on the sphere faded to black, and he was stuck in absolute darkness with only the stars of the universe dimly lighting his ship. He withdrew his arm, and the instant pressurization of the suit kicked in and warmed his body against the harsh cold of deep space. He pressed the button to retract the cable back to the ship. As he was pulled back, he looked at the dark sphere, in hopes of observing some kind of change. The back of his suit nudged the ship's cargo doors. 650.5 continued to stare at the sphere. Lowering his head, he spoke the confirmation codes and the doors hinged open. Even as he stepped inside, he turned around and stared at the sphere through the crack between the doors. He watched until the doors had shut completely—just in case the sphere spurted back to life again. 650.5 walked through the pressure doors and straight to the decontamination room to remove his suit.

As the automated limbs came down from within the ceiling, 650.5 stood on the foot-by-foot platform and let his arms go slack at his sides. He tilted his head down so the helmet latches were exposed. Small lights beneath the machine lit up green and so did the microscopic ones on his suit. The limbs processing his suit blinked rapidly, then stopped. They moved down and forward—grasping his wrists snugly, forcing him to lift his arm toward the roof of the ship. Then the machine unlocked his arms and descended to his waist, where they unlocked the upper half of his suit and disconnected it. Finally, as they unscrewed the waist from the legs, a third limb—much smaller in diameter—came down from the ceiling and hair-thin screwdrivers emerged.

The screwdrivers planted themselves into the helmet and rapidly unscrewed it. 650.5 still had oxygen pumping into his suit because he hadn't yet finished the decontamination process. The helmet and torso portions loosened at the same time; he could wiggle his way free if he wanted to, but he probably wouldn't get far since he was still hooked to his oxygen tube. The two larger limbs ascended and their lights flashed fluorescent blue. The room's lights automatically clicked off when this happened so the limbs could detect any dust particles that might have punctured the suit. Up and down they went—several times. The platform rocked forward and backward and caused 650.5 to lean at a 45-degree angle to scan his rear properly.

After a few seconds the main lights kicked on, and he was in the clear. He slipped out of the suit. Just as the helmet was about to be released and with it, the oxygen tube, the smallest limb hovered inches from his face. It attached a fresh oxygen tube from the ship's main cabin, and 650.5 took a deep breath. The old tube was taken away. He let out a deep exhalation of satisfaction as the weight of the suit was removed from his shoulders and taken to be sterilized.

The limbs unlocked his legs from the bottom portion of his suit. They lifted him out so he was free to traverse the platform. The machine resumed its resting position, softening into the shape of the room. The white floor was spotless as always.

650.5 dragged his oxygen tube and carried his small tank in his arms as he entered the shower. It was the only entrance to the main cabin. "Protocol" is what the on-board AI called it. Two extremely thick doors opened to the showers and locked aggressively behind him. Oxygen was pumped into the room, and once the AI had signaled its approval with that shimmering green light, 650.5 took off his mask and set the tank down near the locker where the rest were kept. The shower opened up to him and he let any lingering unease wash away with the water and hot steam.

She heard the water rush over him from the small cargo window. She had been watching him periodically. She had snuck onto the male community in the middle of her shift so she wouldn't miss the 650.5 encounter of 650.5. She found the logged sheets for the next delivery. She knew he must be a tanker from how he looked. So clean even his feet. That and he was looking up at above her community and she didn't have the faintest idea as to why, she was just following her instincts. She saw the tanker number and 650.5 was written next to it. She snuck onto the tanker and found a hiding spot. Her eyes ached to see the curve of his lips one more time.

The unscheduled stop, the large orb of light that somehow called to him. He had even gone outside and touched the orb. When he had returned, he seemed different. She peeked around the corner and saw him through the clear glass curtain. Resting his head back, he eased into a comfortable position. He was glowing in a fluorescent light; he gleamed like the sunrise—like the first beam of light that broke the silent dark night. She didn't know the word for it, but she knew it was pleasant.

The tanker was still levitating in place. She walked past him and into the airlock space to get whatever he had received. Maybe then he would give her the gift of his lips again. After dressing, she waited until she heard water. The airlock doors would make a sound. She heard the rush of the water again and released the button to the door which withheld space's vacuum.

All was still as she stepped out. The small sun glowed faintly; she used the suit's buttons to get close, and when she knew she wouldn't be able to reach, she got ready to expose her hand to the bitter cold. It was centimeters away. Then, oddly warm against her hand, she felt it. A wisp of air had broken from the orb. It circled her as though it were alive, then darted to her hand and disappeared beneath her skin. She waited a moment, then retracted back to the tanker. Although she focused on the possibility of what he felt—and hoped something would happen to her—there was no change. She closed the doors and heard the silence. No water.

She quickly undressed, skipped decontamination, and ran back to the cargo hold. Peeking around the corner, she saw that he had finished bathing. She looked around the cockpit and found him just sitting down, getting ready to put on his headphones. He was speaking to the onboard AI, instructing it to head home. Sure of her safety, she returned to her hiding place.

Afterward, he landed on the home planet and exited the ship. He dragged himself across the tanker area and down to the planet's surface. 650.5s eyes were heavy. He didn't make eye contact with any of the other Wikums. 650.5 climbed up to his tree house while the second sun was just about to dawn. His body ached and his mind was blurry. He started to dream just as he fell on his wooden floor. It was an odd dream indeed. 650.5 felt himself escape from his body like a spirit.

She woke with a start. Her dream had been a vague series of pictures. Within its confines, she dreamed of the other 650.5. The curve of his mouth was the only clear image she could remember distinctly. The second sun was rising, which meant it was time for her shift to begin. She walked down the community's steps and took the first shuttle. Climbing in, she rode in silence, observing other female Wikums' conversations. It wasn't long before the shuttle landed at the edge of the trees. She exited and headed straight to work.

But she found herself distracted. She looked up at the sky the way the other 650.5 had done when they had met. She stared into the emptiness. Her mind went blank; there were no clues or feedback corresponding to what she was looking at. She felt a terrible feeling: a stony sense of urgency toward that Wikum with the other half-number.

The ceremony of the grays came again, its welcoming vibrations running through the wooden slats of her home. A knock sounded at her door. Opening it, she found the anticipated elder, clasping the ceremonial cloth. 650.5 donned the strip of fabric. Following the elder outside, she noticed the first sun had already been up for a while and the shuttles were coming and going. The urge to see the other 650.5 returned to her mind and stomach with a sharp pain. Her face wanted to stretch and her lips wanted to have caused it. However, around the elder she didn't dare show such a thing. She bit her lip as they approached the males who waited at the base of the community's meeting point, waiting to perform their duty. She scanned the random mass, ignoring those who stared at her as she sought he whose gaze was tied to the sky. Or the ground. The one curving his lips, who she wanted to see so badly.

She couldn't see him. Maybe he was just playing the part too? She scanned the males a second time. A handful had already left with females by the time she reached the base of the steps. The elder left her side and brought forth a Wikum. The number across his chest read "651."

A feeling of brokenness overcame her. It was as though every piece of her being was being chipped off to fly away in the breeze. This male looked like every other Wikum, and that was the worst part.

"650.5, please meet 651."

She tuned out the elder's repetitive speech, and stared at 651. He didn't look anywhere but at her. A sense of duty washed over her brokenness. She extended her hand. 651 took it without hesitation and walked with her to her home. 650.5 was out of options; she would accept the situation and the culture of which she was a part of. She ascended the wooden steps to her home and 651 followed. She embraced him with an emptiness inside her.

Was this how it was supposed to feel? Was this her duty to her planet and people, to work and reproduce to provide her community with more Wikums? Her mind went blank to the movement and friction between them. She lost track of how long they had been engaged in the twists and turns of each other's bodies.

Their hands never found one another. It was like they never wanted to discover each other's fingertips. His lips never budged from their straight line. His breathing vibrated in highs and lows but never synced with her own. When the deed was done, he left her, closing the door behind him. There were no words, no touch. Once his footsteps hit the last step of her home and the world grew silent around her, she felt her eyes burn with intensity.

Her breathing tube shrunk to half its size and created a painful sound—the sort of sound she only recognized as that of a Wikum being strangled or drowning as they fought to breathe. Was this what bringing offspring into the world was supposed to feel like? Her burning eyes went flush with great pain, then were filled with a refreshing sensation as liquid rose to them from somewhere deep within her body. They filled her lower eyelids.

She panicked. Believing something terrible was about to happen, she opened her eyes wider to make room for the liquid's increasing volume. However, she finally gave in to her instincts and let her eyes droop shut. A remarkable sense of calmness ran over her body. The liquid formed a heavy raindrop then quickly painted a single streak down her face until each met at the tip of her chin and dripped, like rain from a leaf, to splatter against the wooden floor. It was so silent she could hear the droplet's echo on the floorboards. She blinked several times, listening to the drops as they fell. It soothed her chest and calmed her breathing.

Someone knocked on the door. Her eyes shot up. 650.5 quickly wiped her eyes and took a couple of deep breaths.

The elder stood at the door. "Congratulations, you have succeeded in furthering our existence in the universe and added more workers to the universe's ever needed supply of fresh oxygen." The elder read from a wooden box that was flipped on its side. She looked up and asked for the cloth back. 650.5 sniffed and handed the cloth over. The elder thanked her for her services and left without any further remarks.

* * *

The day of the ceremony was upon him. He didn't want to go; he knew they wouldn't pair him with the other 650.5 so what was the point? He would see her and want to give her this new thing, this thing he called a smile. And now he had all sorts of things running through his mind. He felt happy and then sad. His thoughts played with the possibilities of his heart and his face expressed them.

He didn't show up to work. Instead, he stayed in his hut for a long time. Knocks would emanate against the wood of his door but retreated after some time when he didn't answer. No forces of authority other than the elders existed on this planet, after all.

CHAPTER 12

‖‖

the first haul

H is brain throbbed with new thoughts and vibrant ideas.
650.5 was afraid to open his door and be seen by the other
Wikums. He couldn't hide forever. He still had a job to do. He breathed
in and breathed out, reaching for the door to his home. Images of what
he would see and experience flooded his mind. Emotions he never had
and words for what they were all came to him as he forced the door
open against the second sun's welcoming light. He blinked against the
brightness, staring down from his tree at the Wikums walking to their
jobs. He followed in line but kept his chin tipped up. For the first time,
he saw hues of various depths and textures where before had been one
bland swath of clouds and sky.

A word came to his lips. He mouthed it silently to himself. "Color."

A voice in his mind responded to his movement around the word.

"Who is that?" he said to himself.

"I am you?" the voice responded, questioningly.

650.5 looked around at the other Wikums, walking in formation
toward the trees. No one paid attention to him.

"Can anyone else hear you?' he asked the voice in his head.

"I don't know. Let's see. Hello!"

The voice screamed, and 650.5s eyes widened. He looked around frantically, waiting for someone to say something…anything. But no one did. It was silent besides the sound of footsteps on the dirt ground.

The voice calmed, then spoke again. *"I guess it's just you."*

650.5 didn't know what to think, so he asked the first thing that came to mind. "What do I call you?"

The voice laughed in his head, and spoke, in between giggles. *"I am you, silly. I am a part of you. Every thought, every emotion you have, I am a part of. There is a word for it, but we will get to that later."*

650.5 smiled to himself and walked out of formation, back toward his tree. While he walked, he spoke to himself without caring whether or not anyone thought him strange. "If you are truly a part of me, 'voice,' then tell me—did you come from the glowing sphere in the sky?"

"Yes, when you touched me, you touched an immense source of energy. You took me in. I traveled through your cells and into your nerves until I found a home right here, nestled within your brain."

"That's interesting, voice. What else can you tell me?"

"I can tell you many things, but you must think for yourself first. Like I said, I am a part of you."

"Very well. What is 'color'?"

"Color is everything that you see around you. It covers everything in sight and beyond. When you look up at the stars and sky, what did you see?"

"I see light, round shapes—the second sun too. Are there different colors?"

"Yes, 650.5. There is an infinite spectrum of colors. Different combinations are always at work to express something more beautiful than what occurs in the present."

"That's…that's…"

"'Fascinating,' is the word you are looking for. We can play with words later. It's something that comes naturally to all species. But for now, tell me about this female Wikum who you are crazy about."

"I'm not crazy."

"No, not crazy in a bad way. In a good way! It's a good thing. Believe me," the voice corrected.

By this time, he had reached the landing pad, and a Wikum was waiting to hand him the order forms. He took them and entered his cargo ship, then took a seat in the cockpit. Once the engines had fired up and autopilot had kicked in, 650.5 sat in his chair and told the voice about the female Wikum and the questions that had taken form in his mind. Then more questions came when he landed back home.

"Voice, why does my heart flutter and my fingers tingle when I speak of the other 650.5?"

"The feeling goes by many names. Its definition cannot be found on any scroll or bound book. It is a creation of something unknown, perhaps magic even. Everyone has their own interpretation of it. You must find your own meaning. Might I suggest we go find the Wikum responsible for such feelings?"

650.5 rose to his feet, cut the engines and walked across the field of trees in the direction of the female community. The ceremony of the grays would be drawing to its end. His fear of someone else making her smile thrashed his legs into motion. He ran, something no Wikum ever did. He felt their gaze as he ran. He felt his heart beat faster than he thought possible.

650.5 hoped he wasn't too late to show her this odd but remarkable voice which was inside him now. He reached the steps and slowed to a walk. He panted as his breathing tube retracted and relaxed frantically. The gray male Wikums were leaving the females' homes. No interactions beyond that took place. The door simply opened, and the males walked out. The females closed the doors behind them. 650.5 knew he would just have to look for the odd one. The odd one just like him.

650.5 walked out of her home and into the open. She started to look for him. Something told her he was nearby. She swam with her arms through the mass of males. She didn't know if it was worth the heartache to look for him only to be disappointed again.

"650.5," a voice murmured. It started low and gradually grew loud enough for her to discern within the crowd. She looked around and spoke softly. "Is that you? Why didn't you come sooner, 650.5?"

The voice went silent.

She twirled and twisted, stumbling into other Wikums, and found the ground shortly after. She sat up and looked around as the male Wikums walked past her. They didn't bother to look down. She brought her knees to her chin and wrapped her long, slinky arms around them, bowing her head as she called out.

"Please don't leave me already. Why do you do this? You gave me this curve with my lips, and I want to feel that again. Teach me how you do it."

"To smile? You can do that on your own. You don't need another being's help to be able smile," the voice returned.

"Why can't I see you?" 650.5 peeked her eyes just above her arms still wrapped around her knees. She just saw the last of the males as they left the gathering grounds.

One male Wikum remained. His back was to her. He was looking at the homes on either side of the community. She dried her eyes but didn't bother getting up. She stared at him. Maybe he was lost?

"It's him, I'm sure of it. It has to be him." She said aloud. "He must have come back for me. Oh, but I did the ceremony without him. I wanted to do it with him. Get up and walk to him—tell him how you feel, even if you don't have the words. Words will come, but this feeling…this has to be explained now."

The voice rang out to her. *"I am your inner voice. Don't be afraid. I am here to aid you in reasoning and debates within yourself."* 650.5 interrupted herself.

"No, I can't. I don't know how to act like he does. He does it so—"

"'Effortlessly' is the word you are searching for," said the voice.

"Yes, I think that is what I meant."

"650.5, it is worse to take a leap into the uncertain than to be stuck in this routine that you see all around you. Like when you fell. Did you see how the other males didn't even react to you? They simply walked around you, not even looking down to check that you were alright. You will give birth to the next generation. Your body encompasses the greatest gift of every species. This is in front of you. This

interaction is so incredibly small compared to who you truly are. Rise and walk to him." The voice's commanding tone made her lips curve up into a smile.

She walked over to him.

650.5 was looking at the homes trying to remember which one was hers.

"Voice, which one do you think she lives in?"

The voice was now his companion, but never seemed to shut off.

"I have no idea; everything looks exactly the same. This place really could use a splash of color. No individuality exists, does it? We will break that cycle."

650.5 felt someone watching him. He turned around, and his eyes rested on the other 650.5.

They smiled at one another. And stared for a long while. When the words finally came to their lips, they both spoke at the same time—not making much sense, the sentences circling on top of each other.

650.5 looked over her right shoulder to see the elders walking up the steps.

The elders spoke up. "650.5, both of you need to come with us. We have been hearing the most regrettable news. The court has been assembled, and you must answer for these questionable behaviors."

She didn't know what to do, other than reach out and grab his hand. She was grateful that this time he accepted her hand and held it tightly. She turned so they were both facing the mass of Wikums and the Original Ten. She looked at him, taking in his small chin and following the line of his lips, then up to his eyes. His gaze was focused, and his eyes narrowed at the elders, who had finished berating them and were now waiting for a response. 650. 5s voice struggled as if a new born baby was creating its first words.

She tugged on his hand slightly to get his attention. 650.5 looked to his left, straight into her eyes as she formed the words. "650.5, whatever you are going to do, I'm with you. I don't know what we will say to the court. I don't know how to explain these feelings. I don't think they will understand us. But I am with you, regardless. I don't want an ordinary life. I would rather be the weirdest Wikum with you than fall in line."

He smiled again and looked at the ten elders as they formed a wall in front of them. "That is exactly why we can't go to court. If you are with me, we must leave. We will never come back. We are too different now. We see the faults of this planet and its inhabitants. We must find a new home where feelings are accepted and the odd and awkward are seen as a spectacular thing to behold and not be ashamed of. Are you ready?"

"Ready for what?"

"We are going to run right through them. They don't know what to do. They will be in too much shock. Or maybe they won't be shocked at all. Either way I know they will simply move aside."

"If you are certain. Let's go!" she responded.

He was certain. He whispered, "Voice, do you think this will work or should we figure something else out?"

His voice came to him. *"Looking at our options, the only escape we have is forward, unless you want to climb the wall behind us?"*

"Nope."

Both of the 650.5s ran toward the mass, shoving past the Wikums, who fell over or stumbled back, unsure what was going on. 650.5 stole a shuttle and blasted across the field of trees, over the male community and onto the ship dock. Hand in hand, they ran to the filled tanker he was supposed to leave with a while ago. He set the controls to manual and they launched into what the voice called the "mid-afternoon" sky.

CHAPTER 13

||||||||||||||||||||||||||||||||||||||||||||||||||

a love that transcends time itself

Asha stood and stepped around his chair before wrapping up his tale. "So you see, Sainath, the two half-Wikums came together and became one. They discovered Tamara's greatest creations. The ones that would be placed in each and every human after a thousand years. Look how far we came from creating you. I mean you don't want to look like a Wikum—trust me. They're gentle souls but not the prettiest."

I interrupted Asha's story. "Wait, why didn't they have names?"

"Because, names didn't exist. Even today, the oldest language is mathematics. Numbers are universal. No matter what galaxy you are in. And weren't you listening? Wikums didn't care much about anything until 650.5 came around, and even after that they still went back to their old ways and ended up being enslaved and destroyed by a galactic war that tore apart that star system."

"I was hoping to maybe see the Wikum world one day. It sounds like a dream even though it was so long ago and on the edge of the known universe." I spoke softly.

Asha laughed out loud. "Why do you think I told you this story? Sainath, you are going to travel to this star system. I have a good feeling Prima is hiding on the old Wikum home, or somewhere close to it within that star system, I'm sure of it. She loved that galaxy. So you see, everything ends. It's the natural balance of life. It's just as simple as dying. Only one or two people ever see it coming."

Asha looked up into the tree, pensively, as if the story meant something more to him. He fell silent, staring into the darkness. I thought about the story and what he might be trying to communicate.

I got that he had told me it was the former home of the Wikums because I would be traveling there, but why provide all that detail concerning the two creatures who were misfits within their society? I wanted to ask but then I noticed how late it was. I should be getting back to the kingdom.

"Asha, we really need some aid. Can you join in the fight?" I said bluntly.

He set out a tea kettle. A vine traveled around the trunk, like a snake coiling around a branch. The wall would move and morph as the vine traveled from one side of the home to the other. It popped forth from the tree—never forcing its way out. The tree opened its walls and let the vine through just to touch Asha's hand. I guessed this was how he stayed connected to the rest of the forest. That snaking vine acted like some kind of relay system.

"Sainath, this is my brother's game," responded Asha. "More importantly, this is his world. We saw the end coming for you but didn't realize the trigger would be pulled as early as it was. We had to act. Apollyon threw this planet together and crafted the environment to be suitable for all creatures. There is still a lot of work to be done. It is not an easy task, starting a world from scratch, resetting history's clock just to watch it unfold the same way. I will help you, but you must leave the war. You must get off-world and find Prima. It is the only way your species will survive past your generation."

I sat down at the table as Asha carried the tea over. The clay cups were warm to the touch and decorated with a splash of abstract color in bright patterns, as if a child had painted them. I took a sip. It wasn't as potent as the stuff he had given me before. This didn't cause any dry heaving in my stomach, thankfully. It was smooth and smelled of raspberries and smoked rosemary. The warm vapors engulfed my senses as I held the cup in my hands. The aroma of rosemary filled the inner tree and calmed my head and weary limbs. The raspberries' potency coursed through my system, reactivating my cells with much-needed energy and focus. A few more sips and I felt ready for a full day's battle.

I sat the clay cup down and looked across the table at Asha. I had never noticed exactly how many aspects of nature composed his body. Maybe it was this new and improved sight Tamara had given me.

Asha had shrunk to my size. I wondered if it was difficult for celestials to shrink themselves. What did his true form look like? Flowers bloomed throughout his body as he drank his tea; his eyes were pure green and pupil-less, rounded in gray wood. Bright green moss and cattails hung to his shoulders like hair. As for his broad shoulders, they looked like a vineyard or the rolling hills of some wildflower meadow. Earthy root clusters acted as hair for his armpits and were scattered above his wild berry lips.

After realizing I was wasting time in admiration, I spoke hurriedly. "Look, I don't have much time. I have already been here too long."

He laughed, "Don't be foolish. By now you should know any time you enter nature, time becomes irrelevant. It moves at a much slower pace here. You have only been gone an hour in the kingdom's time."

I almost spit out my tea. Steadying my cup before it dropped from my hands, I said, "What?" It was the only word I could muster.

Asha laughed again, releasing a hummingbird from its small nest which was tucked away in the oak branches that served as his massive ribcage. Pieces of tree molded together with sharp edges, curving in the natural direction of a halfmoon around his chest. His sternum was made of some kind of bone, wrapped in seaweed and overgrown with vines in a crisscross pattern which was finished with thyme branches. The hummingbird flew around the inner tree, looking for an exit. Asha reached for the door. His arm extended, then it stopped. A crack sounded from the limb, and a gray spring appeared between the green flesh. Then, his arm extended even farther. The only unnatural looking element in his body was well hidden. The door opened, allowing the little bird to fly free. Asha closed the door and brought his attention back to me.

"So, don't worry about time when you are here. What you should be doing is getting ready to leave this kingdom as well as this planet. I gather you didn't take Tamara's advice, did you? What made you choose to stay and fight for a kingdom that isn't even yours?"

I exhaled for a long moment, before responding. "Remember when I came upon your home and you helped me get rid of the darkness in my mind?"

"Of course. That was more than a week ago in your time." Asha replied.

"Yes. Well, it seems that you didn't get it all out."

Asha narrowed his twig eyebrows at me. "Don't tell me, Tamara gave you her gift of sight?"

I looked away from him, but nodded in agreement. His vine hands took hold of my jaw and forced my head to turn and face him. "She knows better than to aid anyone on this planet. What else has she told you?"

"Nothing, other than that she wants me to leave and seek Prima because she holds the world in which I'm supposed to rebuild and start humanity again, but I need to convince her that my species is worth saving more than it is worth extinguishing. I have no idea what I am going to say to Prima. I have never met her, and I guess I was one of her chosen few, gifted to create the next world, but I just don't know because after seeing—"

"Tamara showed you Earth, didn't she?"

I nodded as best I could, given that my head was still held firmly by Asha's vines. He came closer to me. "Yes, the gold rings around your eyes betray the false disguises of celestials. She gave it to you so you would recognize Prima. She is well hidden and will take on many forms before you realize it is her. I agree with Tamara. You must abandon this battle and go search for the planet where humanity should start anew. We thought this would be it, but after this battle in Gregory's kingdom, your race—along with your whole DNA chain—will cease to exist. Think about Apollyon's plan. The sad truth is, humanity was never meant to last past Earth. You, Bayard, and maybe a handful others if they haven't already died from being enslaved, will perish."

The vines let go, and I moved my jaw back and forth to soothe it. "What about Orion and Evelynn? The servants...what if they escape and reproduce far from here and find a way to coexist?"

Asha stood and poured more tea. He turned his head to the side and looked at me questioningly as he held his cup in the air, as though asking if I was still thirsty.

I shook my head, and he continued with his back to me.

"I was hoping you would be off-planet before I had to even think about telling you this, but it seems you need a further push to convince you. Orion and Evelynn are products of this world just like everything else here." I walked away from the door and back to the table. "What do you mean they are products of this world? Were they not brought here like the rest of the humans?" I asked, gripping the headrest of the chair.

"They are here to make you feel welcome and comfortable, and more importantly, to keep you from leaving. I know it's difficult to take in, but that's the truth. They are not real. They are morphed and pieced together from our own memories of the people you encountered in your previous life. Parts of your friends and family are embedded in them so you feel drawn to them. Apollyon knew every human who survived would be sent here, and he had no intention of letting you live. He knew that a descendent of Prima would be the only one that could save humanity. When the time arrived, the rest of us were in agreement that it was time to start again. It's a never-ending cycle." Asha returned to the table. He sat down still speaking; he didn't waste a single breath.

"I will help create the next generation of life. This is how it is. It's why I came in the manifestation that you see before you. I'm just like Tamara."

His hands went to his sternum. With a brush of his hands, the thyme branches shrank, leaving the intertwined, diamond-patterned vines exposed. Asha tapped them one at a time, starting in the middle: a couple of taps with his middle finger, a single tap with his index finger on top of the sternum, then three taps with his pinky at its base, followed by a final touch from his palm pressed along the whole width of his sternum and brushing down the entire length of the it. He moved his hand away so I could watch as the vines released their hold and retracted into his chest. Finally, the bone shard was all that remained.

He spoke to remove the final seal. His voice was deep and sad, a tone I had never heard from him. "Last of the Wikums, I am. Last of the people of the tree, I am. Last of the Soulless, I was. I am Asha, the life celestial. Hear my command and reveal my origin."

The bone shard snapped in a dozen fragments of white bone— falling away from the middle of the chest. I was mesmerized at such a sight: the vines, flowers, worms, dirt, insects, grass, and moss fell away, building onto his shoulders like miniature mountain chains. Inside the cavity of his chest, he was just like Tamara. An empty yet never-ending space of stars and dust.

My new eyes hurt at the sight of him. The inner tree in which we stood was filled with blindingly white fluorescent light. I turned away as the light's intensity grew. A ball at the center of Asha's chest emerged from the far reaches of a galaxy which inhabited his left breast. It grew to the size of an apple. I closed my eyes against the brightness, but I could still see the shape behind my eyelids.

"Sainath, this is a soul. You have it inside of you at this very moment. Not hidden away like mine is. Yours lies just beneath your sternum right in front of your heart. When people feel sad, it is not their heart that hurts, really, but their soul. Your heart is a muscle. It will work day in and day out for you. But your soul will feel every emotion you feed it. Something you can't help, due to your species' trait of compassion. A gift from Tamara, to your kind.

"Orion, Evelynn, that man who was brought in to brainwash you into believing he was your father, and every soldier who has fought by your side—they have all been there because Apollyon has allowed it. If you want to actually live your final days beyond Earth with meaning, leave and seek an audience with Prima. Start a new life. A real life. One that gives your species a fighting chance. One last time."

"I will tell you what—if you pull this off, you will be remembered across the known and the unknown. I will tell your story to the next generation of species which find their inevitable end and must start again. Life is funny that way."

The limbs and vines began to cover up Asha's soul. I felt the heat of the light dispense as I cautiously and fully opened my eyes. I had no recollection of time outside the tree. It could be nightfall back at the kingdom for all I knew. As the moss and flowers found their places on his body, he continued.

"Leave the battle, and head out of the forest. Continue west until you hit the planet's shoreline."

"I can't just leave this instant. What about the kingdom and its people? And Donte is still back there. Don't tell me he is also fake."

"I won't break your heart any further, Sainath. I can tell you are angrier than you are sad about all of this. I'm sorry it had to be said. But you have to leave. What did you think would happen—that you would live this fantasy until your dying breath? Your true parents died on Earth along with Emily and your unborn child! Look at yourself. You are not like the rest of this planet. You have a mind of your own, still. You are not set in a routine like the rest of them. Ever notice that the palace doesn't change? That everyone looks exactly the same as the last time you saw them? Why are all the servants beautiful to look at? Why is every knight a more handsome version of the next? Or how about the fact that your royal knights act exactly the same even when they are not instructed to? Isn't it fascinating that, in recalling the moments spent with Evelynn, the realization dawns that she only spoke briefly to you? If she liked you as much as you like her, wouldn't she have wanted to stay here to protect you? Was she not your 'personal bodyguard', as your Gregory put it? This whole place was built to reflect a fantasy in which you would thrive. Evelynn herself was created to mimic certain gestures Emily had. Part of her even resembles your dead girlfriend. How odd is that?"

I gulped air into my stomach, pushed the chair away from the table, and headed for the door. I couldn't take this anymore.

As I reached for the irregular wooden doorknob, I said, "What am I supposed to do?" I stared at the door. "I should have died with Earth. I shouldn't be here if nothing is real. Except Tom, and even he exists in the form of Bayard for the sake of protecting his life. I have been brainwashed and tortured beyond belief. I thought that this world was just the afterlife. That kind of place. I had no notion to even question who I really was—it didn't happen until my mind started to notice how Evelynn moved like Emily once did.

But then the headaches started. I think that was when I realized something was very wrong with this place. I had a fun time when it came to killing, but if everything was set up for me to succeed then it really doesn't feel like I succeeded at all. In fact, I feel like the biggest phony there ever was. I turned my back to Asha as I felt guilt build up in my chest.

Facing the door so Asha couldn't see, I sniffled. Only after Asha had shone light on what was happening around me on this planet did it become clear that I was beating myself up. I was in so much anguish that tears fell onto the tops of my metal boots. They made a sound like pins falling in a silent cave. Each drop echoed in the hollow tree as the sound bounced off the solid objects that lay randomly scattered about.

"Donte, poor Donte," I cried. He was the one creature on this planet who was made for me. Apollyon took my childhood of horse riding and built the perfect companion. "Where is Apollyon?" guilt boiled into anger. "I want to make him pay for all of this, for brainwashing not only me, but everything else that arrived or was molded on this planet to live a certain way, to hate certain things just because they were trained to. He has taken free will completely out of the equation, and it's simply heartbreaking."

A large hand turned me away from the door, Asha looked at me with eyes hard as bark. "Sainath, you cannot fight Apollyon. If you seek him here on his own planet, he will see it coming before you even get a chance. He has spies in just about every kingdom. Take my advice. Leave this place before your second life reaches its untimely end. You have been lucky in the past, but leave now. Head for the shoreline, before your luck runs out. Leave everything—and everyone—behind you. Bayard already knows what to do. He has been instructed to meet you at the shoreline two months from now, in your time. The shoreline lies just beyond the Owl Kingdom. There is someone there who you must also take with you off-planet."

Asha opened the door and stepped out into the sunbaked canopy of leaves with me. He had been right; time was nothing here. It looked like only a few minutes had passed outside of his home.

"One last thing," Asha cautioned. "Remember to use your sight when you arrive to see Prima. Like I said before, she changes her appearance often. She is the celestial being of creativity, after all. Don't worry, she won't kill you. Or at least, I don't think so. Asha squatted to greet a family of rabbits with a fawn close behind, waiting to greet the forest guardian. Stay calm and remember your inner self. Your Earth self. If you thought Apollyon did a grand job building a world to lose your mind in—you have no idea what things come to be true when facing Prima."

"I understand," I managed. "And thank you for being honest with me."

"It's one of my many jobs. You remind me of my former self, and I would hate for you to go through what I went through to discover who I was meant to be. I went crazy and lost myself a few times before... before becoming what you see in front of you now." He rose as the fawn sprinted back to his mother who stood in the tree line in front of us.

"Asha," I interrupted. "The witch visited me a couple of nights ago, and I asked her who she was. How does she fit into all of this?"

"Don't worry about that now. It's not important."

"It is to me," I spoke softly.

CHAPTER 14

||||||||||||||||||||||||||||||||||||||||||||||||||

never meant to be a king

Asha looked up at the canopy of the trees. A vine came twisting down and wrapped around his arm. He listened to the vine, adding a "thank you" after it had relayed its message. He let go, and it traveled back up the tree.

"I have a feeling we are being listened to," he said. "You must leave immediately. I will heal your body in time, but not here. Once you are safely off this planet, I will meet you after your audience with Prima. Until that time comes, ride west. Do not stop. Sleep on your horse if you have to."

"Speaking of horses," I replied, "I don't have one, as Donte is back at camp. Any other way of getting to the shoreline?"

"Hmmm, right. I scared your mare off. I wonder if my horse and greatest of companions will take you. Let me summon her."

"Her?" I asked as he moved away from his home.

Asha looked around for a second then brought his hand to his lips. Curling two fingers into a circle, he placed them in his mouth and blew. A low-pitched whistle sounded from his mouth.

A tree to our left separated like a gate, revealing a leaf-filled path. A shadow moved between the trees. My eyes darted back and forth, trying to follow it.

Out of the trees sprang a horse made of vines. Its hooves were formed from driftwood and rounded with whorled curves. The body of the horse matched Asha's own coloring, and the vines intertwined in horizontal patterns. The horse cantered toward us, then came to a stop in front of Asha, its right side turned to me.

Its mane was made of wild flowers and river reeds. Its tail was golden, black, and green prairie grasses which trailed so that they almost brushed the forest floor. Its backbone was a single panel of ash wood, wide enough to serve as a functioning saddle. The eyes of the horse were made of chestnuts with fronds of moss-green lacing around the iris. Its nose matched the ash wood panel. I wondered, was it one large piece bent over the nose and spine?

"Sainath, this is my horse. She will take you to the Owl Kingdom. The owls know who she is and will not give you any trouble."

"What is her name?" I asked as I approached the horse and rubbed the rough wooden nose. I felt the wildflower mane and ran my fingers across the living vines that made up her body. Each vine reacted to my touch. Some shifted out of place while others grew to avoid my touch in certain areas. She was composed of all living things. It was easy to see she was made by Asha, even if he didn't admit it.

"She's beautiful," I tried again. "What do I call her?"

"Terra."

"Hello, Terra."

"You don't have much time. Take this." Asha reached down into the forest floor and brought out a large canteen of water which he strapped to a vine near my leg. He touched the earth again, and tree stumps rose out of the ground, allowing me to step onto the back of the horse. Terra stood about five hands taller than Donte, which was not an easy jump to begin with. I grabbed onto the mane.

"Oh, she doesn't like that," counseled Asha. "You won't have to command Terra in the way you would a normal horse. She is highly intelligent as she is a direct extension of myself. I will tell her where to go. She doesn't need food or water. She will get you there in two months' time without stopping. You are taking the longest route possible, but it is also the safest path for you to avoid Apollyon and the Bear Clan. Stay within the trails of wooded areas, and you will be protected. If bears come into your path, just tell Terra 'climb,' and she will give you a whole new speed. I will leave that surprise for you.

"I will send for your other sword. You will need both in Prima's world. Besides, it's one of the few things from Earth that is still real. It will please Prima to see them both. After all, it was her gift of creativity that forced you to craft such weapons. Who knows, they might be the one last thing that aids her in giving humanity a second chance."

Terra walked around the forest floor in the small clearing that Asha had created from his whistle, and the tree gave us some room to breathe. I got comfortable with her pretty quickly. She was more intelligent than I had imagined her to be. I didn't have to do much of anything. She moved at her own pace like she was stretching for a marathon. Limber, she bent with the flexibility of a human's form. She lowered her front legs in a crouch and even did a few high-knee leaps around Asha, like an antelope jumping with grace.

As she did this in a circle, Asha gave me one last piece of advice. "It's important you don't make any stops."

"Who am I supposed to pick up in the Owl Kingdom?"

"He is your ticket off this planet. His name is Nayr. He is the captain of a ship that will sail you to Prima. He is also from Earth, but like Bayard he has disguised himself with Tamara's help. He is also like Bayard in that he arrived before you did. Even earlier than Tom, actually. He was from Earth's continent, Africa, which if you remember, was one of the first to fall in the last world. With all of its major animals gone extinct it became a testing ground for misfired nuclear weapons. The man you are seeking was one of the last fighters of that country. Even though he spends more time in the world's oceans than on land, he is the ally you need at your side. He will aid you in keeping the real and the illusory separate as you travel."

Terra stopped and faced Asha. Gently, he touched her face and whispered, "Come back to me, old friend. But first, keep this endangered species safe. Do you remember where you are going?"

Terra nudged his hand with her nose and turned as a few more trees opened to create a path for us. Asha patted her hindquarters and Terra started in a full run to the west, moving faster than any horse I had ever ridden. Asha kept speaking, but I only caught the beginning bits as Terra skimmed trees, breathing softly beneath me.

It was a pleasant ride. I would be able to sleep without being jolted awake by her jumps because she always landed with grace upon her driftwood hooves. She turned before I could even see a tree coming. I had no control. It demanded total trust.

"Use your sight and see the truth. Goooood luuuuuuuuck." Asha's voice trailed off and the swish of the trees consumed my ears. We rode through the forests for two days before the trees and forest floor relinquished us.

* * *

Terra ran with no disruption to her breathing or pace. Her stamina was unheard of; Asha was right—she wasn't any ordinary horse. She never stopped for food or drink. I continued to sip from the bottle that Asha had given me. It was just above freezing as it slid down my throat, cold enough to keep my mind alert and my eyes open. Most of the journey so far had been filled with blurs of trees and spots of color as we rode faster than even the birds flying overhead. Terra ran through the night.

In the early morning sun revealed the mountain chain crossing. That would comprise the longest portion of our journey. I wanted to stop, at the very least to stretch my legs or empty my bladder, but Asha's strict warning prevented me from doing so. By now Apollyon had probably discovered that I wasn't present on the battlefield; he would know something was up and look to those closest to me for answers. I said a silent prayer for Orion and Evelynn. Even if they were of this world and molded to fit my needs for friendship and more, it simply wasn't right to abandon them. It would be like saying that they had meant nothing to me.

Asha had said he'd see my other meteorite sword returned, after I met this Nayr guy. But who was this fellow? He was from Earth too—at least he was real then. I wondered what the end of the world had been like for him. How had the scene unfolded? Did his family die in his arms? Had he loved someone the way I did? These questions ran parallel to Terra, keeping pace with me as I grew bored of riding. The mind can only take so much of the same thing over and over again before it becomes dull to the senses.

I took another sip of the ice-cold water as the base of the mountain chain came into view. The lush forest and grassy fields turned to snow and ice. Unlike a real horse, Terra didn't waste time adjusting to this new environment. The only change I noticed was her expanding rib cage. The vines shrunk away beneath my feet to stretch over her bones and wrap around my legs, covering them until they were completely concealed. Effectively, I was strapped into her body now. An extra vine unfurled from the ash plank had wrapped around my waist a couple times. I was secure.

The wind lashed our faces and forced Terra to slow down from a full run to a cautious trot. The snow grew deeper to the point of scraping along the bottom of my feet. Terra was strong; she didn't give up. Most horses would have stopped from intense cold at this altitude. We were roughly a hundred feet from the summit. Once we reached it, we would ride along the mountain's spine. It was a jagged trail and a thin one at that, but it saved us from deep snow, factoring in those dangerous gusts of winds which kept trying to knock us off. It was a tradeoff from the looks of it. Terra had me pretty well strapped in. If the wind gusted hard enough to fling me away, we would both go rolling down the mountain. At the very least, we'd lose a few days. At the most, our lives.

Left, right, left, and now the summit was mere feet away. We stopped at the top. Terra struggled to catch her breath for the first time the week long journey and I was already feeling doubtful about our abilities. I didn't know if I would survive the two-month journey across the planet. It hadn't seemed so large when Tamara had pointed it out to me. There was also the added issue of Terra. With Donte, I could communicate through sign language, through the subtle movements of my body. With Terra, I wasn't sure what I had to work with. Maybe speaking to her would be a good place to start.

"Terra, would you mind letting me off here?" I asked, unable to repress the shiver in my voice.

The wind howled back and forth like a paintbrush's bristles against my skin. Terra didn't move, though I could see the forceful gusts rumpling her flank. A vine unlocked itself from around my waist, then traveled up my spine and laced its way around my neck. Fear crawled into my belly. The vine felt like an anaconda coming to wrap itself around my body and suck the life from my flesh. As it curled around my neck it split into three separate vines. One wrapped around half of my neck then inspected me—like a cobra ready to strike. It lunged forward suddenly, striking my throat with enough force to make me cough. I released a cold breath as a cough resonated through my lungs. Now the vine struck my throat vertically, so that its tip flattened along my vocal cords. I exhaled. I felt warm all the way to my lungs, allowing for easier breathing and no pain from the cold. It was surreal; everything around me that I envisioned in my mind had gone foggy; if I tried to concentrate on it, it became less and less clear. I played with my breath, controlling the tides of inhalation, trying to create what I had known for so long growing up on Earth.

The second vine was much smaller. Wrapped around my right ear, it connected to the third vine which rested at the crux of my jaw. The third and final vine stretched its tip across my cheek to rest at my lips, where it locked itself in like a fish hook. With the main part of the vine still attached along my spine, this vine clamped onto the inside of my right cheek. All of this had happened in a second or two at the most. I adjusted my breathing with the vine hook in my mouth. I didn't know if this was good or bad. It was neither uncomfortable nor pleasant. Then I heard a voice.

"Can you hear me up there? Testing communications. Hello?"

I looked from side to side. I could only turn at a hundred and eighty degrees because I was strapped to Terra. There was nobody nearby.

"Down here, man from Earth."

I looked down. I couldn't believe it—the horse was talking to me.

"Forgive me. It took a while…a few days…to get your language right. Being as old as I am, I have spoken countless languages. However, this would be the first time I have acquired this language. Do I speak your native tongue? Am I right?"

I looked down at the horse. Terra's head didn't move; it was fixed straight ahead, facing the mountain range. Her voice rang clear, however.

"Yes, you are correct," I said, still somewhat stunned. "Wow, I don't know how to react. So, these vines you have around my head…they're a sort of direct link to you?"

"Precisely. Now that we can converse, please—no backseat riding. I know where we are going and, come to think of it, from the quality of your saliva I can discern that you are fairly new here. You have never been to the Owl Kingdom. So, get comfortable, and get ready for what might be the longest journey you've ever embarked upon. Sampling your DNA through your saliva, I have learned that your species needs sleep, and my readings along your spine reveal you have a few wounds. Nothing major, but rest will do you good. For the largest portion of this journey I will knock you out. Don't worry—I will wake you if there is something worth seeing other than snow-capped mountains. Are you ready?"

"Wait! I have questions, Terra."

"Sorry, but the sooner we get moving, the better. I sense danger following us up the mountain. Now rest, and let me take command once more."

The vine along my spine crawled to the base of my neck and latched to my neck like a leech. I blinked a few times, then I dropped my head and slept. The air grazed my body as the soft thuds of hooves traveled along a rocky, snow-blown path. I felt Terra's speed increase whenever we descended one mountain, slowing until it was time to ascend the next one in our path.

* * *

I couldn't tell how long I spent in hibernation, but I dreamed of Earth. I dreamed of the trees there—how each one was different, how there were different species which compared to each other the same way we thought of the animals that had once lived by our sides. I dreamed about the colors of each individual phenomenon I remembered seeing. I thought of my unborn child, and how difficult it would be to tell that child that animals like the elephant or tiger had once existed. How was I to explain to a younger person—one who was half of me—that a creature with wings for ears and a nose that stretched to the ground had once existed. How do I explain a large cat, striped with the pattern of waves, as if it were composed of water. It sounded like the stuff of pure imagination.

Maybe the world ending had been for the best. Most of us had tried to ignore all the devastation, Emily and myself included. The majority of my country had tried to ignore the fact that at least eighty percent of wildlife had been wiped out by our own self-righteous hands. Apollyon was right: we had all the chances and time to stop what we were doing. We had time to slow down enough to realize what we were losing in our expansive pursuits. In history classes throughout my life, and through books and times of travel, I had learned that humanity might have started in Africa or the Middle East, depending on a person's belief system. If any of that was true, then we as a collective of people had let down the oldest of our ancestors on the soil beneath our feet. Now their ancient bones and treasures were aflame. They curdled with radiation that would send the levels of emissions rocketing through the roof.

A long time ago, scientists had calculated the two-degree marker. it wasn't until we were three fourths into reaching that dangerous line that we had decided to come together and address the problem. It wasn't until the most recognizable of animals, birds, and ocean creatures were wiped out that we realized we were too late.

And then the pointing of fingers began, by everyone—one nation to another, to another…It hadn't been a pleasant time to grow up. I was born at the beginning. In less than thirty years, Earth had ended its rotation around the sun for the final time. It was the end for me and billions of others.

I dreamed of this. I dreamed of the plane crash and the last moments I had shared with Tom, at that time. I dreamed of my foolishness in thinking I was doing this new planet some good by killing the evil men and women in power, the ones controlling the slave trade. The things I had done, only to now realize I was a puppet in some twisted game to annihilate the last members of the human race. It was to happen slowly, through torture of the mind, before we were slaughtered on the battlefield—just to make for an epic showdown between the remaining humans and the non-humans. I dreamed of the beauty this place had been crafted to reflect. The details that were too good to be true. I should have seen it for what is was instead of acting like everything was okay;

rather than ignorantly believing this was some kind of second chance, afterlife scenario, or limbo.

I dreamed of the celestial beings and their true forms, of the mysteries of their beginnings and who or what they had been before becoming what they were now.

I now slept for many weeks of the full length of our journey. Just how many, I wasn't completely sure. I felt the heat of the sun as it rose and set multiple times. I heard my breathing steady into a rhythm beside Terra's own; her calm state made me more comfortable.

As my dreams shifted from one divided memory to another, I thought about Tamara. I imagined what she looked like when she opened herself up like Asha had done. He was intense. I dreamed of the rich greens and reds residing deep within him. Tamara was much brighter—so much so that I had to look away. Perhaps she was newer, younger than the rest of the celestials. I dreamed of the story of the Wikums and how they had discovered the soul. How those two same-numbered beings whose names escaped me…635? No, there was a half in there. Maybe 670.5? It didn't matter. Or did it?

I dreamed of their appearances. Their odd, naked bodies, only clothed when a ceremony of courtship occurred, totally backward-thinking to my kind. We were clothed in every situation but that. Asha had never finished that story. I would have to ask him how it ended when I saw him next.

Finally, I dreamed of Prima. The many forms she might take manifested in my mind's eye. Tamara and Asha both spoke highly of Prima and the connection I supposedly shared with her. But I had never known it. My slumbering eyes moved rapidly across a vision of the world she might have laid out for the possibility of the next generation of humanity. I dreamed of this, and of the journey through the stars and how everything would look from up there. I had never traveled like that, at least not consciously.

Terra halted. A vine snapped free from my neck, and my eyes shot open. I blinked in the moonlight. The snow was gone, replaced instead with desert floor. I was sweating profusely. I asked Terra to remove the vines. With a nod of her evergreen head, Terra relaxed her hold and the vines retracted, all but the mouth, ear, and throat ones which linked us.

"Those were some intense dreams, young one."

"Wait, you saw what I was dreaming? Isn't that like, private?" I replied, stretching my arms out away from my head.

Terra rustled her leaves. "You are on my back. I am carrying you across vast distances as creatures of this planet pursue us. They are trying to find us and kill you so that your species has no chance of living on beyond this place—and you want me to worry about privacy?"

I raised an eyebrow. "Fair enough, Terra."

"That's what I thought."

"How long was I out?"

"Just a month and a half. We only have about a week or so to go."

"No way." I rolled my eyes. "I'm being serious. Was I out for a couple of days or a week?"

Terra whinnied in annoyance. "I do not understand your joke. I am being serious. You are well rested, yes?"

"Most definitely. I normally eat when I wake up, but I haven't eaten anything for almost two months. I should be dead of starvation."

"Maybe on Earth, yes. Not so here. The liquid has sustained your needs for drink and food. You will eat when you arrive in the Owl Kingdom. Their border is a couple of days away." She broke into a trot as her voice murmured into my ear. Every time I spoke, the vines vibrated down into her ash spine and traveled along that, to her mind.

"If you can see my dreams as I see them, can you read my thoughts as well?"

"No. I can only see what you freely present to me. Your thoughts are safe, your dreams are free, if we allow them to be. If your mind didn't want me to see your dreams it would have erected walls. I have to say, it made my journey smooth, listening and seeing what your world was like. I have never seen "Earth." It seemed like a gorgeous place; no doubt my master created some of the things you dreamed about. I know his work—after all, I am one of his creations, and one of the oldest, in fact.

Tell me, did you ever see the animals that you dreamed of, or were they merely figments of your own mind's creation?"

I mulled it over. "Everything I dreamed was all once real."

"Fascinating. It's a shame that it doesn't exist anymore. Tell me, can you point it out in the night sky? Perhaps one day I may be able to travel there. I know there might be nothing left by the time I get to it as we are practically an infinite number of miles away, but even so."

I turned and looked up, searching the night sky for the faded star I once called home. "I can't see it anymore, but I heard Tamara say... there." I pointed. "It's the star next to that small red dot, about a thumb's space apart from this planet. Head directly toward it and when you reach a strip of stars in a row of three, head for the middle one. Beyond that, you will fall right into it." I hoped I'd remembered her directions accurately.

"The three stars you refer to compose Orion's Belt. I am sure of that. The straight shot from here would mean jumping to another galaxy. Interesting. I will have to travel there when my master no longer requires my presence on this journey. I have seen many worlds—sadly, most in their final state of destruction rather than the flourishing lushness that my master is known to create."

"How will you get there? You can't run there; do you have something to travel in to visit such places? If so, I would love to go with you."

Terra picked up the pace. She broke from a trot to a canter, and then a full-on gallop. We raced across a final stretch of sand, and then, the desert left with its dry breath, and the sweet smell of damp bark greeted us. We had officially entered the Owl Kingdom.

I didn't know what to expect. I had a good feeling another massive ancient creature like Ursa was waiting for us. I just hoped this one dealt differently with its kin than the sly old bear. My mind returned to the battle and fretted over the "what ifs" of it all. Had anyone survived? Had the fakes perished beneath Ursa's claws? Maybe he was already sitting in the great hall, on the wooden throne, painting the walls red with the blood of the innocent.

Redwood trees touching their tips to the stars greeted us as we trotted a narrow path between them. It was still dark, but fireflies gave off enough light to illuminate the outline of each trunk as we passed between trees. Every centimeter of my skin crawled with the feeling of unseen eyes on me; I kept wondering if the owls were hiding at the top of the trees. My new eyes didn't give me any better vision in terms of depth perception.

We walked through the forest until daylight. A ray of sunshine bounced from the redwoods and highlighted Terra's flank. I looked as far back as I could. Terra felt me wanting to turn and let the vines go lax against my legs and waist. It was good to stretch my back.

I looked behind us properly for the first time since the journey had begun. My stomach and intestines were clogged up. I felt very heavy, like I had eaten for weeks on end and never let anything out. I should have asked what that liquid was before drinking it. Then again, I would still probably have had to drink it.

I had hibernated through so many sunrises and sunsets, watching that gold orb claim the sky was like seeing an old friend.

Terra disrupted my moment of bliss. "In regards to what you were asking, about how I would one day travel to Earth—no, we do not have anything that can take us there. If I want to go, I just have to ask my master. Then I will take flight and go. As I am a product of my master, I too am built of the star stuff that composes the known and the unknown alike."

"You can FLY?"

Terra laughed. It sounded like a couple of squirrels playing and chatting. Their fast-paced clicking was Terra's laughter. It was closest to snickering. She stopped abruptly for the first time, forcing my body forward so that I crashed into the back of her neck. A vine that was wrapped around my waist shot out and latched around my shoulders, effectively saving my forehead from slamming against her wooden spine. If I'd hit the wood hidden beneath the wildflower hair, I would surely have been knocked out for good.

In front of us stood a sequoia so large, it made Asha's tree home look like an outhouse. The sun was rising with every silent moment which passed. The light drew my attention to the bigger picture: a quickly expanding forest of massive sequoia trees. Each one was connected by rope-like ziplines. Multiple levels of each tree featured dwellings burrowed into the wood. Large circles formed round doors—greying wooden knobs with four indentations in them carved like the imprint of a claw. I saw shadows flutter within small holes acting as windows, vents, or both, perhaps. Three homes were carved into each tree. As the sun rose higher, I could see deeper into the forest. And more trees came into view, with more homes as far as I could see, until the forest on the opposite side was obscured by distance and became dark again.

Something whistled through the canopy. A spear struck the ground in front of us. Inspecting it, I found it was made of redwood and carved with the symbol of an owl feather which ran along its staff. I couldn't see the tip—it was buried too far in the tundra's moss. Rocks—some small, others larger—came into view, scattered throughout the owls' homes. The screech of a zipline assaulted my ears as a figure swooped toward us. It wore a cape that curved along each massive wing, and attached at the shoulder. A small crossbow fitted to the top of the forearm snapped back as a dart flew straight for us. I unsheathed my sword, but before I could cut the dart from its path, the vine around my waist released and, like a dart itself, shot up into the sky where it smacked the projectile away. Terra had it all, even her own defense system. It only made sense since she was nature in horse form and more importantly, shared a direct link to a celestial. She really was a smaller version of Asha.

The hooded figure detached from its zipline and fell with grace, than rocked from side to side slowing his fall further until he landed softly on the wet ground in front of us. I peeked over Terra's neck to peer at the hooded figure. Bright yellow eyes took up the majority of the face, which inspected us. Another dart was loaded and pointed in our direction.

My hand was still on my sword. Terra didn't move. Her gentle stare was fixed. Her body started to rumble and shake. The vibration traveled throughout my body, and my ears picked up movement behind us. It was the sound of large paws, moving with the urgency of pursuit. It could only mean one thing: polar bears. They had been tracking us for months now.

A disturbance in the air snapped a vine, releasing its hold on my metal boot. A bear jumped over a few rocks and headed straight for us. Terra unleashed another vine, letting go of my other foot. She unhinged the vine in the corner in my cheek and throat. Relaxing the ear vine so I was completely free, she spoke.

Her words echoed with finality. "This is where my journey ends, young one. It has been an honor to serve a new species. Through our journey I have felt how simultaneously strong and fragile your kind must have been to call something your home and witness its destruction. I am sorry for your loss. I bid you farewell. Remember, don't forget your eyes when looking for Nayr. He is sly when he doesn't want to be found. Now grab my mane. On Asha's behalf—and mine too—know you have a friend in the true nature of things. Take this gift from the ancient world of the Greens and Grays. It protected them from space's harsh environment."

It took less than a breath for her to communicate this thought. The vine retracted from my ear and my final connection with Terra was severed. I reached out. The same vine morphed back into a single stem and ran up my arms, covering every inch of exposed skin. The vine that was around my waist climbed to my shouldered and stripped my metal armor off, finding the small spaces in-between the metal plates and covering my back and torso. As the vines finished layering across my flesh in their diamond weave pattern, I looked down at Terra and saw she was disappearing. Everything that made up Terra's outer canvas was now covering my flesh. Nothing but tiny stars in a neural network and a fragment of soul resided in what remained of my friend. Since she was Asha's creation, she was a part of him and therefore, was fueled by a piece of his soul.

Her frame shrunk to nothing—leaving behind wildflowers which planted themselves as they hit the ground. Her mane became lush grass which carpeted the forest floor, and the long piece of ash wood that had formed her spine flattened against my chest, forming a breastplate to complete my armor. I was fully covered from head to toe with vines and bark. I smelled like moss. My feet were free of metal and wrapped with an organic shell of seaweed and moss. I moved silently. Up ahead, the bears were getting closer.

Everything happens so quickly with nature. Even on Earth. You could never stare at the seed and watch it grow. But unwatched…We had had to use technology to catch such moments of transformation. Perhaps it was just this planet and the closeness of Asha's presence, but I found I could finally appreciate such things. With my feet firmly planted, the final vine detached from my ankles and wrapped itself around the small soul fragment, disappearing into the earth in front of me.

"Terra and Asha. Thank you for your kindness and courage. You aided me far more than I expected." I murmured my goodbye aloud as the hooded figure flexed his crossbow. The dot shot forward, and I flinched. Then I heard a groan. Looking behind me, I watched a polar bear scout clutch his bloody eye. The bear landed on his feet with a roar and lunged forward, clawing the air. I withdrew the rest of my sword. Had I been holding it half drawn this whole time?

I jumped back but not far enough away. I needed two swords to bring down such a large creature. Gifting Orion one of my swords to fight the enemy may have been poor thinking on my part. Of course, I was in a good position right now with the other half in my hand anyway. Gritting my teeth, I dodged the paw and sliced quickly at the waist. The hooded figure was closer now—he grabbed the spear he'd thrown earlier and started to tinker with a swath of leather at his hips. The mechanism was a utility belt with small handcrafted holders, their hinged lids wrapped around his middle. He unclipped one of them and pulled out a small object. A whistle? He put it to his lips.

The yellow binocular eyes didn't blink; they merely bore into me as I fought my opponent. "Are you just going to stand there, or are you going to help me with this guy?" I shouted as the double-sided axe came down too close to me. A vine extended from my side, grabbed a rock and swung me out of danger as though I were a trapeze artist in the most dangerous circus of my life. I slashed my blade down—leaving thin cuts in the polar bear's flesh. The vines grabbed rock after rock and tree trunk after tree trunk, saving me from a single blow powerful enough to slice me in half.

Then there was a new sound. I looked around, almost forgetting to watch my weight as my feet hit a tree and jumped off again, treading air as a vine from my left shot straight up and sent me flying toward the treetops. I swung over the bear—missing a throwing axe that came from a second Bear Clan scout in the opposite direction. A newcomer. The vine released, and I fell at full force.

The vines stretched upward, leaving my stomach bare and crowning my head so that everything but my eyes and nose was covered. I exhaled a deep breath and descended a hundred feet from the sequoia tree. I pointed my sword straight out. The vines tightened around my whole body. I felt like they were suffocating me. The vines overlapped and squeezed against one another until they basically became a second skin. My body was streamlined for an effective kill; the vines pulled my limbs close so I cut through the air like a giant arrow let loose from above the tree's canopy. I struggled to breathe, but I knew Terra wouldn't do anything to hurt me. I had to trust she was doing this for my own good. I let my body relax and gave over to the vines to hug me a little tighter.

The bear swung its axe, but I spun in a clockwise rotation and my plant suit tilted me just as the blade came within an arm's distance. The bear had no chance to dodge my blow. I moved in faster than expected, and the force caused me to slam right through his body. The vine relaxed, and I hit the ground on my knees and slid to a stop in the black dirt. I was drenched in blood. The head gear retracted and the vines thickened around my abdomen as they tended to my stomach once again. I stood up and took the second bear's blow at full force. Dense pockets of bark raised in gnarled bumps over my hands. It even covered my palms, as my fist clenched tightly around the dark blade. My hands braced against the impact, but the shock still traveled up my shoulders, vibrating into my lower back as I was forced into a warrior pose, both arms raised in front of me. One leg was bent in front and the other in back—my knees scraping the forest floor. The polar bear was shocked he hadn't drilled me into the ground. He swung his axe again, and once again I took the full blow. This armor was the greatest thing. I couldn't believe how well we connected with each other.

I looked around as the bear tried for another hit. This time I did sink into the earth. No matter the armor's power, I was still only human and running out of stamina. I wasn't sure if I could keep this up for much longer.

I had to move before the next blow came. The vines didn't propel my body out of the way this time. Perhaps they were tired too. I had thought the hooded figure had abandoned me, but then he appeared—running through the trees, small whistle at his lips and cocked spear ready to throw. His eyes shone like two lamps on a street corner as he came into view, his feathered cape flapping behind him.

He blew the whistle. A series of shrill screams filled the forest as the sound bounced around the trees, rebounded, and echoed into my ears. Irritated, I dealt the distracted bear another blow and smacked his weight away with my bark gauntlets. I rolled out of the way and tried the move I had performed multiple times on the battlefield.

The bear saw it coming. "Do you take me for a fool? We know your ways, human!" it snarled through sharp teeth as it raised a foot and kicked me away.

I rolled, letting the vines absorb as much of the impact as they could. I glanced at my chest. There was a thick crack in the ash breastplate. I was in danger now. One good blow to my unprotected sternum, and that would be that. The vines around my stomach made an imprint on the large mark creating a purple hue in my skin, realizing that I had been injured cracking at the edges of the imprint. I stood and raised the black steel in front of me. In its reflection, my image was shown, split in half.

The sky grew dark. I didn't look up to see what had caused it. I already knew. The owls were finally here. The branches waved like there was a forceful wind, from the beating of wings. Giant spears rained down toward my assailant. I relaxed my sword and let the tip drop to the ground. I had a feeling my part in the fight had come to its end. A dozen or so redwood spears impaled the bear from above, landing inches apart in neat lines. The bear had neither heard nor seen them coming.

CHAPTER 15

I fixed my eyes on one of the owls. It fluttered in the air, surrounded by a dozen others, and clutched the final spear in its claws. Then it spun its lower body with such ferocity that I thought its talons would come straight off. It released the spear at a downward angle and let go. The spear came straight down, spinning like a top. No wobble. It was completely streamlined as it cut through the forest air. The bear writhed where he was pinned to the ground—the eleven spears digging into fur and flesh. The final spear joined its brethren, shooting through the back of the head and out the front of the mouth. The bear died instantly.

The flapping of wings quieted to a murmur, and most of the avian shadows climbed the branches above. Their glowing eyes scrutinized me. Then the largest of the owls—the last one still in flight—glided forward and landed in the clearing. The wind gusting from its wings reminded me of the dragon I had fought so many years ago. Indeed, this was the ancient being of this realm. And just like Ursa, it was massive. Just a few feet short of how large the dragon had been, so it was a fair comparison to make.

The second moon shone through the slits between feathers as the ancient being landed in front of me, bringing its wings in. The flapping stopped. Its body was a sight to behold: the feathers were speckled with brown and cream patterns and spots that were incomplete, black circles. These last ones looked like eyes from a distance. The talons were immense. Each one was easily my height. They curved into the ground, leaving deep troughs in their wake. The eyes were large enough that I could have hollowed them out and crafted the sockets' arches into doorways. They gleamed bright like a pair of twin spotlights behind thick eyelashes which curled like tall meadow grass. Its beak curved slightly, ending in a sharp tip which jutted downward. Two nostrils flared; the pronounced shadows were primed for breathing at high altitudes. There was no neck beneath the rounded head. Ears like great horns shot straight up to the sky. The creature was taller than it was round. A hemp cord was wrapped around its right leg, decorated with multicolored beads the size of small boulders and a similarly large, single feather.

The Great Owl looked down at me and tilted its head, as if trying to see me better. The large eyes roamed over my body. I sheathed my sword and dropped into a deep bow to convey respect. The speared bear lay between us and the other corpse, beside the Great Owl's left wing. Other than a couple of scratches on tree trunks, everything looked as it did when I had arrived. Hearing clicking sounds, I let myself look up. The tree homes started to light up. Owls of various sizes came forth from their homes to witness as I bowed to the ancient beast. I felt the ground shudder as it raised a talon free of the earth and extended it as though it were a hand reaching out. I stayed in my bow. I didn't know what else to do. Each ancient being was different. I didn't feel like my life was in danger like it was when I'd met Ursa for the first time. The night was calm. Not even a leaf budged. From the corner of my eye, I could see the hooded figure. He stood in the distance, to my left. It was he who had blown the whistle which must have summoned the ancient one.

The massive talon stopped short in its path. Then, the Great Owl grabbed the corpse and moved it gently out of the way. Spears snapped like twigs under one of its feet. My eyes widened at the pure strength of the bird. The owl standing to my left came running to the dead bear and waved his wings in a circular motion. Two others swooped down like fighter jets and scooped up the body; they clasped both arm with their talons and disappeared into the canopy of the trees. The ancient being stepped forward. My nose picked up the fresh smell of blooming wildflowers and ripe gooseberries. And there was an earthy smell beyond that, something I could most closely compare to mustard seed. The beak opened, and the creature spoke.

"Hello. Who are you?"

It was a female voice. I hadn't expected that.

She reached out a talon and nudged my chest as if poking at a mouse. I stood up straight. I looked up into the unblinking yellow eyes. She cocked her head from side to side, puzzled. It was like she had never seen a human before. There was a row of piercings in one of her ears, which I hadn't noticed until now.

"How strange. You look like a worm, but you are not a worm at all. You have limbs and—where have I seen that armor before?" She looked away and scanned the woods around her. "If I am correct—and most of the time I am—she should be around here somewhere. Ahh, there she is. Terra. I wish you wouldn't disappear so quickly. I would love to meet you sometime." She bent down, taking up the entire space between the trees with her long body. It would take at least a hundred men to fill this clearing. She easily did so, just by going horizontal. Admiring the wildflowers that had once been Terra and the grass that had made up her mane, the Great Owl's voice dropped to a whisper. "Whoever or whatever you are, you must be of great importance for Asha and Terra to aid you in battle." She pressed her beak against the flowers. "I have only seen the celestial beings help one other than themselves once. Actually, I have only heard the story."

"The Wikums story?" I guessed.

The owl nodded, "Has Asha told you it? It's one of my favorites."

I cleared my throat. it had been some time since I last spoke. "He has and yes, it has come to be one of my favorites as well." I enunciated as clearly as I could, but couldn't help trailing off at the end of my sentence. I was mesmerized by the sheer beauty of this creature.

She raised herself to her full height and stepped closer. "You are *clearly* not a threat and can handle yourself well. A friend of Asha and Terra is a friend of mine and all who dwell in my realm. Welcome, traveler. I do not know of your species but perhaps my library has something on your kind. Tell me…wait, no. Don't tell me." Her eyes widened in excitement. "I love a good challenge." Then, her eyes narrowed. "The armor has served its purpose. Out of respect for Asha and Terra, please return it."

"I...I don't exactly know how to take it off." I shrugged sheepishly. "It kind of wrapped itself around me. Terra said it was a gift."

"A gift? Very well, I believe you. Strange-looking creature. Nonetheless, it must come off. It's damaged, and if you want to make use of its full potential, it must be repaired. I have something that should remove it. These devices can be tricky—their magic is older than I am. If you can believe that." She turned away, dismissing me.

Someone appeared at my side. It was the hooded figure from before. He was the smallest of the owls I had seen so far. "Come. Follow me to the library," he commanded in a gentle yet tired voice.

I followed him to the giant sequoia. A beam of light shot up the middle of the tree and its trunk opened like an elevator.

"After you, please," said my companion.

I entered the tree. The entrance automatically closed behind us, and we were alone. It was definitely an elevator in a tree. Who knew or had heard of such a thing? We ascended quickly, in silence.

I already liked this place. For the first time in ages, a clan I had met wasn't trying to kill me. The doors opened onto the treetops. A wide path circled each home, connected by ziplines. From up here, I could discern shapes I hadn't seen from the ground: hemp bridges connecting each tree and a community sprawling for miles. There were owls of many sizes—some bigger and others far smaller. They shuffled about, not paying much attention to me. It was because they had decided I wasn't a threat, I suppose. The homes were decorated with intricate carvings and personalized with names which embellished the doors. Small numbers scratched beneath them served to distinguish one address from another.

As we passed the first home, I squinted to read the name carved into the door. I couldn't pronounce it. The characters were part of a language I had never seen before. Their shapes integrated letters that had odd tails and swooping curves like calligraphy. Maybe they weren't names at all. A large mailbox hung above the door. Just how civilized was this place?

The small owl walked me across one of the bridges that hung from a large tree branch. It swayed like a pendulum as we walked across it. The owl waddled back and forth to keep his balance.

"We normally don't use these," he muttered. "Have them in place for the children. The rest of us swing from the ziplines above."

I looked up. Overhead, the ziplines crossed over us to the next tree. Every once in a while, I heard an owl zooming by, casting its shadow across our path.

The sun was high in the sky. The forest floor was dimmed as the tree's canopy trapped the sun's rays, stopping them from penetrating all the way through.

We made it to the other side of the bridge and found ourselves standing in front of another home. The door popped out of the tree's base as if the houses were there originally, and it was the trees which had grown around them. Some of the homes even had branches going straight through their small windows and out of their roofs. The owls didn't seem to mind the intrusion of nature and its tendency to fill every nook and cranny with leaves and twigs. A staircase on the back side of the tree appeared and we walked up to the top of the sequoia. Every few feet I could feel the baking heat of the sun press into me. I started to sweat and soon realized no homes had been built this high up.

I spoke to the owl, who had stopped just after we had passed the last roof. "I cannot go any higher. It is too hot."

"Follow the steps to the very top," he replied. "There is a zip line waiting for you. Take it. It will carry you across the realm and deposit you at the library entrance where the Ancient One awaits you."

The small owl stepped aside and let me pass him. The stairs were narrow and no guardrail was in place at this height. An elderly owl emerged from his home below us where the guardrail ended. He leaned over the edge before rotating his head in our direction. His eyes were tinted orange, his eyebrows drooped, and where there had once been feathers, only the ridges and dips of wrinkles now remained. His beak was cracked in a few places. He slowly limped toward me, one wing braced against the rail.

"I thought I heard something," he said. "You must be the newcomer. You woke me up, young one. Say, you look like a giant worm with appendages, and just when I thought I had seen it all." He laughed creakily and retreated to his home.

The small owl turned to me. We locked eyes. Then, we burst out laughing. We couldn't help but crack up at the scene that had just unfolded. In this moment, I got a closer look at my guide—this peculiar owl who had aided me on the battlefield. I noticed his eyes. They seemed to be double layered, like a mask. He noticed me staring and turned away quickly. He hurried down the steps, past the old owl's home and around the corner. I didn't give it much thought and walked the final steps around the tree.

I was so drenched in sweat that I left wet footprints on the hot steps. The canopy felt like it was on fire. Finally, the steps ended, and the I found myself on a platform. I stood on the foot-by-foot square; the tip of the giant tree was just out of my reach. A black cable wrapped around a taut hemp cord which stretched downward, at an angle. It wasn't a sharp drop by any means.

It looked like a steady ride. A simple clamp rested in a little wooden box strapped to the tree. I grabbed it. The metal had been painted a deep brown. So as not to reflect any light, I guessed. At this height anything shiny would betray this position. I snapped the clamp over the cord. The handgrip was so large, I could have grabbed it four times, if I had enough hands. Back on Earth, I had never done anything like this without a safety harness. I wrapped both my hands around the clamp's handle. I was sweating uncontrollably. Although I wiped them on my vine armor, my hands kept beading with moisture. This didn't help. The overheated vegetation was causing me to sweat even more. I shook my hands as dry as I could get them and formed fists around the hand hold.

I started to move along the cord. Below, the Owl Kingdom extended: a vast, forested realm. It reminded me of Asha and his abode. I looked behind me. The mountains were reduced to nothing more than small black hills. I took one hand off the zipline while still hanging on with the other; I placed my thumb in the sky, and it covered the whole chain of the mountains. The tint of desert gold didn't extend beyond the width of three of my fingers.

Up ahead, I saw the edge of the realm. It shimmered, almost as though it were covered with a clear film. That was the gateway to the planet. It was my ticket off.

I looked back over to where I was headed. I looked down at the tops of the trees. I would brush against them as I descended. The zipline disappeared into the canopy of trees and I with it. It spit me out near a tree that looked like a tan brick tower. I narrowed my eyes, squinting to discern the numerous homes flying by. I closed my eyes and listened. I heard the prattling of owls below me, the children's squeals as they ran across the bridges. The parents squawked at the fledglings to slow down. The whirr of ziplines coming and going filled the air.

This place was alive with feeling and movement. The ground, on the other hand, was immersed in complete silence. You would think the forest was uninhabited if you walked through it. For the first time, being in a new place didn't fill me with fear. I felt calm. I didn't have any hand signals to give to anyone here. I was all alone.

It was time to meet with the ancient being of this realm. When I had met the Owl Kingdom's representative all those years ago, Gregory had said that they were the smartest species on the planet. I was beginning to understand that now. Only a species as knowledgeable as they were would be evolved enough to live with such freedom. There were no guards stationed at corners. The citizens seemed to form the army, when necessary.

At least, that is what I thought. I didn't see any of the owls from the battlefield below. I wondered—what had they done with the bodies of the polar bear scouts? Did they eat meat or vegetables? A few questions perched in my mind.

CHAPTER 16

||||||||||||||||||||||||||||||||||||||||||||||||||

the library

A s I traveled across the realm on my zipline, the world below came to life. From this bird's eye view, the trees revealed themselves to me. They made me think of Asha and his home. I already missed Terra and her gentle silence, but I also missed how great her company had been during the end of our days together. I couldn't believe I had slept for as long as I had.

But it had happened. And then a familiar urge washed over me. My gut knotted as I brought my legs in, closer to my chest, only to realize that was a terrible mistake. It made the urgency of "needing to go" that much more of a strain on my body.

It was in the mists of the early afternoon, and I was halfway along the zipline. I looked down at the canopy of trees that I would soon be smothered by. I brought my legs in high and tight while clenching my buttocks. The branches and their leaves brushed my whole body like bristles in a car wash. The sun's light disappeared and all around me was pure darkness. All I could see were the yellow eyes of the owls looking up from their tree homes as I passed. I was still clenching. I released one hand at a time and wiped my sweat off the vines that still lay dormant on my body. It now felt like I had been swallowed by a giant snake, and I'm sure that's what I looked like to most of this world's inhabitants. That, or a "worm with appendages." I couldn't believe a species such as this– known for their wisdom and knowledge–had never before seen a human face to face. I wondered what the messenger at Gregory's meeting had told them?

A light broke through at the far end of the tunnel of trees. A small tower of sand-colored bricks stood at the end. I could only see the bottom-half as the ground came into view. I released my legs and my lower gut spasmed angrily.

I was sweating from stress now—not just the heat of the canopy, but also the fact that the sheer weight of my body was being supported by my hands alone for a prolonged period of time. My hands slipped more than once during this new mode of traveling. My feet dragged along the ground as my head pulsed with a heartbeat of its own. My sweaty hands slipped from the clamp around the zipline and this time, I fell properly. I dropped a foot, maybe less, and landed in the grass. I was bent like a table. I was too nervous to stand—afraid my contracted muscles would give and my suddenly active insides would give in and let go.

I knew that one way or another, it was coming out of me. I couldn't move. My muscles were loosening up. I was shaking to the point of shivering as I tried to hold it all in and stand up. My instincts told me to look around for anything I could use as cover—as a makeshift bathroom. A few bushes here and there stood out as though they were screaming, "Take your pick!" I crawled like a creature that had been shot in the leg, dragging myself to the nearest bush. The tower was just steps away, but I knew I couldn't make it that far in my current condition. I grabbed at an exposed root at the base of the bush. Leaning forward, I pulled myself toward it and, using my arms, wrapped myself on the other side. I got on all fours and rocked back into a squat.

Now I had another problem. The vines were wrapped around every inch of my body but my head.

"Great!" I shouted to the forest. I knew I couldn't crawl to the gates. I decided maybe to just let it happen in my armor. Maybe then it would release me? It was worth a shot, and besides, I didn't have any other options.

I didn't have to try very hard. It was coming, no matter my best efforts. I tried to relax my face, and let it just happen. I felt a slight breeze, which I ignored.

It was coming from above. I looked up. An owl's silhouette appeared overhead. It dug its talons into one of the vines on my back and lifted me up. Oh boy, this wasn't going well. The sensation of being lifted so quickly just about released everything I had in me. The owl's voice drifted down.

It sounded young. A boy's voice. "Just hang on a little longer. My leader will know what to do."

I clenched extremely hard and became stiff as a board. The young owl climbed the sky toward the tower. About half way up, a window opened and we flew in. It was dark enough that I couldn't distinguish the moment we entered its dimly-lit chamber from the darkness that consumed my throbbing head as I fell unconscious.

Two spotlights danced in my vision. Were they eyes? Relief washed over me. It had happened while I was passed out. I sat up, looking at the eyes which danced around in the dimly-lit space. The ancient owl was walking down a hallway, and it was dark. I blinked a few times as I adjusted to my new surroundings. A faint line of light appeared down the hallway, barely illuminating her path as she approached me. Her voice echoed throughout the tower, suggesting the vastness of the space. I felt light—cold, almost. I looked down and discovered I was naked. How did this happen?

I looked up at the talons, then farther up, at the bird attached to them. The yellow eyes studied me critically. "Come. Get up. I found some clothes for you."

"Where are the vines? Where is Terra?"

The owl turned and started walking away, thinking I would just follow her. I did.

"Don't worry, the vines are resting, once I saw who it was I brought them here. " she said. "While you were finding your way here, it gave me a chance to find the right scroll. I found the spell to unwrap them. Are you sure you are not a worm? Like, a mutated worm? Because when the vines withered like the near-dead things they were, you looked just like a worm lying there. A soft tube, with feces protruding from one end."

I lowered my head in shame. My cheeks grew hot at the realization that the ancient owl had seen me like that. What a way to represent my own species, huh?

Her wing tips were just above the ground—maybe inches from brushing against it, not much more than that. I looked up as we rounded the hallway's bend. I looked to each side. This whole time I had thought we were walking along a hallway lined with irregular-shaped bricks.

I reached out in the dim light to make sure what I was seeing was actually real. It was no different from being on Earth and seeing an insect or an object that I had never before encountered. I would often speak to myself as I reached out my hand. "No, it can't be real," I would say, marveling. This was like that moment. I felt the ridges of various spines. I let my hand bend completely into the soft ridges. It wasn't brick at all.

They were books. Thousands of books were laid out in the walls of the tower. I looked up. The dim light receded in the darkness of the tower. I couldn't tell how high the books went or for how long. I looked back in front of me, taking in the appearance of the ancient being. I hadn't seen her from behind before. She moved in silence. Her talons were the only sound in the corridor; they made the same tone as tap-dancing, only slower—almost as if the hallway were unfolding in slow motion. I listened as we walked down another aisle of books. I let my hand graze over each tome and loose-papered scroll. Everything was organized and tightly fitted in place. My hand never found an empty space as we crossed to the end of that second hallway.

The ancient owl stopped. My breath rustled one of her wing feathers. She had them folded back so they almost touched. If I had been standing at a distance, she would have looked like one solid piece of decorative wood. However—since I was a mere couple of steps behind her, I could distinguish the palette of colors that composed her body. She didn't have curves like a human being, but her feathers and bearing gave the impression that she did. She spread her wings. I thought with her size she would reach the ends of the tower, but she didn't. In this place, even she seemed small.

Which made me feel even smaller.

"Climb onto my back and hang on. Your clothes are down on the next level." She turned her head in a full three-sixty-degree rotation.

"The next level?' I started to climb her tail feathers.

"Yes, once I turn on the lights from down below it will make more sense. You will be able to see what I am talking about."

"I hope I am not hurting you by walking on your feathers like this." I stepped lightly, careful not to crush her feathers.

"You're not. Believe me. I have carried much heavier passengers in my time. Now hurry along. The quicker I get some clothes on you, the easier it will be for us to talk face to face. There is much to discuss, Sainath."

She took a step forward and we fell with style and grace. Not a flap of her wings was necessary. Seconds passed, and she lifted her body out of the dive in one direct movement and soared lower in a downward circle. She was like a slow twister, spinning downwards to the next level. A moment later her talons reached out, and we landed on the next level. I still couldn't see anything. The small window was high above me now. I looked up at it. It wasn't much bigger than the moon would appear from Earth. The ancient owl bent over and I slid off her soft feathers, so that I rolled off and stumbled to the ground.

It was pitch black and my hands met the ground before my feet. My bare body was even colder down here. It smelled like a cave—like stagnant water and stalagmites. My hand searched around for the ancient owl, it found and brushed into her feathers at full-force. I could tell it was her wing because she used gentle force to guide me.

"Here," she said. "Stand right there, and don't move. I will be back."

I felt a slight wind as she took flight. Then I was alone. In pure darkness. I stuck out my hand just to make sure she was gone. It's an uneasy feeling when you can't see your hand. When there's no way to discern how far it is from your face, that's even worse. Every time I touched my fingers to my nose, I would surprise myself. It felt like a stranger's touch.

The click of talons announced the ancient owl's return moments later. As she rounded the closest corner, the wind confirmed this.

"Okay, the lights should come on any minute. Give it a second. It has been many years since anyone other than an owl has entered this tower. Unlike your species, we can see in the dark."

I couldn't see her, but her voice resounded directly in front of me. I reached out to make sure.

She spoke again. "Don't worry. I am here."

A cranking sound broke the silence. Gears started to move below me, then more—traveling up the wall behind where I stood. The gears turned and turned, triggering other clockwork mechanisms in their path, until they'd reached all the way to the top of the tower. The building was alive; the tower was an inactive machine that had roared back to life. All of a sudden, it didn't feel that old anymore. The dim light grew brighter, then grew in size as it descended toward us. I watched as a pyramid of light came down behind me. I turned around, and saw that I was standing on a ledge. Something that I can only describe as a giant chandelier in the shape of a pyramid dropped from the ceiling, attached to three massive chains which were dragged up by a series of gears. The mechanical cogs were arranged in a pattern on the back wall, just beyond the precipice on which I stood.

"Here, before the light hits you directly. Come away from the ledge and let me get you clean." The owl produced a large bucket of water. It was as big as a bathtub. She lifted it over my head with ease. "Are you ready, Sainath?"

"How do you know who I am?"

Water washed over me like heavy rain. I was engulfed by it. The water seemed endless. I made the best of it and treated it as a shower. I scrubbed the dirt and grime from places I hadn't even known dirt could collect. Then it was over. I shook out my damp hair, letting a trail of fresh water sputter from my lips. The tub was taken away, and I stood there, arms wrapped around my torso as a shiver settled in.

"Right, you need to dry off. That tells me you are not a worm. Which is a good thing." The entire room was backlit by a pyramidal crystal that glowed like a mini star. Its blue light shot a precise ray down every hallway. My senses were heightened from the cold; despite my chattering teeth, I was able to pick out things I had missed earlier. The hallways were organized in a semicircle. In formation, they stood proudly, so that wherever I looked, I could see books. Peeking over the edge, I saw that there were three other levels. In total, there must have been seven floors. Rows of books were laid out vertically, with breaks being the platforms like the one I was standing on. If the platforms hadn't been placed just so, it would be just five columns from the top of the tower to the very bottom.

I wondered if the platforms had been added later. They seemed newer than the columns. The bookshelves were white wood—possibly aspen. The platforms were hewn white marble and bounced the blue light of the crystal down and across the hallways. Before I could step forward, the ancient owl was already in view, swooping down. She moved fast—extremely so—when she wanted to. In the time it took to snap a finger, she'd covered the distance. With a flick of her wings, a gust of wind smacked me like a whip across my body. I was dry instantaneously. She held a nicely-folded pile of clothes.

"I bet these will bring back some memories," she said as she handed me a bundle containing a flannel shirt, hiking boots, and tan slacks. I dressed in front of her. She watched with curious admiration, head cocked to one side and paid close attention as I hooked each button through its corresponding hole. She looked down at her talons and mimicked my hand gestures as best a large bird can. She found it difficult but didn't get frustrated as a kid might. She simply set her talons down and turned her head from side to side as I put on my pants. She brought herself closer to me, sending her talons back so she could bend over without being upended.

She watched me down her beak as I laced the boots. They were a little big, but everything else was spot on. The ancient owl rotated her head from side to side, watching me tie my laces. I thought of my Earth father, and how he had taught me that. *Bunny ears*, he'd called it. Over the years I had developed my own method as many of us do. We are shown how one person completes a task, but sooner than later we find a way that fits our own personality better.

I raised my right foot and set it down so it would be closer to her. She was like a child, watching. I tied the laces as slowly as I could, for I knew she wanted to learn about me, and who I was. I hoped Prima would give me such a chance. It wouldn't be this easy though; Prima had, after all, created a part of me. This ancient owl had never seen Earth, perhaps had only heard or read about it somewhere in this vast library.

I took a lace in each hand and pulled up to tighten the boot on top of my foot. I then laid the left lace over the right lace, forming an x. I raised the laces so she could see. She didn't say anything, just observed even closer. Her breathing was hot on my neck; it reminded me of the dragon I had fought. I then grabbed the marked lace with my left hand and tucked the left lace under my right one to create the first knot. I pulled the ends tight so it looked like a tight braid over the tongue on my boot. With three fingers I grabbed the left lace with my palm facing up, and with the thumb of my left hand I grabbed the right lace along with my right hand forming the first loop. I used my right thumb and right index finger to hold the loop in place. Then I slid my middle finger down the middle—acting as a spacer between both laces—and brought the left lace over the right, tucking the right loop under the left one. With the middle finger of my right hand holding space for my left loop, I tucked the left loop in, simultaneously moving the middle finger just before the left loop passed through. I pulled the newly formed loops taut and set my foot out in the air for her to inspect. I tied the other shoe quickly and stood up.

She backed away and stretched to her full height. "Interesting. You are not a worm, you have appendages. And a multicellular body, coordination of limbs. You have dexterous hands that are very different from mine. You can do what I can, but you can also do much more. Your hands are built for intriguing work. Interesting indeed. Come, follow me. There is much to discuss and very little time to get you prepared for your journey."

I followed the ancient owl down the first row of books.

CHAPTER 17

secrets

Time of day was nothing to be concerned about in the tower. The was no way it could permeate such a place. The single window, high above, swung shut when the gears activated and brought the crystal of light down.

"What is your name? And how do you know my name?" I asked. Only a few minutes ago, you called me a worm with appendages."

"One question at a time," her voice drifted back from up ahead. Her talons tapped against the marble floors, and my lighter tread resounded in a pale echo. She turned and walked down the next aisle to our right, facing the lit crystal once again. It was like a solar eclipse; the sun was the crystal and the ancient owl, the moon, because as soon as we entered the hallway, her figure took up most of the light and the hallway was locked in darkness.

This whole section of books was written in a language I had never seen before.

"Don't worry you won't be able to read any of these. They're written in the lost tongue of a people who lived millions of years ago. Ah, here we are."

She stopped at the beginning of the final hallway, by the far-right end of the tower. Beyond the bookshelf was the tan brick wall, and again, the crystal. In her right talon she grabbed at a book just above my head. It was a large, horizontal tome. I was surprised. I had never seen a book shaped like that before. Most were vertical, of course, and no wider than the two hands necessary to read them. Maybe it was a landscape book? Or one on photography? Perhaps even an atlas of this planet. Now *that* would be helpful.

She grabbed another book. Watching her, I quickly realized that every book was the same length. It made sense. This was *her* library.

"Grab that bag. The one hanging on the hook at the end of the hallway," she said.

I retraced my steps to the platform's landing and looked up. A giant leather bag that could fit a dozen men hung from a silver talon-shaped hook. I looked around for a ladder; I didn't see any way of getting the bag down.

"If you need a ladder," her voice floated back, "put your hands together, rub them back and forth, then clap them to produce a high pitch. I can do it with a tap of one of my talons but you will need to make do. Try that. If it doesn't work, I will summon the ladder for you. Quickly now."

Even from the other side of the corner, I had no trouble imagining her looking right through the bookshelf at me. I brought my hands together and rubbed them violently until I felt heat start to build. Once the friction edged on unbearable, I quickly separated my hands, pulled my fingers back and smacked my palms together.

A short, high-pitched click echoed throughout the tower. Tapping followed—a rapid movement from high above. Now, the slap of wood hitting marble. I looked over to the edge of the platform. To my far left, a wooden ladder descended from the upper levels. It didn't have a face, and yet, it was somehow alive. It walked with one half of its rails moving in front of the other. It skipped over to me.

"Very good. Now just point to the bag," said the ancient owl. "Be precise though—they aren't the smartest of creatures."

I pointed dumbly at the leather bag. The ladder turned and rested itself against the wall. Two spiked clamps extended and hooked themselves into the side of the wooden bookshelf. I swung around and climbed the ladder, took the bag off the hook and nearly fell off from the sheer weight of it. I lost my balance, but some magical force caused the ladder to detach so its rails became legs again, legs which sprang away from the bookshelf to steady my fall. My feet touched the ground, toes first, and the ladder deposited me gently. It flattened back against the bookshelf with a rough noise. It had no face but I could tell it had a gentle temperament. For that, I was grateful.

I dragged the heavy leather bag around the corner to rejoin the ancient owl. She saw me coming and tapped one of her large talons against the floor twice. The bag shook with agitation—eager to be freed from my grip. I let go. The bag swished in the air for a moment, then hovered over to the owl's side. She picked up the book and put it into the leather bag. We continued down the hallway until she stopped and grabbed one more book. We then left the platform. She stepped to the edge, the bag hovering beside her faithfully. I looked over at the ladder, which was resting right where I had last seen it.

"Climb aboard, Sainath. We must now travel to the very top level of shelves. It won't be as smooth of a ride as it was coming down. I will need you to duck your head low against my back and hold on tight. I would hate to lose you. After all, you are a dying species, are you not?"

"I think I might be one of the last of my kind, so yes."

"I had a feeling, but hope still exists. Even in places beyond your reach. Don't give up, for the universe fights for the underdog. Always."

I couldn't help but keep my eyes trained on the ground. I blushed furiously as I passed behind her tail feathers, and clambered up her back. She lowered her neck so she was streamlined for speed. I found a spot snuggled against her well-hidden neck and settled in, bent over. I took hold of the base of one of her feathers. It was easily twice as long as my body. Before I could say I was ready, her wings came up, and my small world darkened. The crystal light was subsumed by her body once more, and her wings started to beat as she fanned them open and let them fall against her sides. The rhythm of her wings started slow but gradually picked up speed. With each rise and fall, we rose up and up, until she shot skyward like a rocket. A few more flaps and we were whizzing through space with great speed. She went full vertical; my legs hung off of her feathered body, waving like a flag to the song of a gentle wind.

Tears filled my eyes and pooled in the corners as we ascended to the top level. I couldn't move my body—the pressure was too great. I hated to think what it would be like to ride her outside the tower, where her flight wasn't controlled by the fixed structures which surrounded us.

Just as quickly as we ascended, we came down. She flew above the last level and glided down to attempt a graceful landing. I couldn't see anything except the feathers in front of me as they fluttered with the delicate movement of a set of eyelashes. We came to a stop on the top level of the tower; this was the seventh tower or the first tower depending on how you looked at it. She bent and let me slide down. I raised my boots in the air so they wouldn't get caught in between her feathers. The marble floor presented itself at the end of her tail feathers. I found my feet this time. The top of the crystal rested right across from us. I turned to appreciate the new hallway of books, but instead found myself staring at a giant planetary system. Something was off. It wasn't my planet's system. Not even my own galaxy, from the looks of it.

"Whoa, what planetary system is that?"

"Come, let me show you," she murmured. "To answer your question of how I know of you, you must understand that my kind is one of the most intelligent species in existence. Half of my brain is always thinking about other things; I found out who you were from the short time that you have been here. I know you are not a worm, and the only record of a creature of your description I believe is in one of these books."

The leather bag floated nearby. She doubled tapped her talon and it floated over and revealed the two books it contained.

"Sit, please." Her voice was kind.

I crossed my legs, one over the other. The planetary system sat to my right and parts of it were above me. A total of twenty-eight planets were visible on thin platforms, all rotating at different speeds. Small gears were concealed under each one, keeping them synced around the center of— not one, but two—large stars. The first was yellow and the second, much larger one was blue. A handful of planets orbited the yellow star while the rest of them circled the blue one. Every color you could image was somehow integrated in one way or another into each individual planet.

A couple of them reminded me of Saturn. The rest I had never seen before.

"Let's see here." The first book was placed between us, and my attention was drawn from the planetary system and back to the task at hand.

"Couldn't I just tell you I am human? Wouldn't that make this easier?" I said. The first page was turned, and a picture of a human body appeared.

"Yes, I suppose that would have saved me some time, but it doesn't mean we still can't learn about it, now does it?"

"I guess," I said as she turned the page on an anatomical study of a skull. She flipped through quickly, without saying a word. Her breath was hot against me with each turning page. She skimmed through most of it. She was a quick learner. She closed the book and picked up the next one. "Now that is finished, where are you from?"

"Wouldn't you rather look it up?" I said with a smirk.

"Humor. Now I know you are most definitely human, Sainath. Get up and come see the planetary system."

She stopped in front of a large work bench, where a few buttons flashed in various degrees of brightness, each one the size of my torso. A talon pushed past my body to press a square button next to my hand. It blinked red, so she tapped it with her talon. Then, it turned green, and the table and the planets stopped rotating.

"These planets you see in front of you are a map to our galaxy. And here..."

She pointed with her left wing tip to the smallest planet on the edge of the solar system. "This is where we are now." She pressed another button which brought the small moon-sized planet to the center of the table, so that it split in the opposite direction from the two suns. Then another button, which sent the rest of the planets shooting high above us, leaving just the blue sun and the moon-sized planet on the table. She pressed the green square again and the table started to spin freely again. The two bodies of matter circled one another as she walked around the whole system, talking to me like a professor.

"The planet that you are on was created by one of the celestial beings—"

I interrupted before she could get halfway around the table. "Apollyon is his name. He gave my people the desire for war and pride. I know this part *far* too well."

The ancient owl stopped and walked back over to me. She said, with a critical glimmer in her eye, "So you have heard the story before. The ancient scrolls dictate that knowledge of such things was forbidden to be known by life in any shape or form. What made you worthy to possess such knowledge? Tell me, do you know the name of the others as well. Other than Asha?"

"I do. There is also Tamara, the celestial being of compassion. And Prima, that of creativity."

"Interesting." She moved closer. "How does all this fit into that small mind of yours?"

"I do not...know." I whispered. She was mere inches from me.

"Open that book," she said without looking away.

I walked over to it. There was no title—it looked like a journal bound in black leather. It was worn and torn in various places, clearly weathered by age.

"If you know all of that, then I think you will be able to handle the contents of that book. After you are finished you can find me at the end of the hallway. Terra's vines are resting there; I must tend to her. Take your time, Sainath."

She disappeared into the shadows at the far end of the hallway. I could make out her silhouette but that was about it. I looked down at the massive journal. It took two hands and all of my strength just to open. I was standing the whole time.

The first page was titled "Earth: Phase One."

I couldn't believe my eyes. It was an entire outline of Earth—its construction, planned proceedings. and little notes from each of the celestial beings: what their tasks were, and how long they had planned to aid my species in our development. I turned page after page until the loose, ancient leaves began to pull away from the binding. Everything had been recorded: how plants were created, land, and animals of every species and origin. I was exhausted from just turning the pages. Two pages slipped out and fell to the floor. They floated just steps away, catching my attention.

I walked over and pinned one down under the toe of my boot. It was badly scarred with burn marks and bloodstains. I dropped to my knees at the edge of the heavy sheet and crawled to the top of it. I pulled myself past the drawing of a burning Earth to a small passage that read the following:

"In the time of greed and corruption, when the land is scorched and the abundance of life has become all but extinct, select the strong willed to carry on to the next home."

A large space was burned out but at the end I was able to discern a few words. "…If the species has been deemed worthy of surviving another lifetime. The notion must be passed by a majority vote of celestial beings."

Deemed worthy to survive another lifetime. What did that even mean?

I looked up at the angled page that lay ahead of me. I crawled to it frantically like a child toward a favorite toy. The page depicted a drawing of what looked like a beam of light traveling between two worlds. It was a sketch—not very detailed—but the concept was clear enough.

I stood up. "Okay, I understand. I get it now; it was all part of a plan, a plan written long before anything actually happened. And yet, they knew *exactly* what was going to happen. Tamara and Asha—even Apollyon—made it sound like it was *our* doing. That we let the planet die." In desperation and disgust, I kept going. "But according to these plans…*their* plans, they let it happen. So, why blame us for it? More importantly, why contact me of all people? Surely there were others more qualified for this kind of journey?"

The owl answered me from the end of the hallway. "They needed someone who they could control. Someone easy to manipulate, and someone with a will strong enough to take a beating and still rise to the fight again. Remember when I said the universe always roots for the underdog? I wasn't just talking for the purpose of making sound," she said softly.

I walked back over to the journal. I had two pages left to read. I turned the last sheet to reveal Gregory's kingdom and a hand-drawn map of plans for other kingdoms. The final page bore the signatures of each of the celestial beings. All but one.

Prima had never signed.

CHAPTER 18

my true purpose

The ancient owl was admiring Terra's vines, which stood in a tall, glass vase. She didn't look away as I approached but asked, "What are you thinking now that you know what that book contained?"

I shrugged. "I don't know what to think. I have been lied to enough on this planet and should have known that something was off the moment I arrived. But I didn't. I went with the flow of things and fell into the rhythms of the world. I kept thinking that the sight of other people should be enough to make me feel at home, regardless of how I was treated. All along I was a puppet for something bigger that I never thought to even consider. Even on Earth, I had thought I was in control of my own destiny. But after looking at that journal, I've realized something. Destiny is predetermined no matter how many roads you carve away from it. You will end up right where you are meant to be. I don't know what to think, beyond that. I'm just ready to do what I have to do so I can lay myself to sleep and wake in death, reunited with my real family."

"I'm glad to hear you've found clarity," she replied. "Come, I must try to spark a connection with Asha through Terra's remains. That's our best bet of figuring out what we will need to send you off the edge. Did Asha say anything to you before you left?"

She motioned for me to pick up the soaking vines. They were heavy but manageable to carry. Water dribbled from the entangled stems, down my slacks, and onto the marble floor. The crystal's light shot vertical rays through the hallways of books as I exited past the observatory table. The ancient owl stepped forward and reached out her right talon, into which I placed the mess of vines. She rested the wet vegetation on a table just a couple of feet from the observatory. Vials of chemicals stood in supports on the table's edge. As she laid the vines along the table, I told her what Asha had told me before I left. By the time I'd finished my story, the vines were completely laid out. The ancient owl started to pick at them with her beak, weaving them until they were latticed together in the two-dimensional shape of a horse's body. She triple-tapped her talon on the marble and the test tubes to my left shook and wiggled themselves free from the metal clamps which held them in place. One was filled with a yellow shimmering potion and the other, with a green one. I climbed atop the table and sat with my legs crossed to better watch her at work.

The tubes moved in front of the owl and hovered above Terra's vines. Very carefully, she clamped two of her claws together, and with them pinched just so, she picked up the yellow tube and tilted it enough that a single drop fell into the green one. The green liquid sucked in the yellow shimmer, but they did not mix. The yellow tube was replaced and the green tube picked up which half emptied itself across the vines. It reminded me of salad dressing. The vines shivered in place, and an instant later, rose to float above the table. The ancient owl set down the tubes and with another triple-talon tap, they returned to their home at the back of the table.

The vines floated just below my chest. The ancient owl whispered to them as if she were talking to me. "Asha, can you hear me, friend? I need some guidance. You dropped off a young man from Earth, I believe. From what he has told me, I am to prepare him for Prima. If this is true, then King Gregory's battle is lost, and we need to move the last remaining humans off the planet."

The vines undulated like an ocean wave then snapped straight. Asha's voice came through, loud and clear. "Hello?"

It was like a magical phone system. It would move in waves to record our message and then snap in place to allow the recording from the other end to come through. Fascinating, to say the least.

"Minerva, is that you?"

"Minerva?" I looked up at the owl. "Is that your name? I didn't think you had one."

She touched her beak tip to my forehead and her hot breath waved through my hair and made me close my eyes. "Yes, though I don't use it much. My clan sees me as an ancient owl and refers to me as such. I only use my name when it's called for. I do not believe in the individuality of names. We are bound together and should live as a collective. I was transported here just like the humans and the rest of the native species I'm sure you will have encountered."

Asha spoke again, and Minerva stepped back to allow his voice to come through the vines. They snapped in time with the frequency of his pitch. "Minerva, I just overheard you talking now. I will clarify as time is of the essence—I can't talk long as I'm busy trying to get Bayard off this planet too. Gregory's kingdom has been overrun by Ursa's forces. Word spread that Sainath fled the battlefield. Ursa was upset and set his full army upon the gates.

"The knights didn't stand a chance. Orion and the royal guard were the last to fall. After a month of slaughter, Ursa himself entered the kingdom and tortured each of the royal knights personally. He did it to discover Sainath's whereabouts. Orion finally broke after two weeks of torture, and told him that you'd sought me out. The bears are in the forest now, slashing and burning it down to find you. Whatever Apollyon has offered them is something of great worth, since he is still looking for you in spite of his victory on the battlefield. Bayard is already on his way to you. He should arrive in a day or two if the bears haven't caught him yet. I am about to head that way as well."

Minerva handed me a scroll. Its edges were tattered and stained. It bore a deep purple seal, imprinted with the symbol of a crown. I broke the seal and unrolled the scroll. It was less than a foot long. The cursive writing was patchy in places where the ink had bled into the parchment.

"It is with great despair that you have been discovered. The bloodline of the kings is in jeopardy. Protect the DNA of the future generation at all costs. The three bloodlines are listed below. You must not fail. You must survive to protect humanity against their greatest threat, *themselves*." My eyes shot across the page. "The three bloodlines must be direct descendants of Asha, Prima, and Tamara. Apollyon is not to have a direct descendant, for obvious reasons. Make haste. The selected DNA must be planned out carefully and our effort put into motion before the advent of humanity's industrial era. This gives you less than 12,000 years to prepare. Make haste."

There wasn't a signature, only characters scrawled in cursive.

"Minerva," I frowned, "what does this mean? Is this what you are trying to do right now? Isn't it too late for this letter to be of any use?"

Minerva shook her head sagely. "The Will of My Father was an ancient order of knights who guarded and watched over those begotten by the celestial beings. Their "offspring" as you might put it. These men and women were chosen by the celestials to track the bloodlines and ensure they remained pure. Collectively, they were more than just skilled fighters—they were scholars, artists, and mathematicians. Every major profession played a role within its ancient order. Many more were scouted as new talents came into existence, with the spark of good will, of course. The letter in front of you is the order's last known letter in existence. If Asha has sent you here, he must know that it is time to get you off this planet, and the celestial beings must have changed their minds about you. It's the only explanation I can think of as to why he would send you to the edge of the planet and more importantly—to me.

"Apollyon must know of this letter. He wants to abolish the bloodline. That would make sense because he wants to create his own, and from the beginning he has been kept in the dark concerning the other celestials' secret. As it read, for obvious reasons he is not allowed to produce a full part of himself in your kind. The results would be disastrous. Small fragments of him have found themselves into the tyrants and dictators of your past. Can you imagine if a full descendant of his was born?"

Minerva shook her head in sorrow. "Follow me. There is a section on the order back here." I trailed close behind as she made her way back into the stacks.

The banded books gave way to scrolls which filled the shelves we passed. The wood here was no longer dark red, sparkling in the crystal's light; this section of the library was clearly no longer in use. All around us were cracked, rough shelving—slanted on the ends as if the number of scrolls shoved underneath each shelf had been placed there for the sole purpose of supporting the weight of the wood. A metal plate caught my eye. Its shine suggested it was a newer addition to these ancient, dilapidated shelves. It read, "Elemental Magic."

Minerva moved in large strides. I wanted to stop and open one of the scrolls but couldn't risk falling behind. At the end of the hallway there was a small table and a wooden trunk.

I had a flashback. That chest was an exact replica of the one in which I had once stored my swords. How could I forget the intricate details of the wood carvings, the Chinese landscape and mythical creatures that I had thought of only as childhood imaginings until I arrived on this planet? I remembered the two animals carved into the wood, with the landscape wrapped around them and the chest itself. The bear was Ursa—no doubt about it now. The moon crest on his head marked him so he was unmistakable. The large owl had to be Minerva, but the head was covered by a helmet of some sort.

A padlock held the chest closed. It looked like it was still intact, formed of a dark, shimmering lump of meteorite. I looked over my left shoulder to address Minerva. "I have seen this chest before. My swords came in it."

"The chest has never been opened," she said. "Only a direct descendant of the celestial beings can do so. Asha brought it here in secret and told me that only when the heir to Prima's bloodline arrives the chest can be opened. Make no mistake, you are the heir, and the other two humans that must leave with you are the other direct descendants."

I interrupted without tearing my eyes from the chest. "Tom—Bayard told me he was taken in by Asha so he must be his direct descendant. That means the human being you are protecting here must be related to Tamara.

"Very good, young one." Minerva smiled.

I reached for the padlock. It was bigger than my hand and the slot for the key was a single slit underneath. It didn't look like a normal key would fit.

Minerva disrupted my thoughts. "Confused? I was too for almost a decade. I even crafted multiple keys to the lock's specifications, but nothing. Until it hit me just now, when you said this chest has a duplicate, just like your swords. Try sticking your blade in the lock."

It was worth a shot, I thought. Then I remembered. "I kind of lost my weapon upon arrival," I grimaced.

"Just misplaced it, young one."

Minerva brought her left wing forward and flipped it over like an unclenching palm. Sure enough, my black meteorite blade rested on one of her massive feathers, winking as it caught the light. I nodded and grinned as I took the sword, then lifted the padlock and drove the blade's tip through the padlock.

As if the mechanism had a mind of its own, it swallowed the sword to the hilt. I let go, astonished at the sight. The padlock lifted on its own and turned the sword as if trying to pick itself open. The sword twitched to the right and then jiggled back to the left and then there was a satisfying click as the lock released.

Minerva and I put our heads in real close, as if the universe's secret was about to be revealed to us, which wasn't far from the truth.

I was expecting to see another set of swords, or some majestic weapon. Peering over the rim, I gasped.

It was a piece of parchment. It was single-sided, maybe two paragraphs long, and covered in writing which had faded over millennia. I didn't recognize the handwriting and to make matters worse, the strange characters meant it was another language I had never seen before.

"What does it say?" I asked without looking up at Minerva.

"How interesting." The ancient owl tilted her head to one side so one of her eyes could properly focus on the page. Quick as a hummingbird's wings, she swiped it up and darted back to the planetary system where her laboratory table stood.

She pressed a couple of switches and a large magnifying glass came down from the ceiling. "Now, let's see here. I haven't encountered this old of a text in a while. I'm going to have to refresh my skills before I can accurately engage with this one. Just give me a moment."

She spoke a few words in foreign languages which I didn't recognize. Minerva raised her head from the magnifying glass, and let the device rise back into the blackness of the tower high above.

"This is one of the rarest pieces of literature I have ever laid eyes on. It's a shame you will have to take it from the library." Minerva hung her head in momentary sadness, then perked up, and asked me to come close. I stopped admiring the texture of Saturn's rings and walked over.

"First of all, this is not just a letter. It's also a map. A map to understanding Prima, I think. It mentions the Wikums' home world and if my knowledge serves me well, then this has to be the Will of My Father decree...? I didn't think any of these survived the First Galactic War. It was written—legend tells—by the two Wikums themselves. Their names were...Hmm, I'm sure I have it written somewhere around here."

"650.5 and 650.5," I replied without hesitation. I stared at the old map-letter, thinking over the Wikum story Asha had told me a few months ago.

Minerva graced me with a bow. "Bravo, young one. Yes, 650.5. They had the ability to see the dull reality of their world. The oldest love story to exist, you could say."

"I guess so, yeah," I said, wishing I had made the connection sooner. "What does the rest of it say? And what about The Will of My Father decree?"

"It was drafted by the 650.5s as a last piece of guidance to their home world. The male 650.5 wrote the first lines to the female 650.5, and by the looks of it, the final words were written by the female to the male. They must have known something that we don't. Legend tells that within the Wikum solar system there is a planet that was created by them. It is said to have been a last resort haven for when all else failed. A fresh start waiting at the far reaches of space. The journey is a long one—over a billion and a half light years from here."

Just then, a shadow crossed the large crystal, momentarily throwing the library into darkness. An owl scout swooped down and landed on the marble. "Sorry to bother you, wise one. Our scouts stationed by the desert front have spotted the Lizard Clan heading in our direction. It might be nothing, but it seems odd that they would travel this far from their borders."

Minerva looked at me. Her eyes narrowed, and she turned her body away and looked straight down at her scout. He bowed.

"It's no mistake," she said. "I thought we had more time. Assemble the border scouts and sound the first alarm to the citizens. Do not strike until I arrive. Thank you, you are dismissed."

The scout nodded and stepped backward until he was clear to fly. He shot up and out of the tower.

Minerva waited until he had disappeared from her sight before returning her attention to me in full. "I must get ready. Give me a moment, and I will translate the text for you so that you may read it on your own."

With a pinch of her talons she reached under the desk and pulled out a piece of paper, dipped a quill into her inkwell, and quickly transcribed the text. At this point I wasn't even surprised. She flipped the paper over the ancient paper, grabbed a thicker quill and holding it at a slant, she took a rubbing of the map. The shading allowed me to see this map that I couldn't discern with my eyes.

She flipped it over once more after she had set her quill down. It now faced me on her opposite side. I grabbed it quickly as if she was handing a child a candy bar or a toy. I read it aloud as Minerva flew around the tower, getting ready for the fight that was headed our way.

"My love, our choices have started this war, and I'm afraid our eagerness to give the gift we have received to the rest of the known species beyond our own cosmos has sparked a dangerous beginning. We must stop fighting the Galactic War. It's all our fault."

I kept reading. "I have an idea, my love. I don't know if I will survive this war. I will be leaving soon. I must flee while I still can. Over the next thousand years I will use my skills and knowledge to toil away for our future; I will build us a new home beyond the reach of war. If you get this, I have already left. You know how I hate saying goodbye. We both know you wouldn't be able to let me go. I'm doing this for the future.

Maybe it won't be ready for our next generation but perhaps it will be a second chance for a species more worthy than our own.

"So, I, Asha, was in the same spot as I am now, searching for a new world. Searching for hope to begin again." I read aloud to myself. The second half of the text was the female Wikum's response, who I was starting to suspect must be Prima.

"As much as it pains me not to see you before you leave, I agree. You and I both know we won't survive this war. Just promise, my beloved— if by some miracle we do, you will find your way back to me. Promise. We started it, so it's only fair that we see it to its natural conclusion. We have lived longer than any known species now. Whatever is inside us has given us incredible gifts to aid whoever we want. With so much power we must be selective. I know you want to help everyone, even those who are unknown to you. Although I agree, I can't simply welcome just any species into our haven. It's too great a risk for our new beginning. I will stay here and wait, and be the deciding factor in who is deserving of a second chance."

As I laid the Will of My Father decree down, my mind felt heavy with the weight of ancient words. The journal made sense now.

CHAPTER 19

||||||||||||||||||||||||||||||||||||||||||||||||||||||

nayr

I felt for Bayard. The witch had told me she would keep him safe if I fought and won the battle. I wondered if she knew I had fled the battlefield?

The ancient owl returned to me and stretched her wing tips then folded them behind her back. If it wasn't for her feathers, she would no doubt look like a human being in anxious wonder. She even started to pace back and forth in front of the table. I sat back upon the table and watched this ancient being do something that was fairly normal for me. Maybe there is a link between us and the animals we surround ourselves with. Maybe I never noticed such behavior because I never expected these similarities—these markers of kinship between my species and others.

After a few moments, something shifted in the corner of my vision. It was the vines. My acute ears picked up the sharp cry of a whistle, and I knew what was coming. Minerva turned to look out the window and then back at the vines. She hesitated. Something told me she and Asha were much more than they both led me to believe. I grabbed my sword and tightened the leather straps around my torso so my my blade stuck to one side of my back. Minerva looked up again. Minerva turned her back to the room and soared straight for the window. Surely, she wasn't going to fly through it? She was only ninety times bigger than the square window frame. Sure enough, she flew right at it, and just like everything else in this tower, some magical force caused the window to expand like an airplane hangar. Even so, I flinched as she sped forward; the window swung open, then resumed its square shape after she'd departed and suddenly I was alone. I walked slowly back to the vines and waited for Asha. I didn't know where anything was, nor did I know how to navigate the library. This place used magic, but I didn't understand it well enough to find my way around.

Minerva had just tapped her talons against the ground. I knew better than to mess around too much. Knowing me, I might cause something catastrophic. The vines seemed to have settled down; since they were dormant, I got up. I walked over to the planetary system and inspected the massive buttons on the far end. There was that button Minerva had pressed to change the planets' alignment. But what did the other ones do? I didn't know the magic in this place but buttons—I could mess with buttons. What's the worst that could happen?

I went ahead and pressed down a blinking yellow light in the far bottom corner. The table started to rattle, and then the gears kicked in, and all the planets went up into the darkness of the tower, so high that even the crystal's light could no longer illuminate their silhouettes. Thoughts rushed through my mind about what might be happening at the edge of the realm. I looked over to check the vines' reactivity. Still nothing. Meanwhile, the gears had kicked in again and the cords and slim discs came rotating down from somewhere above, carrying a whole new set of planets. There were just a handful of them. This solar system was small; a lone white dwarf acted as the sun in the center. The closest planet to it was a lush green orb. Nothing but vegetation filled every inch of its surface area. I had never seen such a planet. Suddenly, it came to a stop, the gears making a slow, whirring sound. Frozen in mid-orbit, I was able to properly inspect the model. Something was oddly familiar about the white dwarf and the lush green planet. I rubbed my chin as I pondered where I might have envisioned this scene.

The vines snapped back to life. My attention—along with my legs— was drawn back to the table. I ran around the small solar system and jumped up on the counter.

"Asha! Asha! It's me. Where are you? Can I do anything!?"

"Sainath, I'm traveling toward you now. I'm just about to reach the realm's edge. Listen carefully. Terra alerted me to the fight, and Ursa is in hot pursuit. I fought off a few of the enemy as they stormed my home but got overwhelmed before I could send a message to you. Apollyon found out from the witch that you had fled to the realm of the Owl Clan. I imagine Minerva is fighting as we speak." Asha spoke quickly.

I grabbed the vines into a cluster and heaved them over to the leather bag. It was on the ground next to the solar system where it had spilled open. The journal was still there, open on the marble platform. I wanted that journal. After all, I had questions for Prima. I took the paper copy and map that Minerva had created for me, but left the original manuscript. It belonged here, in Minerva's library.

The leather bag shrunk as Asha spoke, and I lifted it with ease. The vines became weightless. It was like I was carrying a bag of feathers. I took the cord and wrapped it around my waist so that the bag was like a satchel now.

"Okay, now to get down to the next level we have to summon the ladder. I'm sure Minerva taught you how, right? Otherwise this will take a long time."

"Yes, let me summon it." I put my hands together and started to rub really hard. As soon as the heat became unbearable, I slapped my palms together to bring forth the familiar sound. Sure enough, I heard the tap dance of the ladder's rails approaching. The ladder sprang up to my level and ran forward. Before it could reach me, I pointed to the edge of the platform from whence it had come. It turned its faceless form and tapped danced back, with me following at its heels. I reached the edge just as the ladder went over.

I looked down. The ladder had stretched the entire length of the levels. I was shocked but didn't take time to process my surprise. I stepped onto the ladder, but before I could descend, it retracted. I went shooting down as though I were in an elevator. I hung on for dear life as I fell at a tremendous speed, all the way down to the sixth floor. We stopped just as quickly as we had started and the ladder let me walk down the seven steps to the marble ground. I looked at the many books.

"Okay, you sound like you made it," Asha's voice said through the vines. "Go to the far right, against the tower wall. About halfway along the perimeter, you will find the charts to the galaxy where Prima is. You will be looking for a galaxy titled "twelve", followed by two vertical dots, then the digits zero and eight. Don't ask me about the name. Math is the universal language; it was decided before your kind was even conceptualized. Take the scroll and put it in the bag.

"Next, come back up the hallway. You will find yourself in the Galaxy Species section. As soon as you turn the corner, go to the left side of the aisle. On your left, at shoulder height, there is a book on that galaxy's planetary species. Again, you will need to look for the title that has the same number on it. One number off and you will be in a totally different star cluster. Take that book. One second, let me end this bear's existence. Now move to the middle hallway—the one that is directly facing the middle of the light crystal. This is the galactic wardrobe section. It holds clothes and material from every galaxy. This will keep you hidden from the far-reaching darkness that I am sure the witch and Apollyon will soon summon to track you. Again, look for the same number here."

I browsed the hallway. It didn't look like any closet I had ever seen before. Just more books. I reached the middle where Asha had told me to stop and reached for the book that had the numbered galaxy on it. I should have known as soon as I removed the book. The bookshelf shifted like the small window had earlier. A golden rod shot out, containing robes of various colors and patterns. It spread into the hallway and turned itself toward me, revealing a full rack of assorted clothing.

At the end of the hallway I heard tapping and thought it was the ladder, so I ignored it and started looking through the various robes. Everything was so colorful. A wooden knot tapped my shoulder, I grabbed my sword and swung around on my toes, ready to attack; there was nothing there but a harmless, faceless, coat hanger. It didn't seem to notice my battle stance. Instead, it took out a measuring tape and started taking my measurements. I relaxed a bit and sheathed my sword, standing tall as it recorded my height. It then took a step back and tapped the golden rod to reveal a free space along it. It wrapped the rope around the horizontal robe and in an instant, the robes changed colors and size—shrinking and expanding to my exact measurements. Dark colors saturated the robes like someone had shot pigmented bullets at the fabric. Armor plating protruded in strategic areas. I was liking this now. A utility belt like the one the scout owl had worn wrapped itself around the midsection. I pointed to that robe, the one I liked best. The rest of the robes returned into the bookshelves, and the massive closet shrunk down to just the one robe I had selected. The coat hanger reeled in its rope and measured my sheath and sword, along with the cord around my torso and the leather bag's trimmings as well. It then took the tape and wrapped it around the rod again.

The robe had metal plating and was tinted a deep autumn orange mixed with hues of chestnut and a deep forest green where fabric met armor. The robe had a thick inner layer to keep its wearer warm. Inside the breast flap of the robe were two pockets big enough to hold a couple of human-scale books. They were on the left side. It was a compliment that it knew I was right-handed. It held armored braces that traveled from the wrists to my elbow. On the inside part of my left sleeve—once again—was a hidden dagger pocket. The was the greatest closet I had ever witnessed. Emily would have loved it.

I nodded with approval, because who wouldn't? It was a perfect match to fit my fashion and combat style.

"All right," said Asha. "Once you are satisfied, put it on, and let's get going. Everything else should be waiting for you on board the ship."

"How do I get to the ship from here?"

"Well, through the window of course!"

"Gotcha. And how exactly do you expect me to reach the window?"

"By using the ladder? I presume you have been there long enough to understand that there are mystical powers at work, right?"

"Yes," I conceded.

"Good. Summon the ladder and get going. I'm meters away now, and I sense pressure on the ground ahead of me. I must go now, Sainath. If I don't make it to see you off, I'm sorry for all of this. Truly, I am. If I had felt how I feel about you now when I had first heard of you, I would have never agreed to let everything get this messy. Know that I was once in your shoes—unaware of what was going on around me, believing myself the odd one out. You are part of a remarkable species, and I want you to know…" his voice trailed off through the vines as the ladder stretched at a sharp angle to accommodate my passage.

It clamped to the windowsill near the crystal. I had already traveled halfway with the ladder retracting toward the window when Asha's voice fizzled out.

I knew the Bear Clan had caught up. He was fighting them. I imagined the wrath of the Forest Guardian throwing verdant punches at the bears. I reached the window the same way I had reached everything else in this place: with water falling from my eyes and my cheeks flapping from the force with which things moved in here.

The window opened just as my fingertips hit the windowsill. I didn't see what happened to the ladder as the window didn't stop my momentum. As I fell through the sky, I looked down and saw the peaceful tree homes. I looked up at the realm's edge. I heard the clashing and saw the darkness of wings and flashes of weapons making contact.

There was Minerva. She was an immense force, a sight to behold—easily twice as big as Ursa himself. That would be a battle worth seeing.

My skin felt funny. I glanced at my arms. The robes were morphing. They spread from my armpits along the outer edge of my legs. They had become a wingsuit as I fell. I started to slow down and began to glide toward the battle. A couple of owls flying by gave me strange looks, but didn't intervene. I guess what Minerva had said to them when I first arrived still held true. They flew ahead as I trailed behind. The tops of the trees came at me fast, and I braced for impact.

End of chapter.

* * *

I spread my body out as far as I could, to slow myself down and push into a glide as the treetops brushed against my skin. I felt the urge to tuck and roll but the massive branches would do more damage if I did. One of the bears saw my arrival and threw a tomahawk in my direction. It whooshed at me with great speed. I rolled to the side, the ground inches away. I fell to my knees. The tomahawk landed a few feet short of its target.

It was chaos on the ground. Minerva swooped to the ground to fight as much as possible and drive the attention away from me. She was fighting five bears at once. I looked to my right as I reached my feet and unsheathed my sword. I gripped the tomahawk in my other hand.

A few other bears were fighting the scout owls and the guard owls who were raining their spears down from above. This was dangerous. I had to keep an eye on Minerva, the scouts, and the spears hurtling haphazardly through the air. Everything had to be taken in, all details accounted for in real time. The last thing I wanted was to become a shish kabob.

The entrance to the realm was before me, so I could easily see the landscape changing as it became more and more of a battlefield. The line I had crossed between the desert and the forest snaked across the horizon. Was that Terra crossing over in the distance, Bayard on her back? He looked like he was already engaged in the fight. He punched the snout of a bear as it lunged forward, trying to wrap slavering jaws around his forearm.

I felt the ground shake and give. Its restless trembling told me Ursa's army was not far behind. I flipped the tomahawk in my hand and threw it back at the bear. He was now fighting an owl. Minerva's shadow passed overhead, and time slowed. The tomahawk met its mark in the bear's neck. I started to run toward Bayard.

Then found I couldn't move. Immense talons grabbed my back and lifted me off the ground.

"What are you doing here?! I told you to wait in the tower until I returned."

I didn't need to look up at my captor to know who it was.

I watched the battlefield from above as we gained altitude and shouted against the wind in my face. "I did wait. Asha called and guided me. I didn't have any reason to stay in the tower. I couldn't let you fight the army that had vanquished the kingdom I was supposed to defend. This is my fight."

"I expected you to heed my command, young one. I have to get you across the realm and to the ship. If you die here, this fight will have been futile. My clan will have perished for no reason. You must find a new world for humanity."

I swallowed a cool air bubble. "I want to make sure Bayard is okay. And Asha should be here any moment. We must go back! They need our help."

We stopped ascending. Minerva didn't say anything. She slowed her wings down to maintain a steady beat, as though she were a helicopter hovering in place.

Finally, she spoke. "Asha will be angry if I don't get you away from here. Even Tamara would be unhappy, to say the least. And the celestial being of compassion will not be very compassionate with me if you die on the battlefield."

"Look. Your only knowledge of my species is what you read through that journal about my world," I argued. "Let me show you that I am more helpful on the battlefield than standing on the sidelines. You want me to live, then let me fight alongside you! Trust another species for once, you old bird."

She gave a sigh and circled the battlefield as a white cloud emerged from the desert dust.

The enemy had arrived with his army. "Let me fight with you," I pressed. "You don't have much of a choice now. You need all the help you can get!"

"There is always a choice, young one," Minerva said. She sounded tired. "I will trust you for a few minutes. But as soon as there is a clearing and the rest of my army arrives, you must flee to the outskirts of the realm."

The ground came into view as the bears' rounded bodies and roars spread across the forest. Minerva let go as her talons touched the moss floor. Sunrise was announced with the high scream of a whistle, which came from the single owl scout I had encountered when I'd first arrived at the Owl Kingdom.

This scout was the smallest of owls. He emerged from the forest, blowing his whistle and hurdling bears as he pulled two daggers from his utility belt. He moved faster than I could. He made quick work of the first bear he encountered on his way toward us. Just as I took a step to face my own approaching enemy, he had already downed one and was moving to assist Minerva who clamped her beak around one of the bear's legs and swung him into the sea of white fur that had circled us when we landed. She cleared the circle and gave us some breathing room as the army on the horizon came to a stop. My ears picked up the almost endless beating of wings flying in from the west.

By now the sun was in full view, and the sky had darkened. Minerva's wings opened over me. I could hear spears reflecting off her thick feathers. She was protecting me. However, her wings gave my presence away as the bears around us were speared into the ground. The sky cleared, and many of the owls fought on the ground, going toe to toe with the bears.

The owls were highly intelligent. They studied the bears' tactics and welcomed them with slaughter in return for traveling such vast distances. I could still hear the cries of war shooting up between the trees as I made my way away from Minerva. I could hear another wave coming through the forest. Owls swooped down from overhead and joined the ancient one's side. They formed a line of defense in front of me.

There was the owl with the whistle. He came gliding down and cocked his head to one side. "We will hold the line for as long as we can. It will buy you time to get clear and a head start. Make for the edge of the realm."

I nodded but stood my ground. "I'm staying with you."

Those eyes shone back at me—those eyes that were slightly off from the rest of the owls. The tremble of stampeding paws shook the loose dirt from my boots. I still had the leather bag strapped to my waist. Terra's old body was there, but still no movement and certainly no voice. I couldn't see with all the owls zooming through the trees.

"I have to find Asha and Terra first," I replied. "There is a friend traveling with them. I also need to find a human who is hiding in this realm before I can leave this planet. That is what has been asked of me. Now please, like I told Minerva—let me stand with you."

The small owl said, "Terra is nowhere to be seen, and Asha is at the far end fighting off as many of the bears as he can, all to buy you time to get to safety! Now is no occasion to be stubborn. None of us would be here if it weren't for you. You brought chaos here."

He went on. "I was told you would show up. That your blood had something to do with humanity's rebirth. With you we might have a chance to live another generation, but none of that will be worth a damn if you are dead! Put your fancy sword away, and start running."

I looked at him. I mean, I really looked at him, for the first time. I squinted. He had betrayed himself with one word—one simple word that sparked my curiosity. I finally saw it.

He wasn't an owl at all. His luminescent eyes were magnified through lenses. Small lights lent them their yellow hue. His wingsuit was far more detailed than mine, with the actual texture of an owl's feathers, rather than a simple woven cloth that harnessed the wind's power. Each feather had been individually designed and inserted. I wanted to reach out and touch it, like a fake plant or flower which from an arm's length looks like real until your touch reveals plastic leaves and paper petals. The owl in front of me was like that—an authentic, believable fake. The talons looked real enough, their sharp ends digging into the ground.

The owls were engaged in combat all around us. As the small owl was about to turn away, I grabbed him by the shoulder.

"What do you mean by 'we'?"

The owl bowed its head. He took his right wing and tapped the base of his neck. Clamps that were hidden under feathers released, and he grabbed what appeared to be his own head only to reveal it was a mask of great artistry.

"I am the final human you are looking for," he said. The red-haired face wore a thin goatee. It belonged to a young man around my age and weight. I could tell the armor made up much of his mass.

"Are you Nayr?"

"I am. I have been waiting a long time for you, mate, hanging on to an old story I found in a journal. I wasn't sure if I should try to make a living instead. The ancient one found me and took me in. After she discovered my identity, I was shown the journal in the tower. She created this disguise, and for close to twenty Earth years I have lived in these woods. Just a couple of years ago I became one of the highest ranked lieutenants for ground and air operations for the ancient one's forces. Minerva's forces."

The battle was happening all around us. As a bear lunged forward, we moved in tandem, standing back to back as we slashed down the assailing bears.

We shouted to keep the conversation going. "That is her name, though she did tell me, everyone in this realm calls her the ancient one due to her great size and wisdom." I dropped a bear to his knees as my sword came up over my head, then down. I sliced the skull clean through the middle, split his brain in half, and segmented his tongue.

Hot blood sprayed my face as Nayr replied. "I never thought she had a name. Just thought she was like the celestials, you know? Made of something beyond anatomy the way we comprehend it."

We danced around each other, taking out bear after bear in quick succession. My sword kept a safe distance between the bears and the two of us, as Nayr edged into the discomfort of close combat. Getting into the face of his enemies, he stabbed their eyes from behind while I used my sword to slash their legs so they toppled like trees.

We worked in unison. It reminded me of the royal guard—that natural syncopation evident in how well they worked together. Even if they were products of this planet and possessed a mere fraction of human DNA, I still respected them for whatever they were.

Nearby, Minerva pulled a spear from an impaled bear and pinched it in her talons. She flicked it between two claws.

The spear came in fast above my head. I heard it break the sound barrier among the trees, bouncing so much noise throughout the clearing that it was tough to triangulate what direction it was coming from. It was way too powerful of a throw to have come from anything small. Sure enough, my wondering was answered as the spear flew past us. It hit five bears in one shot, knocking the fifth bear into the ground.

Nayr and I looked down the line of dead bodies. Minerva's voice rang out from the other end of the line. "Nayr, it's time. Take Sainath with you, and head to the ship. What you have been training for is finally here. The army's last wave will arrive shortly, with Ursa at the helm. I won't be able to watch over you like I have done in the path. Humanity's fate rests with getting Sainath to Prima. Now go!"

We both shook our heads and sheathed our weapons. Nayr was still in disguise as he put the daggers in his utility belt. Just as I slipped my blood-soaked sword in my back shoulder, the ground trembled and a dark shadow materialized behind Minerva.

"Behind you!" I shouted, reaching out with my hand as if I could pull her away from danger. But I wasn't close enough. Ursa landed a blow with his right claws—sending Minerva toppling to the ground.

I screamed in rage and ran at Ursa like I'd never run before. "Looking for me!?"

I leapt upon him. The ground below shot up like a volcanic eruption and an equine figure came out of it.

"Terra?" I said in my mind as another bear claw slammed me to the ground and disrupted the link between me and my sword. I landed against a redwood, pain blooming somewhere within my left rib cage. I was pretty sure Ursa had shattered three of my ribs with one swing. Minerva was right. If we wanted to live, we needed to leave right now.

Minerva. I looked up. There she was, fighting Ursa. Two giants. Two ancients. A king and a queen. One who fought for power and the annihilation of a race and the other, fighting to give a second chance to a species that was alien to say the least.

Nayr came running to my aid. "We have to go now, mate! Can you walk?"

I looked at him as if that was a challenge. "I can do better than that," I wheezed as my ribs touched one another in ways they shouldn't. "I can run."

I stood up carefully, using the redwood as a support for my back. I took a step forward, but fell to the ground.

"Put him on my back, and let's get moving."

I knew that voice. It was Terra. She galloped past us, slamming into a bear and knocking him out, then circling to face us again. She looked naked without her vines. Only parts of her head were covered with moss and grassy growths. Her body was a skeleton outline of branches and twigs. She looked like a zombie version of herself.

"Terra, you look a little rough," I wheezed. Her vine earbud reached me and I let it get firmly attached as her voice reached my mind. "Here, I have something for you."

"There is that sense of humor I missed," she neighed in my mind. "Quickly now. Throw the vines over my back, and they will do the rest. Should only take a moment. Get on as soon as the vines integrate. I carried Bayard all the way here without the support of the vines and it was absolute torture on my legs."

I looked down. Large logs stood in place for her thighs, curving like sapling trunks. Her shins were smaller branches, while twigs acted as hooves. I grabbed the vines—which shrunk to an apple-sized ball, almost like yarn—and tossed them onto Terra's back. The ball moved as if magnets were pulling it in multiple directions. Then it went still, and the vines snapped up from their spherical hold. Like baby snakes they quickly found their routes along Terra's body and grew in width and length. They spread quickly as another bear came toward us. I walked around Terra, clutching my chest and trying my best to conceal a limp. Putting any weight on my left side sent shockwaves of pain coursing through my rib cage. I inhaled a shaky breath and reached for a sword which didn't exist. I looked around where the two ancient beings were biting at one another.

The sun's rays glinted off the black meteorite sword, where it lay in the grass. I went to retrieve it. I started to half-run-half-fall in that direction. The bear who had spotted me closed in. A dagger whisked past my ear lobe and stuck the right leg of the beast. Nayr sprinted past like the shadow he was and took his place against the enemy. A body's reach from the sword, I collapsed. Nayr and the bear were on my right side, about ten steps away.

Without looking back, Nayr yelled, "Only one of us needs to make it to Prima. You are so stubborn, mate. You keep insisting in fighting when humanity's fate rests in your hands. Now I must give my life to make you realize how vital your existence is, Sainath."

"Don't you dare die on me, Nayr!" I shouted from the ground as I crawled across the blood-stained grass. I grasped my sword by the hilt and used it as a crutch to bring myself to my feet. I tried to breathe. The breath felt scattered—I could feel it breaking off in various directions inside my chest, places where air shouldn't go. Wiping the blood from my lips, I broke into a run. I ignored the pain as I staggered up behind the bear. Nayr had its full attention. I jumped and brought the sword down between the shoulder blades, severing the spinal cord and ending the bear's existence.

Terra raced up to us. Her weight and beauty had been restored to their former glory. I didn't need the communication vine to tell me what she was thinking; her body language toward me said it all. "Let's go."

Without arguing, Nayr helped me jump up on the tall horse. I reached out my hand. "Come on. You are supposed to join me," I wheezed from the corner of my mouth. I cradled my left side with one arm. Moving hurt.

"I will meet you there," Nayr replied. "I must find Bayard first. He is the final human left on this planet. I can fly just as fast Terra. Now go." He looked around, perceptive as a hawk. "All of the bears are after you. None of them will recognize me under my armor's disguise. I'll see you at the ship."

He turned and ran past Minerva. She was busy with Ursa. She threw him against a sequoia. There was a loud crack. The tree fell in slow motion. Terra turned on her haunches and sprinted away. The battlefield became a blur in an instant. Vines roped across my waist and Terra's vines got to work reestablishing our link. A new vine approached my rib cage and locked around it. This vine pulsed red and white. I had never seen anything like that. I said as much to Terra, through my mouth vine.

"It's a medical vine," she responded. "The red and white pulses are sending small vibrations into your bone marrow to activate your growth cells. By the time we reach the end of the realm, your ribs will have reknit. They will be stronger. Now rest. A week-long journey awaits at the end of the realm. I won't be able to run as fast as usual, since much of my energy is being used to heal you. I can only run at about fifty percent of my total speed."

I let my shoulders relax. "Thank you, Terra. For everything."

"Oh, how did you like wearing me?"

"The armor was amazing; I had never worn armor with a mind of its own. It literally saved my life."

I continued to tell Terra about the spectacle of the battle, my first encounter with Minerva, my zipline adventure, and the magic tower. After what seemed like hours of me talking while she listened, the night sky and the first moon made their debut on the horizon. The stars' lights were hard to see as the canopy of the trees obscured the planets from our view. Hopefully, we were hidden from Apollyon and the witch too. That witch, I wasn't too fond of her.

I had broken our deal; I did still want to see Emily and be reunited with her. I wanted all of this to be over. But for some odd reason, I was meant to survive the destruction of my home world. These celestial beings had lied to me—but not entirely. I didn't know whether to be angry with them or trust their vision.

My conversations with Asha and Tamara had given me insights into new perspectives, as well as a clearer understanding of my purpose. I still had my promise to Tamara to uphold. All I had to do was visit Prima and convince her that humanity deserved a second chance. I would aid the beginning of a new world. Assuming she accepted. She might refuse and kill me on the spot—ending humanity for good. We would be relegated to the realm of memory by whatever creation might come after us.

I let go of the question of "why me." The journal explained everything that I needed to know. It had been written way before I was born; my name and occupation didn't matter. It was my blood. Something deep within my ancestry apparently meant I would be able to handle the trials and tribulations which awaited, like both the journal and Asha had stated. The DNA had been in the mix before I was even a thought. It really was pure chance that I had become the chosen one.

Cawing interrupted my thoughts. I turned my head, and the vine holding me upright went lax, giving me room to move a little. "Great," I said. "Just as I was getting sleepy. I had literally just thought about sleep."

Terra said, "Don't tell me. It's not just your average crow behind us. I take it there are three of them?"

I resumed my position on Terra's back, but kept my ears perked up in case the crows came any closer. "Yup. Three of them. The witch and her decoys are right behind us and closing in fast," I said. "Go ahead— remove the medical vines, and reclaim your energy. Let's try to lose them."

"My thoughts exactly. Get down and make yourself horizontal along my back. It's going to be a bumpy ride."

Before I could react, the main vine on my back forced me down; I buried my head in Terra's wildflower mane. The rest of the vines retracted from me. From my peripheral vision I watched them spread out, brushing the trunks of trees as we raced through the forest. No surprise—Asha must be alive and well, because he was aiding us. I felt his presence in how the trees moved out of our way, giving us more than enough room.

However, the more I thought about it, the more I wondered at his strategy. Shouldn't the trees be trying to conceal us from view? Instead, they opened up their canopies, and gave our position away. Was this Apollyon's doing?

I kept my head down as the vines stretched and snapped. They ossified, becoming rigid as bone. Then, they shot out layers of leaves. My eyes widened at the sight of wings sprouting between Terra's shoulder blades.

The mouthpiece was no longer in my mouth, so there was nothing to quell my amazement as I shouted, "You can fly!"

She could hear me but without the mouthpiece, was unable to respond. Instead, she threw her head back with joy and sent her sprint into a whole new gear. The waves of wind created by her speed rustled through my hair. The vine around my waist split away so they could trap my leather boots, holding me more sturdily in place. Terra's wings beat against the air. And then, we were in the sky. From where my head rested on her neck, I watched the canopy of the trees collapse back in, smashing two of the crows. The lead crow just barely escaped. It still trailed behind us—this time keeping its distance.

CHAPTER 20

||||||||||||||||||||||||||||||||||||||||||||||||||

heartache for hope

I stayed low. Terra's green feathers fluttered with each stroke. It was fascinating to see such a thing. Terra climbed through the sky until the air became so thin that the witch didn't have a choice but to return to the forest where the altitude was bearable. I was surprised that she hadn't tried to throw herself at us.

It was the end of the day by the time we leveled off above the clouds. Terra only brought us below them when she felt secure enough to descend. The end of the realm beckoned in the distance.

I finally saw the edge of the planet close up. It looked like a dock. Ships of various shapes and styles were tied by rope and chain to the stones that formed its shore. Lights hanging from tree branches lit our path down to the docking area. The last of the forest canopy fell away beneath us.

Terra's hooves touched cobblestone. I dismounted quickly. How in the world was this possible? And why would ships—of all things—be hanging off the planet's edge? Terra followed closely behind but waited on the dock as I stepped up onto one of the ships. The sails were tied against the arms of the mast. The ship I had boarded was mid-size. A much larger one was moored next to it, followed by several small fishing boats. This one was cream-colored and fashioned from sturdy-looking wood. I couldn't see the front of the ship from where I stood.

It had definitely seen better days. The main deck's birch planks had been smoothed and polished to a high shine to hinder any sort of decay in the wood planks. However, the upper deck was made of planks of elm. A patchwork job. Perhaps it had been added later.

Those planks were much smaller. They'd been cut into panels to fit the upper deck. I walked up the four steps and turned to my left, where I expected to see the wheel of the ship. Instead, there was a black leather chair. Like the kind you'd see in a barber shop, except this one had armrests and a duct-taped head rest, and was drilled into a track nailed into the deck. These tracks ran from one end of the ship to the other, and were paralleled by a metal rail which ran along the back side of the ship. The chair faced a panel of buttons that resembled the one in the library. I stood in between the panel and chair and looked back toward the forest, hoping Nayr would spot us. The ship was composed of a main mast and a foremast. Both boasted four equally-spaced sails. The last one was just beyond my reach. Two sets of ratlines hung on either side of the masts.

Turning my back to the captain's chair, I glanced over the metal railing. Where there would usually be a rudder, there were four hollow tunnels, each the length of an average man's height. They resembled exhaust pipes—the kind a rocket would have. I looked up at the sails.

They weren't ordinary either. A stitched pattern was woven into the cloth. Cables intertwined around the masts of the ship and disappeared below the deck. "Fascinating" was the only word that formed in my mind, uttered moments later, to myself. What did it use for fuel? I had expected to see a rocket of some kind; instead, I was standing on a sailboat floating off the edge of a planet.

The trees shifted. A moment later the sound of heavy flaps announced Minerva's arrival. She broke through the green. I ran off the ship, knowing she would chastise me for not staying there. As I approached the tree line, I realized something was wrong. Blood dripped from her right wing as each flap painted the trees' canopy crimson. A drop the size of a backpack splattered beside me as she passed overhead, looking for a spot to land. I stopped, frozen in place. What should I do…what *could* I do? I was supposed to be on the ship, ready to get off the planet. But I had to wait for Nayr to arrive. Then I heard a familiar roar.

Ursa. He wasn't far away. A few scout owls perched by the forest's edge. I ran back toward them, watching Minerva come down. One of the scouts landed in front of me and shouted, re-awakening my legs from their temporary paralysis.

He shouted again as I closed the space between us. "What are you still doing here?"

"I just arrived a minute or two before you did, honest. Ask Terra."

A rumble coursed through the ground. It came from within the forest. *Asha?* I thought to myself. *Was he alive?* Either that, or there was an earthquake.

The owl scout met up with Terra who was already in position to slow Minerva down, just in case she landed too close to the edge of the planet. I arrived just a few steps behind. Her body language told the scout to back off. Minerva stirred up a cloud of dust as she came in for a rough landing, her eyes barely open. She fell to the ground while her feet were still in the air. Her weight shattered the cobblestones, and her back made a concave dent in the dock. She didn't move.

I ran to her. The other scouts circled above as citizen owls came pouring from the forest and crowded around her limp body.

"Back off. Give her some room!" I shouted, shoving through the stunned and stone-faced owls. I broke through the crowd and walked slowly to her. My hand rested on her feathered body. I let my hand search her breast for the rhythm of a heartbeat.

As I passed the curve of her wing where it folded against her body, I felt it. Her heart stuttered weakly, and she gasped for air. She had maybe a couple of hours at best. Something crashed to the forest floor somewhere behind us. Ursa was making short work of the trees.

The scouts who circled overhead formed a line between Minerva and Ursa. The citizens did the same; they had nothing but their clothes and empty, weaponless wings. The armored scouts took a stand, pointing their spears in defense as the citizens behind them did their best to not look terrified. Ursa emerged from the forest's edge, his white pelt illuminated by the first light of sunrise.

I didn't care about him. I knelt down next to Minerva. She felt cold. She rolled over and opened one of her eyes to look at me. Her left eye was a black bruise. I had never seen her eyes close under any circumstances. Her thin lids fluttered slowly as she rolled over, getting her talons underneath her.

She coughed, then whispered, "What are you doing out here? Get on that ship *now*. I have just enough strength left to hold him off while you launch."

She coughed again. Her left wing acted as a crutch; she used it to brace herself as she got to her talons. She turned to face her people. Her head was still inches off the ground, and her whole body shook as she tried to stand. I threw my arms around her beak and looked up the bridge of her nose and into her one good eye. It was fully open but clouded with pain. I bent my knees in a squat so I could wrap my arms around her beak. I lifted it off the ground, straining my back. I went light-headed from the weight and the pain in my still-fractured rib.

"I will carry you if need be. You are not dying on me. Over eight billion of my own people have already perished. Lower your wing, for goodness sake. Let me fight instead. I don't know how to sail or fly that ship. I'm waiting for Nayr to get here. I can't do it alone. The two others aren't even here. I can't make this journey alone. If, by some miracle I figured out how to fly the ship, that isn't a good enough excuse to leave like this, knowing I wouldn't be the kind of leader the world requires me to be. I'd be a coward who abandons friends. Let me help."

I let go of her beak as she seemed to want to open it. A stream of blood trickled down my legs as she struggled to speak. "Young one, you must survive the journey. Leave." Her eye was wild. "This world was never meant to be your journey's end. Your journey is just beginning. Now go!"

She got up on her talons, as I walked up beside her—hoisting her left wing above my head so it wouldn't drag on the ground. The sun was at our backs, cresting the distant treetops.

"You humans are stubborn, huh?"

"Damn right we are." I forced a smile. "Last I heard, the universe liked that about us."

Just then, Ursa barreled through the owl scouts. He was here for round two with Minerva. I dropped her wing, the anger rising in my stomach as I felt her talons shiver with exhaustion. I walked in front of the ancient owl. Then I drew my sword and pointed it at Ursa. Taunting him. The citizens backed away, creating a ring for us to fight in. Minerva rested at one end.

Ursa lunged at me "Fool! Bow down, and I will give you a quick and painless death. Let me end your species quickly so I can lead my victorious army home!"

"Ursa, that is enough," I shouted. My voice cracked, but I kept my sword trained on him. Sunlight caught the blade and reflected light back at Ursa. Squinting, he slowed momentarily.

"I played your little game on your land and won fairly," I continued. "There is no need for this. If I wanted to, I could have started war in your kingdom, but I didn't. If I had known you would take advantage of my kindness toward you and your offspring, I would have ended your vile and disgusting reign immediately. Your rampage of this planet's kingdoms ends before I leave this planet!"

"Little bug, you have no idea what it took to get to where I am," he smirked. "I have lived over five of your lifetimes. Apollyon has promised my kind status at the top of the food chain as long as I stop you from leaving his planet. He knows you are going to see Prima."

Ursa moved out of the sunlight, stopped, and then started circling me. I moved with him, keeping my sword pointed in his direction. The ground beneath me shook, and I was certain Asha had arrived. Then I heard his voice, and with our next rotation, saw him.

Asha stood next to Terra, his large tentacle arms severed in multiple places all the way up to his shoulders. A bite mark on his rib cage revealed the glimmering orb within his chest. One of his arms rested on Terra's back.

"What are you still doing here, Sainath?" he shouted. "Get out of there. You should have been long gone by now. Maybe your species does deserve to die for being this stupid and not listening! Do you realize how many of us just died for you?" Frustration rose in his voice. "The owls who surround you at this moment—they don't even know who you are or what to call you. Yet they have fought to the death for your cause. Some have used their dying breaths to make sure all know the mission at hand: *get the worm with appendages to the boat.* I hope you know what you are doing! I have slowed Apollyon but he is on his way now. My forest will keep him at bay, but not for much longer."

Asha turned his back to me. Terra bowed her head but kept her eyes on me. I could imagine what she would say from the dejected slope of her snout: *I can't watch this.*

I was too preoccupied to respond. I circled Ursa a second time. He charged, I rolled safely away and got to my feet, and we resumed our tango.

"So, you want to know what Apollyon wants?" he said, with a menacing glimmer in his eyes. "Don't you get it? You are *extinct.* Nothing more than a stink bug. I heard what you did to my kind too, back on your world. You hear that everyone," he roared. "His kind wiped us all out!"

I felt many eyes on me. Even Terra looked up. The tables had turned. Ursa had gotten into my head. It was all he needed, even if for a second. He charged. I rolled but this time—I lost my balance and Ursa took advantage. He charged again, merciless. I sliced at the paw coming for me and managed to create a deep gash. He let loose a roar which echoed across the dock, but quickly regained his composure.

He spoke to the crowd, trying again to get under my skin. "Many of you here have no idea what this creature with limbs is about. Let me shine some light on *exactly* what his species has done to each and every one of us, on his own planet." He slowed his pace. "You were put in charge of your planet, Sainath. Because of your upright position and your higher intellect. And what did you do with such power? You watched helplessly from nearby as your world melted away. You have an old saying, 'Actions speak louder than words.' Isn't that correct?"

"Yes," I said, just above a whisper.

"My kind couldn't speak your language on Earth. They were defenseless. But didn't their starving children and dwindling numbers speak loud enough for you to hear?"

He circled closer. I was having trouble keeping my guard up. He forced my steps closer to the center of the circle, which was growing as his voice grew louder. The truth hurt me, but it hurt those around us even more. The sad thing was, the hardest truth was still to come. I scanned the eyes of my allies; they were watching with a mixture of rapture and betrayal. Some had lowered their spears to listen to the enemy. Was I the enemy now? Ursa spoke louder—with greater confidence—now that he'd won the crowd's interest.

"My kind perished, but guess what, owls? He also let you go extinct. Oh yes. Long before my kind was stuffed and exhibited in museums, you had become a thing of legend. They poisoned your food supply. The rodents and plants which kept you alive became too toxic to eat, thanks to their constant dumping of nuclear and chemical runoffs from their industrial farming methods. Their ever-growing population grew fat while your families starved. The chemicals permeated the seeds of plants and trees you depended upon. You digested the same poisons that killed your chicks by the thousands until your reproductive cycle broke down. Then his people created stories and myths about you to tell their children. Tell me, owls! Who is the enemy now? Are you willing to die for this species—a people who has killed you off once already?"

I curled my lip and bit hard until blood flowed. I was beyond angry with what he had said. The worst part was, he was right. My species had decimated the polar bears and destroyed the owls along with numerous other animals both on land and sea. I felt outnumbered; I could feel my body telling me to make a run for it.

Sensing my nervousness, Ursa charged. I slashed again at the paw, but he grabbed my sword in his jaws. There was a sickening crack as the meteorite blade snapped in two. I staggered back, falling on my rear. Ursa backed away. He was standing on his hind legs and looking around him, searching for a weapon.

One of the owl scouts was holding a double axe, stolen from a fallen bear. Ursa reached for it, and the owl offered it up. I was defeated. I had lost the support and belief of the owls. I looked back at Minerva. She was watching with her one good eye. The owls maintained an opening in the circle for her beak, which rested on the cobblestone dock. She was close to death; her eye growing glassier by the minute.

I caught her eye. "I'm sorry," I mouthed.

"You want to know what Apollyon told me?" Ursa said. He was getting arrogant now, worked up from the crowd's attention. He looked at the double ax, then to me, chuckled and dropped his weapon. "This weapon is too good for you, human scum. Let's see if I can still knock the wind out of my enemies."

My movement slowed as he slashed and lunged at me like I was a fish in a river. I was exhausted. I tried to dodge him but a large white paw clamped around my waist. It pushed me down so that my shoulders dug into the cobblestone's rocky bed. I had to survive. I brought my arms up to cross over one another as he punched them repeatedly, burying me a few inches in the ground with each strike.

"After you left, he came to my kingdom," Ursa continued. "He told me everything. What was already written must come to pass, of course, but if I were to kill the last of your kind, he would make me master of the world. I will be the dominant force on this planet. My species will thrive once again. When I bring him your head, he will give my species the gifts that were bestowed upon your undeserving kind. Can you imagine what I will create with such a gift?"

He loomed over me. I couldn't feel my arms. I'd had the wind knocked out of me so good, I struggled to breathe; I saw stars and then everything went black. I couldn't move. What was the point anyway? There was the sensation of something being heaped around me. Dirt, probably. I was a good foot in the ground. I lost track of time; Ursa's words were the only indication of any sort of temporal progression. And it would all be over soon. I'd be with Emily again. I smiled. I could let him end me—end the celestial bloodline.

No. I had to go on.

Ursa spread his arms to the crowd. I braced myself for the sound of applause. Nothing. The crowd was silent.

A single owl shouted, "What about us? What makes you any different than them? How do we know that you won't just wipe us out too?"

I forced my eyes open in time to see Ursa lower his arms. "Silence!" he roared. There was murmuring among the crowd.

I crawled out of my own grave, groping the cobblestone with my aching fingers. But there. I clutched the two pieces of my sword. Slowly, my muscles screaming, I got to my feet. I clenched the two halves of my blades tightly. I took a deep breath, and my chest exploded with pain.

"It doesn't matter who the dominant species is," I spoke out wiping clods of dirt from my face and mouth, "The same cycle will continue."

Asha was the first to turn at the sound of my words. Terra peered into the circle. Minerva shoved her head forward like a sea turtle, using her wings like flippers to drag her wounded body nearer. I regained a smidgen of confidence.

I scanned the horizon. Still no sign of Bayard or Nayr. I couldn't rely on them to back me up. I was on my own. My voice cracked as the saliva caught in my throat. I put my broken sword behind my back, then shoved them into my belt and brought my hands forward across my chest just as Ursa turned to face me.

I no longer feared the massive bear. He was alone. His army was already rotting in the forest and across the planet all the way to Gregory's kingdom. His offspring were gone. The only females—if any were left alive—wouldn't last long without their ruler.

"You see, it doesn't matter," I coughed. "It doesn't matter if it's the polar bear or the owl, or a single tree. Without anything to keep them in check, the dominant species will always become a virus running wild, replicating at the expense of everything else. The scariest thought concerns adaptability. Without checks on a species, it will adapt and come back stronger and more intelligent than before. That is why it will never work, Ursa. No matter what deal Apollyon may have promised. He lied to you. If you continue along this path, you will find yourself in my shoes soon enough. If you want to fight the enemy, fight the very celestial who promised something that would only ever end in destruction. Only ever end in you blowing this planet and yourselves up, and thereby ending everyone's existence."

I stumbled around in the circle. The axe fell to Ursa's side. He swung it back and forth, trying to decide what to do next. I appeared unarmed to him. Keeping my back to him, I was careful to seem as unthreatening as possible, which wasn't hard to do, given the state I was in. I picked the dirt from my ears clean as I kept calm. His sense of smell was far superior to his sight. I had to remain in control.

I felt the tension of the crowd shift. Suddenly, Asha stretched both his arms behind Ursa and grabbed him around the waist. Ursa clawed himself free, but Asha got a second wind and grabbed at him again, pinning the ancient bear in place. I dashed forward—finally revealing the two broken shards of my sword. They were sharp. In my right hand I held the hilt, and in my left, the fractured blade. Pumping my arms, I launched myself up into the air and stabbed both ends of the sword into each side of the massive neck. I saw his eyes roll in their sockets and his tongue slip from between jagged teeth. Blood spurted and warmed my hands. Ursa tore free from the vines. I heard them snap a second too late. His massive claw closed around my neck. My own eyes started to roll. He was weakening, but not fast enough. My esophagus was burning as he crushed it. My eyes rove around the crowd, seeking any escape route. No one moved.

Asha was losing his grip; Ursa had freed himself from all the vines. Terra came running up from behind, but Ursa wasn't fooled. As Terra tried to come to my aid, Ursa brought his leg up—ripping more vines— and kicked her in the neck. Terra went flying across the circle and slammed into Minerva. I punched at the paw around my neck. Each hit sent shockwaves through my oxygen-deprived brain. Everything was going sort of fuzzy.

A cry resounded somewhere in the forest. It sounded like hope. I forced my eyes open with my last shred of energy. A sharp whistle blew, and I knew it was Nayr. The small owl ran forward, stripping off his disguise as he moved. The owls gawked in disbelief. They had probably never suspected that a human had been living among them all this time.

Nayr shoved his way through. A bright light momentarily blinded me, and lit up the landscape around us. Ursa must have seen my shadow stretch from the light, because suddenly, I was being thrown to the ground. I would have mere seconds before he reoriented himself and grabbed me again. I gasped for breath, trying to get my brain to stop screaming for oxygen. I shielded my eyes with my hand and squinted.

There was only one being capable of producing that sort of light. Tamara.

The owls didn't know what to do, so they bowed. Minerva got up again, shaking from head to toe because her muscles hadn't yet regained their strength. Nayr helped me to my feet, his spear in hand.

"I thought you were dead." I said.

Tamara came closer, blinding all of us but Ursa.

Nayr spoke to me. "Not yet, mate. Remember, I'm the only one that can fly that ship behind us. I know I have said this before, but are you ready to finally get off this planet? Also, I brought a friend." He nodded to Tamara.

"You bet I am," I nodded. "With Tamara here now, I feel better about leaving." Then I remembered Minerva. I walked toward her as quickly as I could, given the state I was in. Her glassy stare was fixed somewhere beyond us—beyond everything.

"Minerva..." My voice faltered.

Nayr put a hand on my shoulder and led me away, under the crumpled arch of her wing.

We crossed the wooden plank to the ship's deck. I pulled my arm back from Nayr's shoulder and leaned on the handrails for support. We were finally a good enough distance away that I could open my eyes fully. In the dim light, Tamara towered over everyone and everything. She was half as large as one of those sequoia trees. She grabbed Ursa with one hand and brought him toward Asha, who summoned massive roots from one of the trees nearby. They tangled together like bars and held Ursa in place. A sharp vine removed my swords and plugged the puncture wounds they had made. The bleeding might have stopped, but Ursa was in no shape to put up any semblance of a fight. Not against the celestial beings, anyway.

The scout owls scattered now that the excitement was over. Nayr was already unhooking the cables that kept the ship from drifting into space. Tamara moved in our direction. She stopped at Minerva and wrapped her arms under the ancient owl as if she were picking up a baby or an owlet. She spoke with great admiration in her voice as she raised Minerva into the air so they were face to face.

"Minerva, thank you for watching over the last humans. I know we asked without giving you time to consider the options. I am sorry to have brought such danger to your home and people. My thoughts and prayers are with your fallen warriors. I have repaired some of the damage on my way through your kingdom."

I walked away from the rail and disembarked. "Can you save her?' I asked. Tamara stood tall as a tree. Her body pulsed like a faint star. Her glowing white eyes met mine.

"I cannot. She has lost too much blood, and over half of her soul is already in the Unknown. The best I can do is take the pain away and let her rest in peace. I will have to watch over her people now and try to hold off Apollyon. He will arrive shortly. You must turn around and board the ship, Sainath."

"Thank you for coming to my rescue," I replied. "Did you deal with the witch too?"

"No sign of her," said Tamara. "I have a feeling she will find a way to Prima. After all, she did create that abomination. Your final questions must be saved for her."

I heard Nayr shout from the captain's wheel. "The engines are primed and ready. Launch is in thirty seconds. Wrap it up, mate!"

I waved for him to give me a second. "May I see Minerva one last time?" I asked. "And did you happen to see Bayard on your way over?"

Tamara fell to her knees. She reached forward so Minerva was at my level. I brushed her beak carefully as I gave her my final thanks. Tamara cupped her hands around Minerva. The Great Owl's one eye lost its glow. Tamara whispered something unintelligible beneath her breath—ancient words in a language long gone. Her breath blew across Minerva's corpse in a gentle wind. A bright light exploded in her hands, and Minerva's feathers fell to the ground like leaves on an autumn day.

Minerva had turned to stardust. Tamara opened her hands and released Minerva from her owl form. A pure white bird—no larger than a finch—gathered from the stardust and perched on the edge of

Tamara's finger. With a quick flutter of wings, she flew around us. She rested between Terra's ears and said something to the horse, who neighed happily. Asha lifted a finger which she landed on next; his vines sprouted vibrant leaves around the little bird. He looked at me and nodded back to her. She flew around the ship to Nayr. He gave her a high five—her wings fluttering against his palm.

She finally circled me from head to toe, then stopped midair. She looked into my golden eyes, then came in close to my ear and spoke my tongue. "Young one. It takes great courage to stand up for what you believe in, especially when everyone around you doubts you. Take care on your journey. You might need this, as space travel is not in your DNA."

I smiled as she spun around me again. She shook a shimmering white dust around my head. A thin, see-through blanket covered my frame, and a glass visor crystalized around my head, attached to a breathing tube. This curved around into an oxygen tank fitted across my back. With a final wink through my glass shield, she soared out of view and into the night sky. She was gone.

Tamara shrunk down to my size and motioned me toward the ship. "It's time, Sainath."

I walked with Tamara by my side. Her white dress covered her as she met my pace and adjusted her size. "As for Bayard," she said as we boarded the ship, "he will find his own way there. He was badly injured at the border, and I'm afraid he won't live to see your final destination."

"What do you mean not fit for travel?"

I turned around to look over Tamara's shoulder. There was Bayard, walking through the clearing of the forest. A crutch supported his left arm and his right leg was bound in bandages. I left Tamara's side and ran to Bayard. I embraced my friend with gratitude. At his shoulder was the unmistakable hilt of my second sword. With a broad smile, he hobbled toward the ship.

"I'm glad you could make it, old friend." I said, as he stopped short and turned his shoulders to the forests.

"Well, let's get going. Don't be misled by how slow I am. Apollyon is not far behind," Bayard said, searching the forest line with a furtive glance.

Asha came up to the ship and wrapped me in a hug. His arms were like vines, or perhaps, Wikum arms.

"Sainath, I know you will make it through to Prima," he said. "After all, you have encountered me, and Tamara, and many other non-human entities. You have grown so much in the five years that you have been here.

"You will venture to the oldest part of the known universe; it will look desolate and depressing. Look for Prima on a planet similar to Saturn. It holds a second ring, which moves in the opposite direction. It is the Wikum home world…my home. Tamara and I have both given you our greatest gifts. I never thought I would work so closely with one of our greatest creations. I have to admit, we have broken countless rules to get to where we are at this moment. Even now, I feel the ground speaking. It tells me that King Gregory and the rest of the kingdom are coming this way. They are moving because of you. Now get on that ship, and believe that your true destiny lies in your heart. Keep it beating, and keep fighting even when it seems like all hope is lost."

I let Asha's words fill my mind as he finished talking. He squeezed me tighter than ever. It felt like I was hugging a tree. The smell of bark, vegetation and wildflowers filled my body with bliss. Finally, his arms relaxed, and I drew away from my celestial friend. I walked back onto the deck. Bayard was getting settled in with the help of Nayr, who had taken off his owl disguise. His red hair blew in the wind.

"We don't have much time," he said. He didn't look up as he walked to the panel by the captain's chair.

He sat down and commenced a system check—flipping switches on and off as the ship croaked and creaked to life. Tamara spoke to us as a group, and I took a seat near Bayard below the main mast, facing Nayr and the control panel. I looked up at the massive solar sails of pearl white and silver as Tamara's voice settled upon our ears.

Bayard was strapped into a leather chair that had been brought up from the ship's second deck. Nayr tied cables from the main mast to the chair. He attached a harness around his torso, then linked it to a retractable cable, for additional protection. Bayard only had one good arm now and wouldn't be able to hold onto anything for long. He reclined against a pile of sandbags stacked two feet high, so his legs would be supported. Even though the spirit of Tom had left him, I still saw signs of this old identity in Bayard. Perhaps now more than ever.

"Very well, this is goodbye then. To the three of you—you are the last of your species. Prove to Prima that you are worthy of a second chance at life." Tamara gave me a meaningful look. "Use your eyes, Sainath. She will try to deceive you with her many forms. She is the harbinger of creativity. She will use your strengths against you. Stay focused on the task at hand. Get some rest, all of you."

Tamara left the ship. We all nodded. The ship began to rise as the solar sails were released from their chains and unfolded to their full extension. I reached out and touched one; it was made of tightly-wound fibers and felt like metal instead of cloth, even though it had looked like fabric from a distance.

I was standing as the ship rose. My heart started to beat harder. Something deep in my gut told me to run toward the rail as the ship started to rise away from the planet's edge. I did. Looking down, I waved at the celestial beings, the saluting owl scouts, Minerva's shining form—a fairy-bird of pure light.

And then, through the forest came my knights. Orion dismounted and ran to the edge of the dock, screaming, "My King, we will never forget you. Thank you for seeing us beyond ourselves."

He tore off his armor and revealed his mechanical insides. Asha was right; he was a product of this world. The rest of the knights followed their captain by tearing their armor off to reveal their robotic insides. Their true selves.

I shouted back to Orion and the knights. "It doesn't matter. You will forever be a friend, and if I ever become a man of power again, I will select each and every one of you as my guards. You are the truest of friends, human or otherwise!"

Orion waved and bowed in a show of deep respect, before walking away from the dock. King Gregory arrived and just when I thought the goodbyes couldn't get any harder, a voice called out. A voice so familiar it almost sounded like Emily.

Evelynn sprinted forward with her horse. She reached for the ship, even though it was now far beyond her grasp. I extended my hand to her own, which was nothing more than a quickly shrinking dot below the ship. I had to squint to see her figure as we reached the upper atmosphere and clouds began to cover our trail. I yelled, knowing she wouldn't be able to hear me. I ran to the retractable cable boxes that were bolted to the main mast. Hooking them into my harness, I ran toward the edge of the rail. I didn't give my safety a second thought.

"Are you crazy?" Nayr yelled as I ran at the rail.

I hurdled it, swinging my body over the side and diving back to the edge of the planet. "You bet I am," I shouted.

Terra saw me plunge toward the ground. She broke into a sprint and sprouted wings to catch up to the ship. Evelynn saw me free-falling toward her outstretched arms. She heard Terra coming and leapt onto her back as the arboreal horse flew by. My cable went taut and jerked me back toward the ship. The cable started to automatically retract, but Terra followed my trail back to the ship's deck. Her hooves touched the smooth wood, and I unclamped the cord just as Evelynn jumped to hug me.

"Sainath, I thought I might have missed you. I'm sorry I couldn't be there to fight by your side when Ursa attacked. I'm even more sorry that I wasn't here in the owl realm when you defeated him."

She let go quickly and looked around, fighting the urge to cry. Always that fearless persona to uphold. She walked to the opposite side of the ship, the one facing away from the planet. The empty void of darkness stretched out in everlasting starlit emptiness.

Evelynn swallowed back her tears again. I joined her at the ship's rail. I knew I would tear up too, if I looked at her.

Her voice was calm. "We came as fast as we could. My true assignment along with Gregory and most of his army was to fight Apollyon on his own turf. We lost a large number of our troops—too many men. We knew our time with you was coming to an end. We just didn't know how to tell you the truth about this planet. We knew you wouldn't take it well."

She pulled her eyes away from outer space and fixed them on me. "I knew you would fall for me. I was created to look like your Emily. It was hard for me, too. I knew this moment was going to be difficult. I'm sorry for leading you on…I tried to fight Apollyon. At first his plan sounded like the best way to aid humanity. Little did we know it was all a lie to get you to the kingdom so Apollyon could remove you from the equation for good."

I looked down at the metal railing while I collected my thoughts. "Are you a machine, like Orion and the knights?" I said, looking her straight in the eye.

She paused. "Not quite. I'm more human than you think. Look." She turned to face me and unzipped her armor. The material beneath her clothes looked well enough like skin. But Orion had that too. Evelynn pulled at an invisible seam and folded her skin to the side, revealing wires and flashing circuits. Yet there were bones and joints in there too. Her heart was a human heart.

I reached for her face with my left hand. "Evelynn, it doesn't matter anymore. Don't you see? I found this all out from Asha. I learned the truth—that I'd been manipulated into following a path that had been laid out for me long before I wound up here. Even though it hurt at the time, I no longer care. What is done is done. I have to say, this is nothing like what I thought life would be like after humanity was wiped out. Why am I still alive? That's life, I suppose."

I shook my head. "It all seems fine on the surface, when you are fighting like crazy to survive just below. I'm thankful to be alive, and, in part, glad to have seen things people of my kind could only dream of in the deepest parts of their imaginations. I understand now more than ever what I must do. The three of us have a duty to our species, and if it's in our DNA, then so be it. I will do what I can."

A neigh announced that our time had come to an end. I gave Evelynn one last hug and helped her mount Terra. I caressed the beast's wildflower mane one last time. A vine came toward me, and I quickly opened my visor, making sure my breathing tube remained intact. It attached to my ear and grazed my esophagus, and Terra spoke to me.

"Goodbye friend. May you find that which you seek. When you are ready to see Earth, I will be waiting. If things don't go as planned, remember—you can live the rest of your soul's journey with you beloved. Nothing to lose, but a lot to gain. We will hold off Apollyon for as long as we can to give you a head start. Stay vigilant, and follow your instincts. Remember, you are dependent upon one another. Use that to your advantage, for the universe loves stubborn hearts. Safe journey, Sainath."

With that, the vine retracted. It happened before I could reply. I shut my visor as she flew away from the ship and back down to the planet. I watched as the girl and horse vanished below the clouds' cover.

The sun gleamed at us and the solar sails stretched out as if they were alive and following the sun's light, as flowers often do. I walked back to Bayard, who punched me playfully, then strapped myself in. Sitting in leather chairs and looking out into the sky reminded me of how we had started this journey back on Earth on that last flight, following a dream that there was a safe place for humanity to start again. How crazy was it to think that we hadn't ended up anywhere near where we had wanted to be?

I had a feeling Bayard was thinking the same thing in that moment, as his damaged body acted out the final scene in that plane. I reached out as if I were holding a yoke, mimicking him.

He turned and shot me that unforgettable smile. "Seems like a familiar sight, don't it?' he said, adjusting his visor as the stars came into view. The planet was now far below.

I watched Nayr do the same with his over-the-head straps. "Three, two, one."

Nayr flipped a switch, and the main engines ignited, propelling us forward with great speed. My feet started to rise beneath me. Another switch was flipped, and a dome closed over our heads. I brushed my hand against it as if I was feeling the ceiling of a home. It reacted to my touch; its texture was like a live blanket, wavy and textured. My feet touched the wooden deck, and my visor retracted. I looked over and saw Bayard unhooking his mouthpiece.

"It's all right, mate. It's safe to breathe now. That blanket above us is like a mini atmosphere that circulates the air and filtrates it, bringing oxygen back to us," Nayr explained. "Imagine it being a giant translucent plant that doesn't look like a plant."

We all laughed. I removed my mouthpiece and the oxygen tank. Nayr stepped away from the wheel and did the same.

This was it. The final leg of the journey with the three humans left in all the universes. Our mission was to talk to one celestial being and prove that we deserved one last shot at existence.

I walked to the bow of the ship. Bayard had gone down below, to rest his broken leg and of course, find something to eat. Nayr punched in some coordinates, and we shot through space.

I looked to my right, off into the distance. Three stars of Orion's belt were just barely visible. I thought about Earth, and how it might look right now. I thought about the Unknown and the deal I had made with the witch. I wondered what she would say about my half-fulfilled side of the deal. I wondered why Tamara and Asha were both so concerned about the many forms that Prima might take to distract me. I had plenty of questions. Hopefully, Prima would answer them.

I thought about Evelynn and how she was doing—if she had already fought Apollyon or if she had been killed by another in the interim. This world that he had created, this false hope he had put in my head. The cruel training he had forced upon all the humans that had been brought here to be slaves as punishment for their actions on Earth.

Was it really *our fault* if the celestial beings had planned it all along?

I reached into my leather bag and flipped through the journal again to inspect the signatures. They had lied and manipulated me, but after spending time together, they had come to my aid, saved my life, and in the end, turned their backs on their own kind to save a dying species. Three left of eight billion. Three lives. Three souls hoping to spark a second wave—a generation of humanity. Three strands of DNA. Three different personalities. Three uniquely-talented individuals.

I put on my breathing apparatus, attached the retractable cable to my waist harness and walked to the edge of the ship, where I sat with my feet dangling freely into space. All around, a protective field buffered the ship from its surroundings, so I wouldn't slip off. Stars, planets, asteroids, nebulas—it all slipped by. I got nothing more than a glimpse at the speed we were traveling. As we flew at lightspeed, I thought about my past life.

Asha had said that the trajectory of our lives is planned out before we are created. I believed there was some truth in that. That no matter how many different side trails we take and no matter how far we find ourselves from the main path, we will eventually end up where we are meant to be. I thought about the faces of friends who had helped shape me into the person I had grown into. If I had to guess, I was in my early thirties now. Technically, I had more than half my life ahead of me and yet, I had survived two planets only to learn my journey wasn't even close to ending.

I wasn't even sure what to say to Prima. Perhaps the story of the Wikums had some hidden meaning I had yet to grasp. After all, Prima and Asha were the rebel Wikums who had fought against the stagnant, rigid customs of their people. I wondered what Prima's world would look like. She *was* the celestial being of creativity. Maybe everything would be flipped on its head, in a topsy turvy kind of way.

The thought of the Unknown scraped at my curiosity too; if the opportunity arose, would I have the mental strength to dive headfirst into a world which even the celestials themselves didn't dare travel to? Maybe it was time to pray and reflect on Emily, to build a treasure box in my mind and lock up all our memories together. To say goodbye. Even now I didn't feel like my former Earth self.

How small-minded we are, to think there is nothing beyond our own planet and our own species. When I was a child, I talked to the trees and plants and the insects that crawled on the ground. These funny insects, with too many legs. I would ask simple questions of ants that traveled long distances to clear their paths. Expecting an answer, I would repeat my questions again and again. Nevertheless, as I grew older, I stopped talking to things that didn't respond. Is that an adult thing to do? To ignore the quiet things, like trees and plants? It took the destruction of my own planet and a war on another one to open my ears to the things I had once shared an intimate connection with as a child. I wished I could have played in the dirt a little longer, and built makeshift homes from twigs and leaves for bugs, collected spiders and traced their mysterious webs, and picked a blade of grass just because I could.

It had taken me almost half my life to learn to love the world. Sure, Apollyon's planet was a war-torn one, but it had held its secret until the very end. The same secret that Apollyon whispered into my ear in a nightmare that had kick-started this whole journey.

He was right; a hero arrives at the very last minute, *not* when they are needed the most. It didn't make much sense to me then, but now I saw it perfectly. In every struggle I had faced, just when I was on the brink of giving up—relinquishing my last breath—a hero in some form arrived to bring me back to my feet. To remind me that that moment was not where I was meant to die. Yet my image of an Earth hero then was no longer my image of one now. A hero was a woman in an olive dress. A hero was a four-legged creature, a true friend. A hero was a knight who fought beside me, against incredible odds. A hero was a celestial being who changed its heart to aid a species far less worthy or powerful than itself. A hero was a mythical owl filled with wisdom, who gave her life for a battle on her doorstep that wasn't hers to fight. A hero was a blessing in disguise, one that took many forms. For all the wrongs Apollyon was known for, I couldn't help but be thankful for the lessons he had taught me.

I walked back down to the main deck and strapped myself in. Nayr was looking over his charts. My eyelids flickered, and my right hand reached for the hilt of my sword. I wrapped my fingers around it, as it was the last artifact from Earth, and let the buzz of lightspeed cradle me to sleep.

Prima, here we come.

End Book Two.